Grace in Glasgow

Seduced in Scotland
Book 3

Matilda Madison

Dearest Reader;

Thank you for your support of a small press. At Dragonblade Publishing, we strive to bring you the highest quality Historical Romance from some of the best authors in the business. Without your support, there is no 'us', so we sincerely hope you adore these stories and find some new favorite authors along the way.

Happy Reading!

CEO, Dragonblade Publishing

Prologue

Lismore Hall, Scottish Highlands, June 1856

"THERE HE IS," Grace Sharpe said, standing on her tippytoes to gaze across the ballroom at her Aunt Belle's seventy-sixth birthday party. The man she had been searching for all evening was speaking to her brother-in-law, Graham McKinnon. "Excuse me, Faith. I'd like to thank him in person."

"Wait," her sister said, a note of hesitation in her eyes. But then, she shook her head. "Good luck, Grace."

Grace grinned, acutely aware of the trepidation in her sister's voice, but Faith needn't worry. All Grace wished to do was thank Dr. James Hall for taking her on as a student. She had been trying for months to gain acceptance into any university that would permit a woman to study medicine, but alas, every one of her letters had been rejected and she had to submit to studying under Dr. Barkley. He was a fine mentor, but as Grace had hopes of working in the bustling city of Glasgow as opposed to Glencoe, she needed a teacher who lived in the city. As a former student of Dr. Barkley himself, Dr. Hall had agreed to allow Grace to shadow him over the next six months, or so her aunt had said, and she wished to thank him personally.

Skirting around the crowded ballroom, Grace was careful not to make eye contact with anyone, particularly gentlemen, as to avoid being asked to dance. Although she had helped facilitate this birthday celebration for her aunt, she had no intentions of participating in the festivities. Not when her future was hanging in the balance.

Lifting her chin to peer over guests' shoulders, she silently cursed her short stature as she saw the familiar outline of Dr. Hall who was now talking with a group of men near the back terrace of the ballroom. Unlike the other men in attendance, Dr. Hall wore slacks as opposed to a kilt, a mark no doubt of his modern professionalism. Grace was bolstered by his dress, believing that if a man didn't possess an affinity for tradition, he would undoubtedly champion her in her prospects.

"Dr. Hall?" she spoke, causing the man to turn.

Grace had braced herself when the doctor turned, his gray-blue eyes landing on her with curiosity. They had met, briefly, several times over the past year, ever since Grace and her sisters had been removed from London after their grandmother Alice's death and resettled with their aunt in the Highlands. Ever since the first time their eyes met, Grace had to remind herself to exhale.

He was attractive, more so than most, but what was curious about it was that it affected her. She was never distracted by good looks or charming words. In fact, Grace had been around much handsomer men before, men who outranked Dr. Hall, but there was something about his straight nose, near black brows, and the perplexing scent of lime that hovered about him wherever he went that made Grace aware of his imposing presence.

"Miss Sharpe," he said with a charming smile. "A pleasure to see you."

Grace ignored the silly giddiness she felt in her stomach. He was taller than most, though not as broad as her brothers-in-law, but far more pleasing to look at, at least to her. With dark brown hair that was clipped close to his head, as well as a short beard which had become fashionable in the last year or so, he appeared every bit professional.

"And you. I was wondering if I might have a word with you? I'm not sure if you were able to speak with Dr. Barkley yet, but—"

"Ah, yes," he interrupted, shooting a speculative glance at the company around him as his charming smile faded. "Let's discuss that over here."

His hand came up to her elbow and the barest of pressure landed against the back of her upper arm. The warmth from his touch caused her pulse to flutter, but she was quick to ignore it. As a student of the body, physical reactions were commonplace and as expected as the sun rising in the east and setting in the west.

Dr. Hall escorted her out of the ballroom, across the semi-filled stone floored hallway. As large as Lismore Hall was, it was still rather small for all the guests that had come to the celebration. Still, Grace was aware of the separation she and the doctor had from the other guests.

Stopping just behind the grand stone staircase, Dr. Hall's hand fell away from her arm and he exhaled.

"I must tell you, Dr. Hall, that I admire your bravery," she said, continuing her previous train of thought.

The doctor's dark brows cinched together.

"Bravery?"

"Yes. When I first started shadowing Dr. Barkley on his rounds, he tried very hard to, well, dissuade me, for lack of a better term. He was firm in his belief that women didn't possess the stomachs nor the devotion that the study of medicine requires. But I was steadfast in my determination and I proved to him that such ideas were antiquated and while it will take years, if not decades to change the hearts and minds of our fellow countrymen about a woman's right to study medicine, I just wanted to say that I feel very privileged to have your support." She exhaled soundly. "I'm so very grateful that you're allowing me to work under your practice in Glasgow."

It was truly a dream come true for Grace to be allowed to shadow a doctor as prominent and well respected as Dr. Hall. While Dr. Barkley was the primary physician in Glencoe and the neighboring villages in this part of the Highlands, Dr. Hall was a police surgeon in a metropolitan area. The advances in science and medicine that he was able to see and experience would further her education in ways she could not yet imagine and it was her greatest desire to help people.

But the expression on the man's face seemed conflicted. Grace tilted her head, sure that she had surprised the good doctor with her extensive speech.

"You'll have to forgive me," she added quickly, shaking her head. "It's just that, I'm terribly excited to continue my work and while I will forever be indebted to Dr. Barkley, I believe my strengths in medicine would be best utilized in a surgical atmosphere."

"Miss Sharpe—"

"And I know," she interrupted, lifting a hand as if to apologize. "It will take years to learn and prove myself, but I am determined."

"Miss Sharpe, I regret to inform you that I disagreed with Dr. Barkley's idea of having you shadow me in Glasgow."

For a moment, the smile on Grace's face was frozen. Surely she hadn't heard him correctly. She blinked.

"I'm… I'm sorry?"

A shadow of pity passed over Dr. Hall's face and the laryngeal prominence of his thyroid cartilage moved up and down as he swallowed. Or rather, his Adam's apple.

"Dr. Barkley and I have spoken extensively, and I unfortunately will not be able to oversee your studies in Glasgow. What with my work for the police there, as well as my own practice, I don't have the time for a student to follow me." He paused. "Nor would I, in good conscience, allow a lady to shadow me. Not in that city."

Grace blinked again, his words barely registering as her hopes and dreams were once again dashed, like glass shattering on the floor. How many rejection letters did she have upstairs in her room? Dozens, if not more, all from colleges and universities that had refused her entry into their schools, all because she was a woman.

How many times must she suffer because of her sex?

"I see," she said softly, her eyes unfocused.

"I am sorry that I did not have happier news, but you must know, it would be near impossible."

She nodded and when she didn't speak, he turned to leave, his arm very nearly brushing against her shoulder.

The dismissal was enough to sting, but something within Grace's chest seemed to snap and she turned on her heel.

"Twenty-one schools have rejected me, Dr. Hall. Twenty-one. Every single medical school in the country."

The tall man turned back, his blue eyes piteous beneath his black brows.

"There are only twenty schools that teach medicine."

"Oh yes," she said with an exasperated bob of her head. "I applied to one in Italy as well."

He frowned.

"I am sorry for that, Miss Sharpe, but—"

"All of who accepted me when I reapplied under the name of Andrew Sharpe." She paused, hoping to let that information sink in. "I am not arrogant, Dr. Hall, nor boastful, but I am capable. I have a mind for medicine, my experience and abilities are demonstrative of that and if I had just…" She swallowed, fighting off the building emotion. She needed to quell it, control it, lest he use it against her for being dramatic or hysterical. She inhaled and exhaled slowly before continuing. "If I had just an opportunity to show you my abilities, I promise, you would not be disappointed."

"I'm sorry, Miss Sharpe," he said firmly. "But my answer is still no."

No. It was the vilest word in the entire English language and yet one that seemed most attracted to her. No, she couldn't study to be a doctor. No, she wasn't clever enough for medicine. No, she wasn't fit for doing the thing she loved most in the world.

She was forever having to prove those no's wrong.

Out of the corner of her eye, she saw the doctor approach.

"It was not my intent to make you cry, Miss Sharpe."

"Cry?" She laughed, worried for a moment that she was, but thankfully the water in her eyes was dispelled by several blinks. "Sir, there is nothing in this world that you could do or say that would make me cry." She cleared her throat and squared her shoulders before staring him straight in the eye. "It is no matter. I'm used to rejection."

To his credit, Dr. Hall appeared fully focused on her in that moment, as if he were debating something internally. He opened his mouth to speak, but Grace held her hand up once more to silence him.

"Please, Dr. Hall, whatever it is you're going to say, I pray you keep it to yourself."

"I was just going to say—"

"I am not your student and there is nothing outside of medicine that you could say that would interest me." She gave him a tight smile as if trying to convey that she was not bothered in the slightest. "Excuse me."

Grace was quick to move away from him, grateful that the hallway had become crowded.

"Miss Sharpe, wait," he called after her, but she did not stop.

She would not waste a single moment more in his presence and what's more, she needed privacy.

Stepping quickly over the flagstone floors, she was down the hall and in her aunt's private study, locking the door behind her should she be followed.

The quiet of the room was in stark contrast to the rest of the house that was buzzing with activity. And just as she convinced herself that she was just going to have to pursue her studies from yet another angle, a wayward tear fell down her cheek. She immediately wiped it away, angry at herself for giving in to her hurt feelings.

She was used to rejection, used to everyone telling her no or that she wasn't capable. Well, everyone outside of her family. Her sisters had always fanned the flames of her passion, but there was no use for it apparently, because she could not pursue her dreams. Ever.

Another tear fell and then another. Frantically and furiously, she kept wiping them away, but then they wouldn't stop coming.

A sob escaped her mouth, and for the first time in a long time, she allowed the full weight of her misery and disappointment to wash over her. She was forever meeting with obstacles too high and yet she continued to pursue her dreams.

What was the matter with her? Why couldn't she learn?

Just then, the door to the study shook, causing her to jump away from it.

"Miss Sharpe?" The muffled voice of Dr. Hall called from the other side of the oak door. "Miss Sharpe, are you in there?"

She shook her head, knowing fully well that he couldn't see her, but still having a need to answer. After another shake or two, the door handle stilled and Grace could hear footsteps fade away into the music on the other side.

Thank goodness she had locked the door, she mused as she bit her bottom lip. For whatever Dr. Hall thought to say to her, she would have been all the worse off if he found her crying.

He truly was an unfeeling man, just as his aunt had described him. Mrs. Fletcher, better known as the Witch of Glencoe, had been a close friend of Grace's ever since she had arrived in Scotland. When she had confided in the older woman that she wished to study medicine, it was Mrs. Fletcher who had first suggested her nephew. When Grace hesitated, as he was an attractive sort close to her own age, the old woman had reassured her that there was nothing to fear from Dr. Hall, as he was incapable of possessing amorous feelings. He was an incompatible soul, which was just fine with Grace, as she always considered herself incompatible too, and she had become confident in the idea of studying under him.

But not anymore.

Grace exhaled slowly through her nose, taking deep breaths to calm herself down. She could not let yet another setback ruin her evening. This was a celebration for Aunt Belle, her seventy-sixth birthday after all, which, according to Grace's eldest sister Hope, was a very important milestone.

Moving around the room, she sought out the small cart that Aunt Belle kept next to her desk. Reaching for a crystal decanter filled with water, she poured herself a glass and dipped her fingertips in, moving the liquid around her face before moving toward the fireplace.

In a few moments, once her face was dry and not so red, she would return to the ballroom and avoid both Dr. Hall and Dr. Barkley, lest her true feelings be exposed as they were far too close to the surface.

Instead, she would stand next to her aunt and offer what support she could for the rest of the evening and tomorrow... Well, tomorrow she would come up with a new plan. Somehow, some way, she would figure out how to see her dreams come true.

Even if it was the last thing she ever did.

Chapter One

Four Months Later...

D R. JAMES HALL peered out the window of his home that sat one street over from the Woodside Crescent in Glasgow as a black coach carriage carrying a number of trunks came to park behind one of the fashionable houses. Within moments, two male servants, dressed in dark blue coats, began unpacking the vehicle, as a number of maids and footmen exited through the back door of the terrace house and began helping unload all that had been carried from Lismore Hall.

James frowned, dropping his hand from the sheer window hanging as he turned around to face his mentor, Dr. Barkley, who was finishing his breakfast of poached eggs and toast, seemingly completely unaware of what a mess he had caused.

"This will be a travesty. You must know that," James said as he moved around the dining room table, taking a seat at the head of the table to finish his coffee.

"You're far too concerned with the rest of the world, James. You always have been," Dr. Barkley said, taking a sip of his tea.

James glared at him and the older man lifted his brow as he swallowed.

"I'm not concerned about what others will think of me, although I will not pretend that inviting a lady to shadow me won't cause a certain stir in my professional life, but surely you must admit that this little experiment of yours will only lead to failure. On both our parts."

"If either of you fail, I will put the blame solely at your feet."

"Why is that?"

"Because it will be your failure as a teacher to guide a student." He pointed his fork at James. "You've had dozens of successful students when you were teaching at the university."

"But I never had a lady student."

"And as I've assured you, at least a dozen times over, Miss Sharpe is as bright a mind as any." The old doctor placed his teacup on the small saucer before him. When he spoke next, his tone was gentle, if not a little sad. "Besides, that's not entirely true, is it?"

"What isn't true?"

"You've had a female student before."

James's hand paused midair, the coffee in his cup nearly spilling out, as a familiar misery crept up his spine. It wasn't fair for him to bring her up and James was actually surprised that Dr. Barkley had even done so as they never spoke on the topic of Catriona.

The mere remembrance of her name caused him to shift uncomfortably in his seat, but he would not be deterred. He took a sip of his coffee and placed it down on the saucer.

"I did not say that I never had a female student. I said I never had a lady student. Grace Sharpe is an earl's daughter, a lady of first society." He picked up his fork and pushed the last lone sausage on his plate back and forth as he spoke. "Everyone knows that members of the ton are incapable of hard work."

Dr. Barkley laughed.

"My, what a snob you are."

James sneered at him.

"Am I? Tell me, who do you know that was born into such a world that has ever put off their leisurely lifestyles and chose to work instead?" When the doctor did not answer, James smirked with vindication. "You can't think of anyone, can you?"

"The Marquis of Eneshire was rather helpful in the pursuit of artifacts during an archeological dig—"

"I don't mean people who throw monies at their hobbies. I

mean people who take up their own hands," he said, raising his. "And work with them."

"Do not discredit the patrons, James. It's at their discretion that many a science and art is studied."

"Which is criminal, in my opinion."

"Criminal or not, my reformist friend, it is the way of it." Dr. Barkley pointed at his friend. "And do you see now why I thought you a fitting teacher for the Sharpe woman?"

James scoffed.

"I'm no reformist."

"Says the man who believes schools should be socially funded."

"If there was ever a way to advance a society, it would be through education."

"If you truly believe that, then you wouldn't find any issue with Miss Sharpe searching for a teacher."

James opened his mouth to argue, but snapped it shut when he could not think of anything else to say. It was true that he believed in education for all, not just the well to do, but he also staunchly believed in the lacking character in members of the ton.

Perhaps it was because he himself had grown up so poor, or perhaps that he understood where he would be without the support of someone more financially stable than himself, but the truth was that his distrust of the ton was more personal.

James leaned back in his chair and lifted his gaze to the plaster ceiling. There was no use in trying to convince Dr. Barkley that he was wrong, particularly when he was so keen on the girl. If he had any wit about him, James would refuse the old man outright, but even as tempting as an idea as that was, James knew it was an impossibility.

He owed his entire practice to Dr. Barkley, nae, his entire life to the old man, as he was the one who first took an interest in his future when James was a lad.

Sighing, James glanced down at his plate and stabbed a sausage link with his fork. Yes, he would do this favor for his mentor, but he'd be sure to let him and everyone else know just how ridiculous he felt about it.

A lady as a doctor… It was preposterous.

"Very well," he said, annoying even himself at how mulish he sounded. He cleared his throat. "But do not be surprised when this goes up in flames."

Dr. Barkley shook his head.

"How can it? Miss Sharpe is of sound mind, better at handling a scalpel than even you, I might say. As long as you teach her everything you know, I daresay she may be one of the leading physicians in Scotland one day."

James laughed incredulously and stood up once more. He pushed back the curtains again and peered out his window, spying as the last of the boxes and cartons were carried off inside.

"I wonder by what divine intervention you've managed to see to it that my house should sit directly behind Lady Belle's."

"Divine intervention? Nonsense," Dr. Barkley said as he himself stood. "I told you five years ago when you bought this place that it was very near Lady Belle's home."

James made a "humph" noise as if to say he didn't believe him, but then there seemed to be some movement in a second story window. It seemed whatever room Miss Sharpe was in would be directly across the way from his own bedchamber. Squinting, James saw a mop of dark curls, tied up above a peach-colored gown, darting from one window to the next and back again, as if she were hopping about the room. There was no doubt in his mind who this woman was, and as much as he scowled, he felt a flicker of excitement pulsate through his body.

That, of course, meant nothing. As a man of science, James had long since learned that matters of attraction were animalistic in nature. He could sooner stop his stomach from rumbling when it was hungry or wet his mouth when he was parched. These were basic needs and aroused feelings weren't any different. In fact, he'd rather be aware of it now than be surprised at some other point in their time together.

But it was still interesting. He found the resolute woman attractive. It was her determination that had caught his attention in the first place. Not her hair color, nor her shapely, healthy form, but her clear voice and the perfect enunciation of words like *latissimus dorsi*, as he had heard her say nearly two years ago when they had first met when Graham MacKinnon had been shot.

Yet ever since their discussion at Lismore Hall several months prior, he had found himself thinking about her from time to time. When he had dashed her dreams, the lady did not cry or beg or make a scene. She merely stated that since she wasn't his student, she didn't have any reason to listen to him. He had found it amusing, if a little rude, and had gone off to find her to tell her so, but then he hadn't been able to find her again that night.

"It looks as though they've arrived early," Dr. Barkley said, pointing up at the window.

"Were they not supposed to arrive the day after tomorrow?"

"Yes, but you know Lady Belle. Her desires change with the wind," he said fondly. "I suppose she's eager to set her charges up in society."

James glanced at his friend.

"What do you mean?"

"Well, Miss Arabella Scott has been placed in Lady Belle's charge for the season and she and Miss Sharpe will be participating in town life. It was the only way Lady Belle would condone her niece living in the city."

James stepped back from the window, appalled.

"And when is she supposed to fit in a social life? As my student, I expect her full and utmost attention. I will not have her slacking because she is too tired to attend me due to some hangover from an opera the previous night or carousing at some ball until all hours of the morning."

Dr. Barkley's brow lifted.

"And here I thought you weren't excited about having a student."

"Excited? No. But if I'm to have one, then I will have her undivided attention."

"Well then, you might discuss that with Lady Belle the night after tomorrow. You've been invited to dine with them."

James nodded, turning away from the window once more. He had received an invitation from Lismore Hall about a dinner at the end of this week.

"Oh, but what's this?" Dr. Barkley said, peering out the window himself. "It appears one of the lady's footmen is on his way here."

Both men made their way away from the window. Within minutes, James's housekeeper, Mrs. Cramer, entered the dining room followed by a youthful footman with black hair and serious eyes.

"Dr. Hall? A message from Lady Belle Smyth."

James reached for the letter.

"Thank you."

The footman bowed and hurriedly left, followed by the housemaid. Tearing the edges of the envelope with his fingers, James unfolded the missive.

"Well, it seems our presence is required earlier than the day after tomorrow," he read, gazing up. "Lady Belle is feeling somewhat jolty since her arrival to Glasgow."

"Jolty?"

"It's what she's written."

He handed the note to Dr. Barkley, who let out a laugh, nearly startling James.

"That woman will do anything to have her way," he murmured before handing the note back to James. "Unfortunately, I've not the time to attend her here. I've already been gone too long from Glencoe, and I must leave before noon if I'm going to make it there before nightfall."

James tilted his head.

"You wish me to see her alone?"

"You are her other physician."

"This is not a home visit about her health and you know it. She wishes to lay out her plans and bully me into agreeing with her."

"I daresay the lady has her work cut out for her then. Dr. James Hall is rarely bullied into anything."

"Except by you, or my aunt." He lifted the note. "Or Lady Belle."

"Come now, my boy, what is it Mrs. Fletcher is always saying? Trust your travels?"

"Trust the journey," James corrected him, knowing the elder man knew exactly what Aunt Flora's mantra was.

She had been repeating the same words to James since he was eight, when he had been sent to live with her after his parents' deaths, both of whom had passed away due to consumption. James had been visiting his cousins south in Dumfries when they received word about their deaths and he was immediately put in a mailing carriage and sent to Glencoe to live with Aunt Flora Fletcher. Trust the journey had been her way of trying to teach him to combat his anxieties about the uncertainty of life and death, a topic that he had obsessed about in his youth and likely influenced his desire to become a physician.

"I doubt my aunt's folk medicine will help me with this."

Dr. Barkley wagged his finger, as if tsking a school boy.

"Do not disparage your aunt's belief in the old ways. She has proved time and time again that her little spells work. Remember, the best physician is also a philosopher."

James rolled his eyes. He hated when Dr. Barkley quoted Galen to him, particularly when it made perfect sense. Still, he argued.

"Just because she couples a few words with medicinal herbs and good feelings does not make her a philosopher." He shook his head. "It's the power of persuasion, not magic."

James had been dealing with his aunt's eccentric beliefs and reputation for over twenty-four years. It had been difficult growing up in Glencoe as her nephew, especially when he first arrived. Some children had taken it upon themselves to tease him and throw rocks at him, led by a local farmer's son named Angus. Of course, when Angus broke his leg, the whole town blamed it on the Witch of Glencoe.

Life had gotten easier after that, as the other children had suddenly become afraid to tease him, but there had always been a distinct look in the people of Glencoe's eyes when they saw James coming. It wasn't until he was a proper physician did they start treating him with respect as opposed to fear and even still, there were whispers about his healing abilities being linked to his aunt.

He had been trying to outrun their skepticism for years.

"Placebos are effective. And if it helps the locals of Glencoe to believe that she's some sort of witch, well, why not? It keeps her relatively safe from anyone who would cause her harm. Half of them are terrified of her and the other half go to her for remedies when they think I've failed them."

"I don't know if trusting the journey will help me in this situation."

"I promise, it will not be nearly as bad as you believe it."

James would have loved to believe Dr. Barkley, but if there was anything he was sure of, it was that things rarely ever turned out for the better for him. Every time he had the idea of searching for the bright side of things, or being an optimist, he was always met with the cold hard facts of reality. His mentor and even his aunt had recently begun to be vocal about their worry for him always being so gloomy, but it wasn't that he was a pessimist. He was a realist. And if there was one thing he knew for certain, it was that Miss Grace Sharpe was going to upend his life.

Chapter Two

"GOODNESS! THIS HOUSE is impressive," Arabella said to Grace, as she leaned over the polished banister in the foyer. While Aunt Belle and her faithful manservant, Andrews, took stock of the study at the back of the house's ground floor, which would be converted into a bedroom since Aunt Belle had trouble climbing stairs, the two ladies followed the middle-aged house maid, Mrs. Stevens, who had been instructed to show them their rooms. "I've never seen such dark colors used for wallpaper. And there's so many statues and busts. Your aunt must be a great collector."

Grace smirked at her friend's wonder as she held a small, three-legged tabby cat to her chest. Arabella had held the kitten most of the way to Glencoe, while Aunt Belle slept and Grace had read a series of her aunt's pamphlets on a housing crisis that was currently sweeping the country, particularly in the cities. The severity of what she had read caused her a bit of anxiety and so she had put down the politically charged paper and picked up a cat instead.

"Look at that painting!" Arabella said, pointing to a sizeable portrait of King George IV. It was a profile painting of the former monarch, his hair upturned in regency fashion. Arabella bent slightly backwards. "That's him, isn't it? Your aunt's former lover?"

"Yes."

"He must have cared for her very much to leave her such a

collection."

In truth, Aunt Belle cared very little for the art world, and these relics that lined the walls were actually bits and pieces of the private collection of King George IV. Her aunt once having been the favorite mistress of his majesty, Grace was curious to know if these pieces had been gifts from the king or, if rumors were to be believed, pieces that he had lost gambling. Though whether he had lost to Aunt Belle or she had gone off and bought them all back from their winners, Grace did not know.

"Aunt Belle is an enthusiastic collector of things," she said, as she bent down to let the cat go, as they reached the landing.

Aunt Belle was a collector, of newspaper clippings and gossip pages, but mostly she seemed to collect people. Friends and family had been elusive in her young life as the mistress of the king and she had come to cherish those close to her, having been particularly pleased when Grace and her sisters had come to live with her nearly two years ago.

"This will be your room, my lady," Mrs. Stevens said as she opened a door at the end of the hallway. It was south facing, and the bright midday sun shone through the glass windows that stood floor to ceiling along the front of the house.

"Oh, my goodness," Arabella gasped, spinning around the room as Grace followed. With cream and yellow striped walls, the room was a vision of sunshine and loveliness. The canopy was covered in lace that matched the curtains and bedding, and fine maple furnishings practically glowed in the bathing sunlight. "If this isn't the prettiest room I've ever seen!"

Grace smiled politely, but there was something odd about this room. A melancholy took hold of her the moment she entered and it wasn't until moments later that her usually fast mind realized why.

This room was decorated in the same delicate style as her grandmother Alice's home in London.

It shouldn't make her so sad, especially since she often missed her grandmother, but being in Glasgow to study medicine, well, that would have been an impossibility with Aunt Belle's sister. Grandma Alice and Aunt Belle were vastly different in their manners as well as their approach to life. Where Alice had been strict and steadfast to the proper, upper-class upbringing of gentle bred ladies, Belle had insisted on free thinking and independent spirits. While Grace was thankful to have been blessed with such an aunt, it made her feel guilty from time to time, to think of what her grandmother would have thought of her choices.

"Shoo!" Mrs. Stevens said as the three-legged kitten began to scratch at the bedding. "Go on, get."

"Sorry about him, Mrs. Stevens," Grace said, quickly approaching as she scooped him up. "He's a bit anxious from the carriage ride."

"He's only got three legs. What good is he?"

"Oh, but he's very good at catching mice. Even more so than the other cats kept in the stables at Lismore Hall, but I think it is because he's trying to prove himself. Isn't that right, Penguin?"

Mrs. Stevens blinked.

"What did you call him?"

"Penguin. Mr. Penguin, considering his coloring," Grace explained. "He's been following me the last two months, since he was born. One of the stable hands wanted to drown him, on account of his deformity, but I couldn't let him. Now, he won't leave me be."

"Right, well, come along," Mrs. Stevens said skeptically to Arabella, whose eyes hadn't come down from the ceiling.

"Wait," Grace said, stepping in front of her. "Arabella, you wouldn't wish to stay in this room, would you?"

Her friend frowned.

"Oh, but I shan't. This is your room."

"Yes, my lady. Lady Belle specifically said that this was to be your room. It overlooks the crescent gardens. See?"

Grace and Arabella walked to the windows and sure enough, the gardens were in perfect view from the cushioned settee.

"I know, and I appreciate that, but the sun, you see. It bothers my eyes the way it reflects off the pages of my books and I do intend on doing a lot of reading while we are here. I think a north facing window may be gentler on my vision."

A single brow on Mrs. Stevens' face rose as if she didn't believe such nonsense, but Arabella reached for Grace's hand.

"If you are sure?"

"Quite."

"Then of course I will," she said cheerfully. "What luck! Now, let us see your room."

Mrs. Stevens led the way, back down the hallway to the rear end of the terrace. This room was square, with deep pink and mauve wallpaper and darker, heavier furnishings than the first room, but Grace was pleased. The windows overlooked the street behind theirs, with a handsome row of white stone terraces that went all the way left and all the way right.

This was perfect. No distractions would cause her to abandon her studies when they became too difficult. No vague haunting of her grandmother scolding her for bringing books to the dining room table. Yes, a room in the back of the house was just what she needed.

Deciding to change out of her traveling clothes, Grace waited for a maid to brush out the wrinkles of one of her gowns that had been brought up in a chest that had arrived only an hour earlier. It was a simple white dress with tiny peach-colored blooms that was perhaps too lightweight for the weather, but it was one of Grace's favorites.

"May I help you, my lady?" Mrs. Stevens offered. "Or mayhap Bethany here might assist you."

"No, thank you. I can manage on my own."

The housekeeper didn't move while the maid Bethany glanced at her.

"Are you sure, my lady?"

"Yes, very much so. Please."

Grace held her outstretched hand toward the door and waited until both Mrs. Stevens and Bethany left, closing the door behind them. Sighing, she began to unbutton the front of her dark green travel gown when a small, silver locket bumped against her palm.

Pausing in her undress, Grace held up the piece to inspect it as she did nearly every night. Mrs. Fletcher, her friend who was often called the Witch of Glencoe, had given her the locket not a week prior. She had insisted Grace wear it for good health and while there was a crease that curved around the oval piece, Grace hadn't been able to open it. She doubted there was anything in it save for a sprig or two of water mint, one of the many herbs she had once gathered for Mrs. Fletcher when she was studying under Dr. Barkley.

Bringing the locket up to her nose, she inhaled. It reminded her of the wide-open spaces of the Highlands and she was grateful to have such a wonderful gift, though she kept it hidden beneath her clothing. Mrs. Fletcher had made her swear to keep it secret, and always willing to entertain the old woman, Grace had agreed.

Once changed, Grace headed downstairs to inspect the rest of the house that was to be her home for the next six months.

The house was wider than their London home, but shorter. For instance, it only had two floors above the ground level, but it was equipped with a dining room, sitting room, study, library, and a parlor where one could receive guests. The study, of course, had been transformed into a bedroom and it was there where Grace found her Aunt Belle.

"Oh no, none of this will do." The seventy-six-year-old woman stood, shoulders pulled back beside a small hump that sat at the back of her neck. "Andrews? Help Chauncy move the bed away from the window. Ah," she paused as she noticed Grace. "My dear. How did you find your room?"

"Ah, very well, thank you," Grace said, unsure if she should mention that she had switched bedchambers. "Aunt Belle, since we're a few days early, I was wondering if we might take a walking tour around our part of this city?"

"A walking tour?" Belle repeated, glancing down at her cane. "I'm not sure I'd be much use on a walking tour."

"Actually, the exercise will do you good."

"Oh no. Don't you try and bully me like Barkley and Hall. I don't care if you are my grandniece; I won't be taking orders from you." Grace waited patiently. "Besides, we're having company this evening."

"Who?"

"Dr. Hall, of course."

Grace blinked.

"Dr. Hall? Is coming tonight? But I thought we wouldn't see him for at least a few days."

Aunt Belle frowned.

"That doesn't sound like the excited reaction I was expecting from someone who has begged nearly every doctor and school in the country to let them study beneath."

Grace was momentarily frozen before her head shook and she offered a false smile.

"Of course. It will be good to see Dr. Hall. We could perhaps speak of my training before starting."

Aunt Belle grinned.

"That's what I thought you might—wait, Andrews, no, I don't want that table over there." Belle rolled her eyes. "Come, let me do it."

"Aunt Belle, Andrews can handle it."

The manservant picked up a small maplewood end table and waited for Belle's instructions. There was never a more devoted person to Belle than Andrews. Their constant companionship likely added to the amusing back and forth that everyone was often privy to witness. Belle was demanding and pushy, although she refused to go anywhere without Andrews, trusting him above everyone, and Andrews was nearly always silent and appeasing, although he did on rare occasion advise Belle when he was staunchly opposed to something. Like the time in Italy, when Belle was supposed to have surgery. She had been petrified at the prospect of being cut open and tried to leave their villa to return home. Andrews had insisted upon bringing her to the doctor's theater himself and guarded the door until said surgery was over. It had saved her life, but Belle had been stubborn in her forgiveness of Andrews for that, although he didn't seem to mind.

It didn't happen often, but Belle would always reconsider if Andrews had something to say. Again, though, that was rare indeed.

Grace peeled out of the room, uninterested in all the reasons why an end table should be wherever Aunt Belle wanted it, and instead went to find the library, in hopes of finding the books that she had sent ahead of time.

Of course, they had arrived two days earlier than when they were supposed to, but before she could reach the library, a knock at the front door caught her attention. Pausing, she lifted her hand to the doorway and waited to see who had come to call.

"Yes, sir," Mrs. Stevens said as she opened the door wide for the guest to enter. "She'll be right along. Won't you come into the parlor?"

The tall, familiar form of Dr. Hall entered into the foyer, his cool gaze finding Grace's face instantly. He stalled as he spotted her and Grace had to remind herself to breathe, and in doing so she smelled the familiar citrus scent. Why did he always smell of limes? And why she should suddenly feel under his inspection, she did not quite understand, but then she lifted her chin and squared her shoulders before marching up to him.

The gentle wonder in his eyes turned contemptuous as she reached him.

"Dr. Hall," she said with a slight curtsy. "I did not expect you until the day after tomorrow."

"Aye, that's when I expected you, but Lady Belle has requested me."

"So I've just learned."

"She doesn't fare very well doing long trips?"

"I wouldn't say that. Aunt Belle did splendid on our return from Italy last spring. She has stated that she feels far better since her surgery and traveling does not make her as weary as before."

He squinted at her.

"Perhaps then you would like to examine her?"

Grace smiled but shook her head.

"Oh no. Aunt Belle is your patient and I do not envy you for it."

That seemed to have an effect on him. He blinked.

"You don't?"

"Goodness no. Aunt Belle requires a more enduring bedside manner than I'm readily available to give. Dr. Barkley, in particular, is good at talking to her endlessly about, well, whatever it is they talk about."

Dr. Hall took a step toward her, hands behind his back.

"Lady Belle can be difficult on occasion."

Grace laughed, ignoring the sudden upturn of Dr. Hall's mouth.

"You are being gracious," she said as Arabella suddenly came bounding down the stairs.

When she saw Dr. Hall, however, she slowed her steps, reaching the landing with a delicate refinement.

"Dr. Hall. It's so nice to see you," she said with a curtsy as the doctor bowed. "Are you here for Grace?"

Although everyone knew that Dr. Hall was to take over Grace's training, the words seemed to bounce off the walls on the hallway, echoing in the strangest way.

"Er, no, well… No, that is, I'm here for Lady Belle. At her request, I should say."

"Oh," Arabella said happily. "Then let us wait for her in the parlor."

For some reason, Dr. Hall glanced back at Grace, as if waiting for her to say something. Unsure, Grace nodded and led the way.

The parlor was another room that seemed disjointed from the rest of the house, just like the bedchambers. The walls were covered in a slate gray wallpaper that was almost violet, with bird motifs speckled every few inches. It was strange that the ceiling was also covered in this wallpaper, giving the room a cave-like feel, dark and curious.

Grace was staring up, taking in the room, as Arabella spoke.

"It's so nice to see a familiar face in the city," she stated as she sat in a high-back wooden chair across the table from the sofa where Dr. Hall sat.

"I thought you were excited to meet new people? Not from our little valley, or at least, that's what your brother said."

Grace glimpsed at her friend, whose cheeks were colored from embarrassment.

"I did not say that."

"No? Well, you must forgive me. I never took Logan for a liar."

Logan Scott was good friends with Dr. Hall, had been for years, and it was obvious that he was teasing Arabella. Unfortunately, she seemed more affected than she should.

"Well, perhaps I said something similar to that."

"Oh, was it something similar?"

"Yes, but you must know I didn't mean you. You're practically a Glaswegian at this point and I'm very grateful to have such a close friend to oversee our stay here. Particularly since you're already acquainted with society here."

Grace, who was always more eager to observe than to speak, particularly since Dr. Hall tried to cut her hopes in half several months earlier, noticed a small pulsating muscle at the back of his jaw. Something Arabella had said annoyed him.

"Yes, well, I'm not very good company when it comes to society." He paused; his cool gaze lifted to Grace who stood just behind Arabella before refocusing his attention on her. "I find it distracting from my busy schedule."

Did he think Grace wouldn't take her studying seriously? She frowned, just as Penguin's little black and white form caught the corner of her vision. She made the smallest of sounds and instantly the cat came running toward her. When she glanced back at the doctor, he had an expression of disgust on his face.

Did he not like cats?

"Oh, but you must make yourself available to us once or twice. For introductions, and for, well, your own pleasure of course."

"I assure you, Miss Arabella, my pleasures are rarely found in the company of ballrooms or theaters."

"Where can they be found then, Dr. Hall?" Grace asked.

For a moment, no one spoke. Arabella looked expectantly at the good doctor, who seemed irritated by Grace's question. He was practically glaring at her, although she could have sworn for a moment she saw something in his eyes. Something primitive.

He opened his mouth as if to answer, when Aunt Belle suddenly appeared in the doorway.

"Ah, there you are, Dr. Hall. Come, I believe I've been feeling somewhat feverish since my arrival."

The doctor stood and made his way toward her, as Grace followed.

"Have you? Why didn't you mention it to me?"

"Because, my dear, as brilliant as you are, Dr. Hall is still a doctor and you are a student."

Grace didn't like her answer, but then she really didn't like the condescending smirk that flashed across Dr. Hall's face before disappearing.

She took a step forward.

"You still should have told me."

"And what would you have done for her, Miss Sharpe?" Dr. Hall asked.

"I, I would have checked to see if she was warm and if she was, I would have sent her to rest."

"Nothing else?"

Grace looked back and forth between her aunt and the doctor before realizing that this was exactly how Dr. Barkley spoke to her when she would visit with him to see patients that were too sick to come into his office for a visit.

Diagnosis was her specialty.

"Yes, and observe her for twenty-four hours."

"You wouldn't use Walburg Tincture?"

Grace's eyes widened. She knew of the secret fever tincture, and had learned about it in one of Dr. Barkley's letters with the German doctor and she had discussed it with him at length. She really shouldn't be so surprised that Dr. Hall knew about it, but rarely did she discuss medical knowledge with anyone except for her former mentor.

"No, as Walburg Tincture is really more for tropical fevers. Besides, since Dr. Walburg refuses to disclose what is in his tincture, it's deemed unreliable here in the United Kingdom and wouldn't be a viable treatment, especially without having first made a complete list of symptoms the patient would be exhibiting."

The small jaw muscle twitched again, but this time Grace found that she rather enjoyed it. He was annoyed again, probably having expected her to fail his questioning and she took perverse pleasure in proving him wrong.

Without a word, he turned back to face Aunt Belle.

"When did you first experience feeling warm?"

"Just before we arrived," she said, her voice oddly pleased. "But as I've likely overdone it with traveling and rearranging my study into a bedchamber—"

"I beg your pardon?"

"—why don't you stay for luncheon? Then we might have a better idea of what the next few months may bring."

"Ah, while I appreciate the offer—"

"It is not an offer, Dr. Hall," Lady Belle said with an authority that would grate every Scotsman's nerve. "Come. Mrs. Stevens has informed me that they'll be serving momentarily. And Grace, I should advise you that your Penguin will not be permitted in the dining room during meal times."

Dr. Hall turned.

"Your what?"

"My cat. His name is Penguin."

"Mr. Penguin," Arabella added, though for some reason the

added mister made Grace feel like a child in front of this very real, professional man.

"I see."

With a lightness of foot that seemed to only appear when she was feeling delighted about something, Aunt Belle turned and left, leading the way to the dining room. As it was informal, they followed her, one by one, into a brightly painted room at the front of the house. Yellow walls, paintings of flowers, and lace-covered windows met them, causing Grace to frown. Why was each room so different in style? It was as if two completely different people had lived here and had divided up the rooms and decorated them to each other's tastes.

Grace and Dr. Hall both reached for the seat to Aunt Belle's right, just as they both pulled back.

"It's yours, of course," Dr. Hall said stiffly, pulling the chair out for Grace.

She bobbed her head in thanks, feeling Aunt Belle's eyes on her.

Once everyone was seated, the servants began to plate a various array of Scottish and English foods. To Grace's horror, she was served a slice of haggis, a food she had thankfully avoided in her two years since coming to Scotland. But now as it touched the other small groups of food on her plate, she felt her appetite disappear.

"Now, as you know, Dr. Hall, we've come to Glasgow for two reasons. One is so that Miss Arabella and my niece get the opportunity to mingle with society. It does not do well to keep such pretty, clever girls in the country, especially since they are the perfect age to make matches."

Dr. Hall stabbed a piece of chicken with his fork.

"I am no matchmaker, Lady Belle."

"Of course you're not, and we are not searching for one. We simply require your presence a few times. I am already well acquainted with the societal families in the city, but you know so many people, as patients and otherwise, that we would be grateful for your perspective."

"I suppose I may do what I can, but really. I'm not a very good judge of character," he said, focusing on Grace. "And I care very little for social gatherings."

Well, that was fine with her. She didn't like social gatherings either.

"Yes, so I've noticed. Now the second reason, and likely the more important of the two according to my niece, is Grace's education. She has been studying under Dr. Barkley for nearly a year, ever since we returned from Italy last winter."

"Yes, I know."

"And it was very gracious of you to allow her to continue her apprenticeship under your guidance, and try as I might to understand Dr. Barkley and my niece, I'm afraid I can't quite comprehend how this apprenticeship will lead to her being crowned a doctor."

"No one will be crowned, Aunt Belle," Grace said. "And I've told you at least three times about the Apothecary Act."

"Yes, but will that not make you some sort of barber surgeon?"

Grace opened her mouth to reiterate the terms of her apprenticeship, when Dr. Hall suddenly spoke up.

"Under the Apothecary Act of 1815, a person is required to train for a period of five years, under the instruction of a licensed physician. They are required to learn everything they can about anatomy, botany, chemistry, psyche, *materia medica*, and finish with a six-month residence at a hospital. If they can complete their apprenticeship, they will be given a license to practice medicine, under the Society of Apothecaries." He paused, his cool eyes scanning each of them. "It is an aging practice, one that will hopefully be fully replaced by the earning of medical degrees through university in the next decade or so, but as Parliament has yet to pass legislation, it is the only way a woman can achieve the title doctor, as the fairer sex is not permitted in such schools."

"Yet, Dr. Hall," Belle said with a little wiggle of her head.

"The fairer sex is not permitted, yet."

For the third time that day, Grace noted his jaw twitch. He really did not like that he had been forced into this position and while Grace was sympathetic to him, aware of what being forced to do something one didn't wish to do was like, she couldn't find it in her heart to regret it. If Dr. Hall had been bullied into this role, she would simply have to prove to him that it wasn't a bad idea. That she was a studious pupil who didn't take hard work lightly.

"Of course," Dr. Hall said after a moment's pause.

"What a dear you are to take my Grace under your wing," Aunt Belle said, patting him on the hand. "I trust I could count on you to see to it that Grace is used to her full potential."

Grace coughed into her napkin at her aunt's words. Surely she could hear how bad that sounded? Thankfully, no one seemed to notice.

"But I'm afraid I will not be a very gracious teacher," Dr. Hall said as the tops of her cheekbones turned a shade of red. Aunt Belle frowned. "I take my work seriously and my patients are the most important people. I will require your niece to put this work above all else, including her social life."

"I will not have any trouble with that, Dr. Hall," Grace said, leaning forward. "I am here to learn."

"But only because I allow it," Aunt Belle interrupted. "And you will participate in society if you wish to continue your studies. That is the stipulation that you agreed to, is it not?"

Grace frowned.

"Yes, Aunt Belle."

"Come, do not sound so miserable about it. You will thank me one day for forcing this." She turned to Hall. "I daresay you both might benefit from this little arrangement."

Dr. Hall smiled, but it was not genuine. How Grace knew, she wasn't sure, but his contempt was written all over his face. She hoped he wouldn't let his dislike for her or their situation spill over into her apprenticeship, but then she remembered what Mrs.

Fletcher had told her. That as boorish as her nephew could be, Dr. James Hall was truly devoted to his craft and wouldn't allow his dislike for a situation to color what needed to be done. After all, Grace was going to be known throughout the city as Dr. Hall's apprentice and that alone would cause the doctor a good amount of pressure to make sure her tenure was successful. At the least, Grace didn't have to worry about being sabotaged.

"Dr. Barkley mentioned that you were handy with a scalpel," he asked, breaking her from her thoughts.

"Yes. I've a talent for it."

"My dear, do not sound so sure of yourself. It is unbecoming."

"On the contrary," Dr. Hall stated. "Surgeons should have an unwavering confidence in themselves and their abilities. Do you, Miss Sharpe?"

"Yes. I do."

Dr. Hall's gaze lingered on her face for a moment before he nodded.

"Very good. But I assume you've only ever used your skills to drain infected wounds? Not assisting in amputations?"

"Oh goodness," Arabella said queasily, bringing her napkin to cover her mouth.

"Dr. Hall, please," Aunt Belle hissed.

Grace leaned forward, excited.

"Have you attended many amputations?"

"A few."

"Oh goodness," Arabella said again, standing up. "I don't think I can hear any more."

"Really, Grace. Dr. Hall, while at this dining room table, I refuse to hear such discussion. Save it for your rounds."

"But that's next week," Grace pouted, unable to help herself. She was so interested in what he was talking about.

"I'm sure Dr. Hall wouldn't mind having you a few days early. Isn't that right, Dr. Hall?"

Although it was difficult to see his color change due to his beard, Grace noticed the bridge of his nose change several shades before answering.

"I don't know if that's such a good idea."

"Oh, posh. Grace is desperate to start."

"Tomorrow is the day I make rounds in the East End, near Gallowgate."

Aunt Belle's eyes widened slightly as she watched Dr. Hall.

"Oh. I see. Well then, perhaps next week is better. It will allow her to settle into her place here."

"I can go to Gallowgate," Grace said earnestly.

"Gallowgate is a slum. It is overcrowded, dirty, and dangerous." He shook his head. "It's not a place for gentle born ladies."

Grace placed her fork on the table with deliberate slowness before glancing up.

"Is it a place for a doctor?"

"Grace, if Dr. Hall believes it is too dangerous, then perhaps you should wait."

"Is it a place for a doctor?" she repeated. Dr. Hall's lips pressed together, seemingly unwilling to answer, but his silence spoke volumes. "Then it is a place for me."

"Very well," he said, standing up. "But I won't have you robbed. Wear your plainest gown. Or if there is a servant here who has something dark you might wear, perhaps that. No adornments, jewels, pins, or otherwise. You'll wear your hair back and covered. Hopefully you'll be mistaken for a woman of faith, so at least they'll leave you be. Do you understand?"

"Yes."

"Won't she be safe with you, Dr. Hall?" Arabella asked.

He looked at Grace.

"Aye. But we shan't be too careful. Until tomorrow, Miss Sharpe. Be ready first thing in the morning."

"Yes, doctor," she said. Then he was gone. Grace glanced at her aunt, who had a confused expression on her face. "Aunt Belle? Are you well?"

"Hm? Oh yes, dear, it's just that..." But she didn't explain.

Instead, she shook her head and forced a smile that didn't reach her eyes. She leaned toward her niece. "Be careful tomorrow, Grace. I'd hate to think… Of what could happen—"

"Have no fear, Aunt Belle. I'm more aware of the world than most women in my position. Besides," she said, glancing at the doorway where the doctor disappeared. "Dr. Hall will protect me if anything untoward should happen. I have full faith in him."

"So do I," Arabella said with a definitive nod. "There's not a better man in all of Scotland for our Grace."

Chapter Three

IT HAD TAKEN James all of two minutes from leaving Lady Belle's home yesterday to come up with a plan to scare Grace into reconsidering her apprenticeship with him. Gallowgate was not only one of the poorest neighborhoods in Glasgow, but one rife with disease. Crooks, thieves, women of ill repute, and more had descended on that part of the city; well, not so much descended on as had been forced there. It was one thing to be a country doctor, who took care of expectant mothers and fevers and farming accidents. It was another thing entirely to come to a city, teeming with sickness and the morally depraved. The Gallowgate barracks, for instance, were overpopulated and crowded, with dozens of "sporting women" moving in and out of their own volition.

Usually, James wouldn't have even considered bringing a lady like Grace to a place so dangerous, but he had an idea. If he could scare her enough to the point where she would admit that this work was too much for her, he might be able to avoid teaching her altogether.

But when he arrived at her house just as the sun was rising the next morning, he found a determined, if not a sleepy looking Grace, waiting for him. She was dressed in a faded black gown that covered her from toe to neck. Her hair was parted down the middle and pulled back, and a lace bonnet covered the ball of hair at the back of her head.

She appeared as severe as well as someone so eager, and

James found himself unwittingly embarrassed by the determination in her eyes.

"Good morning, Miss Sharpe," he said as he climbed out of the hackney.

He held the door open as she climbed in and he waved to Mrs. Stevens, who grimaced at him before turning back in through the doorway.

"Good morning, Dr. Hall," Grace said as he settled back across the hired hackney from her, the scent of cool, crisp mint distracting him for a moment. "I trust that I've dressed to an acceptable standard?"

He tried to push the pleasant aroma out of his mind. Mint, in particular water mint, was an herb that his Aunt Flora had always used in his teas. It reminded him of the mountain streams where he played as a boy, but this wasn't the time or place to reminisce. Instead, he focused on answering her question.

"Yes, you have."

Seemingly pleased, she sat with her back pin straight as the hackney made its way through the city. They rode mostly in silence and while they rarely caught one another's eye, James couldn't help but glance at her from time to time, wondering why she seemed so calm. Remembering his first visit to Gallowgate, he had been rather nervous. He had only been in Glasgow a day before Dr. Barkley insisted that they visit all of the slums of the city, every day, to drive home his belief that the study of medicine was the study of humanity. He had been particularly philosophical ten years ago, when he had taught James and though they had some healthy debates on the practice of medicine, the reason for practicing never wavered. It was to help their fellow man, regardless of their lot in life.

He stared at Grace as the fringe from her wrap shook as they drove over cobblestone.

"May I ask you something, Miss Sharpe?"

She stared directly at him.

"Yes, Dr. Hall."

"Why do you want to be a doctor?"

Apparently, that had been unexpected as she blinked at him before glancing away.

"Dr. Hall, I appreciate that you do not think I know my own mind, but I assure you, I know what I want, and no amount of trying to convince me otherwise will be fruitful."

"I do not mean to talk you out of it. I simply wish to know your reasoning behind such a decision." She gave him a disbelieving expression. "You could be a nurse. There are some brilliant nurses who do your gender a justice."

That was perhaps the wrong thing to say, as Grace's mouth pressed into a flat line and she glanced back out the window before answering.

"Every and any argument you have about this is not new to me. There is nothing you could say that would make me miraculously change my mind. I have heard them all, dozens of times."

"But I asked you a question."

"Which you followed up with a suggestion, one you undoubtedly believe to be helpful. It just tells me that you're more interested in your own opinion than finding out anything about me." She shook her head. "If you don't want to know why I want to be a doctor, then I will not tell you. I've no desire defending myself for the next six months against your *helpful* suggestions."

James did not move, but instead stared at her. This was insubordinate behavior, to say the least, and if she were a man, he'd remove her from studying beneath him, yet it bothered him that she thought he didn't want to know her reason for becoming a professional woman.

She had to know it was abnormal. How many working women did she know? How many did *he* know? Very few and even then, it was always a topic of discussion.

Leaning forward, he rested his elbows on his knees and the movement caught her attention. How curious her eye color was, he mused for a moment. Were they amber? Hazel? He didn't know, but he cleared his throat before he spoke.

"Tell me. Why do you want to be a doctor?"

She stared at him for a moment and he was surprised that he was waiting to exhale before she sighed heavily.

"I want… No, I *can* help people," she said slowly, seemingly choosing her words carefully. "I have a mind for it. And what's more, it interests me. How some bodies react to illnesses, how others don't." Her brows cinched together as her eyes unfocused. "I've been very interested in the spread of fevers for as long as I can remember and I've been so sure that, if I could follow a sickness, somehow I could map it out and learn what is needed to prevent it or cure it." She shook her head. "I understand anatomy. Bones, muscles, skin. It's as plain to me as the English language and… I don't know… I feel it is a calling to help people. I can help people," she said again, her eyes meeting his once more. "I want to help my fellow man and I think I should be allowed to do so, particularly if I'm skilled enough."

Well, at the very least that was the answer he had hoped to hear, but as he watched her, he was momentarily lost. Her eyes were amber, he decided. Pulling out a small glass vial from his breast pocket, he opened it and placed his forefinger over the opening. Tipping it over, he made sure the pad of his finger was saturated before he dabbed the citrusy oil beneath his nose.

Grace stared at him curiously, but before she could ask what he was doing, he tipped the glass again, rubbed the oil between his forefinger and thumb and leaned forward. Without asking, he gently pinched Grace's top lip. She inhaled sharply, but she did not move. Instead, she remained perfectly still, her eyes completely focused on him. He swallowed hard.

"W-what is it?"

"It's to dampen the stench," he said as the hackney came to a stop. "I use it when I visit patients who aren't in the best of sorts. Decay can be a foul smell. Shall we?" he asked gruffly as he opened the door and climbed out, grabbing his large leather bag as he did so.

The pungent scent of rotting vegetables, mixed with other foul wastes, was magnified under the morning sun, but diluted somewhat by the lime oil he had rubbed beneath his nostrils. Their first stop was the tenant housing for the factory workers' family. What had initially been a clever idea for cheap housing had exploded into quarters too tight to house whole families. It was a breeding ground for illnesses.

Grace's hand touched James's forearm as she exited the hackney. It was inconsequential, really. He hadn't even realized that he had held his arm up for her, but then she removed her hand and he felt suddenly untethered, as if he was just about to have a cup of perfectly made tea and then dropped it on the floor without sampling a drop.

It was most puzzling, but then he didn't have time to wonder about it. Reactions were human, after all, and she was about to have a number of them once they entered into the building.

Even though it was early, nearly all the men had already left for their factory jobs, save a few who were ill or injured. Grace was silent as she followed James into the building and directly to the first door. He knocked.

A woman, not much older than Grace, who was holding two screaming babies that appeared to be twins, opened the door. Another child, a boy, hugged the woman's legs.

"Good morning, Mrs. Monty," James said. "How are you?"

"It's the bairns. They've both got fevers and were up all night. Poor Mr. Monty barely got a wink of sleep."

"Let me see one," James said. "Miss Sharpe, take the other."

But the woman, who readily handed off one red-headed child to James, twisted away from Grace as her small son scurried across the room, dropping to his knees beneath the window where a number of small pieces of rubbish were lined neatly against the wall.

"Who's she?" Mrs. Monty asked.

"She's my assistant for the day."

"Assistant? A woman? Like Mrs. Muller?"

"Who is Mrs. Muller?" Grace asked.

"She's an elderly woman, one of the workers' mothers. She acts as a sort of nurse in our absence."

"*Our?*" Mrs. Monty repeated. "Wot you mean our?"

James glanced at Grace, who had a clear, impassive face.

"Miss Sharpe is studying to become a doctor and she is quite good with fevers. I'd let her see your bairn if you want Mr. Monty to get any sleep tonight."

Although visibly hesitating, Mrs. Monty handed over the baby, who wailed even harder having been placed in a stranger's arms. To her credit, however, Grace appeared unfazed as she laid the child down on the only small mattress in the corner of the room. The little boy stood up from the floor and reached out his hand to her.

"What do you have there?" she asked gently as he dropped a small, cone shaped piece of wood with a rusty nail in it.

"It's a spinner."

"Is it?" she said, inspecting the roughly made top toy. She held it up so that James could see. "Impressive little toymaker, isn't he?"

"I didn't make it," the boy said.

"Charlie, stop it. Let the woman work," Mrs. Monty scolded as the boy went back to his makeshift treasures.

"Are there any rashes? Has their diet changed?" Grace asked matter-of-factly as she lifted the nightgown.

"That one has little red spots on his back," the mother said, tension in her voice. "But the other one doesn't."

James and Grace immediately looked at one another. Blisters and a fever could be one of two things. Either it was varicella, a relatively harmless illness, or smallpox, a deadly sickness that could wipe out hundreds of people if allowed to spread.

"His back, you say?" James said, noting that one of the only few deciding factors was that smallpox showed up on the palms and soles of the patients. James bent over Grace who had the child on his stomach, pointing to a small cluster of spots. "Are there any on their hands and feet?"

"No," the mother said.

"Have there been other spots before these?" Grace asked.

"Yes, some on the legs, but they've disappeared a bit now."

Grace turned to James.

"It's likely varicella then. Smallpox lesions usually show up all altogether."

"Smallpox?" the mother repeated in a frantic hush. She reached for her baby, snatching her away from Grace. "My babies don't have smallpox."

"I know, I was just explaining—"

"You'll have us kicked out onto the street if you say that too loud." She glared at James. "Are you trying to get us booted from here, doctor?"

James lifted his hands, in an attempt to calm her down.

"It was a mistake, obviously, but the good news is the babies will likely just need rest for the next few days. I'll come back before next week to check on them, if you'd like."

The woman hesitated, her eyes on Grace.

"Alone, I should hope?"

He sighed.

"If you wish."

"Yes, please," she said pointedly.

James was quick to give her a tincture of chamomile.

"This is for the itching. Just dab a little on a clean cloth and wipe down the lesion."

"Yes. Thank you, doctor."

"You're welcome," he said, closing his bag and he made his way to the door.

Grace left first, and waited for him as the door closed.

"I didn't mean to say that out loud," she said. "I mean, I did, but I didn't know she could get in trouble."

"You'll have to learn to keep your voice down," James said as close to her ear as possible, ignoring the scent of sweet mint that seemed to cling to her. "These people are suspicious at best and hostile at their worst. An outbreak, even the suggestion of one, could see an entire family attacked or thrown out of their rooms."

"That's awful."

"It's a reality."

"Is there something we can do? Someplace they can go?"

"I fear the only place they can go is worse than here."

The misery in Grace's face was telling, but it wasn't something James had time for. There were at least ninety families that lived in the building and at least eighty required his attention.

"All right?"

"Yes," she said, shakily at first, but then firmly. "Yes."

"Good. Just remain quiet if you can. These people can be apprehensive."

Grace nodded again as another woman, a Mrs. Hader, waved James over.

"Wot's this?" she asked, staring at Grace. "A lady doctor?"

"Yes."

"Madness that is," she said, before crowding James. "Er, have you heard? Two more graves been dug up over near St. Mungo. They saying body snatchers be doing it, but I think something more sinister than that is going on."

"Is that so, Mrs. Hader?" James said, glancing back at Grace.

She tucked her head to the side as if to question what she was speaking about, but James gave her a small shake of his head. If either of them asked Mrs. Hader to elaborate, they'd be stuck in her rooms for half an hour.

After setting a dislocated finger, they went to the next room.

"A woman doctor? Are you mad?"

And that was the third time out of eighty-eight other times that James was questioned about Grace. It had started to aggravate him after the tenth time, enraged him around the twentieth, and made him aware of how exasperating it must be to be questioned constantly around the fortieth time. By the sixtieth, he realized that even with this small glimpse, he wouldn't ever actually understand how much Grace would have to put up with as a female in this profession.

Thankfully, Mrs. Muller had no such comment.

"'Bout time they start allowing us to be doctors." The elderly woman elbowed Grace as James restocked her medical cabinet with bandages, salves, and the like. "Having been doing all the work all along."

"I suppose," Grace mumbled, an oddly charming blush touching her cheeks.

She really must have heard every opinion a dozen times over since she started studying with Dr. Barkley. James himself knew at least a dozen doctors who wouldn't have stood for it and likely would have left the profession altogether if they were questioned as much as Grace already had been, and yet, still she was willing.

It was impressive. The tenacity of this woman with amber eyes made James thoughtful. After finishing up in the tenant building, they went next door to visit the barracks where they treated fourteen men with fevers, six with boils, and twenty-two who were suffering from various wasting diseases. One man actually lunged at Grace, who was quick to sidestep him, and then promptly scolded him for being a poor patient, much to the delight of the other soldiers. James had to restrain himself from grabbing the ill man, but he kept his composure and by the time he and Grace returned to the hackney, he was contemplative.

Why had he had such a visceral response toward her? Surely it was because she was the niece of someone who had been a patron of his since his youth, but a part of him wondered if that was completely true.

"You did well today. Better than I expected," he said as the sun set across the city.

Grace's tired eyes opened and she grinned, a genuine, exhausted grin. One he knew well, but seeing it on her made his heart begin to beat erratically.

He shifted in his seat.

"I mean it. You didn't let the inane questioning distract you from the tasks at hand. You were aware of your surroundings the whole time and correct in all your diagnoses."

"Thank you."

But he hadn't told her all this simply because he wanted her gratitude. He wanted her to know that she seemed far more capable than he had originally believed. But perhaps that would be insulting to hear and for the first time in a long time, James couldn't think of what to say to fill the silence.

Grace seemed unaffected and after he dropped her off at her house, he was consumed with the idea that he couldn't speak the usual nonsense he spoke with patients to fill long silences. But then, maybe she liked the quiet.

Peering out the hackney window as the night settled over the city, James tried to ignore the sudden wish to know everything Grace Sharpe was thinking.

※

Chapter Four

G RACE'S ENTIRE BODY ached the next morning as she woke. Stretching, she felt the low humming of Penguin's purring vibrating against her back. The pulls and twinges in her leg muscles, sore from having been on her feet all day. It was odd that she felt so tired, considering how much she used to walk in Glencoe and the surrounding area near Lismore Hall, but different activities made for different muscle groups and apparently standing without much movement otherwise disagreed with her.

Yesterday's visit to Gallowgate had certainly been eye opening, but Grace had come out of it reinvested. Never had she been surer about wanting to be a doctor in her entire life, and while it would certainly be difficult to gain the trust of the locals, she believed she was more than capable of doing so.

Whether Dr. Hall believed that or not, however, was still up for debate.

As Grace got up and dressed herself in a pale-peach morning gown, she wondered what Dr. Hall's impression of her was after yesterday. She hadn't let her emotions show on her face and was rather stoic after she made the mistake of mentioning smallpox to Mrs. Monty. But as far as assisting him, Grace thought she handled herself rather well. She was quick to aid him when he requested it, had set a broken finger, and tended to several cuts that were on the verge of becoming infected, and she had even managed to remove a boil off an elderly gentleman's foot, a task she had been quite proud of considering how efficient she was with a blade. She had even expected the doctor to comment on her talent, but he barely spoke the entire ride home.

Peering absentmindedly out her window as she brushed out her hair, Grace leaned against the large sill. Penguin jumped up, demanding scratches behind the ear, which Grace readily gave him just as her bedroom door opened behind her.

"Oh, my lady, come away from there," Mrs. Stevens said. "You mustn't be seen half dressed for all of Glasgow to gaze at."

Grace smirked.

"Half dressed? I'm completely dressed, except for my shoes, but those below cannot see my feet from this angle, can they?"

"Your hair is down."

Grace twirled her fingers around the medium brown curls that framed her face and shoulders.

"So, it is. But that hardly makes one undressed."

"It's not done. Not in polite society, as I'm sure you know. Now come along, and sit. You've more hair than most English ladies I've managed."

Grace pushed herself off the wall and walked to the vanity table where a small silk cover chair sat before it. Sitting promptly, she tilted her head back.

"What do you mean, I have more hair than most English ladies?"

"'Tis a known fact that English ladies have verra fine hair, in both weight and texture. But this," she emphasized, lifting a strand of Grace's hair so that she could see it reflecting in the mirror. "This is thick and proper. Might you be a touch Scottish or something else?"

Grace laughed.

"I don't believe so. My father was an earl, and as English as they come. My mother too."

Mrs. Stevens shook her head.

"Ah, well, there's something about you. Something not entirely tame."

"Tame? How do you mean?"

Mrs. Stevens began to section Grace's hair into pieces, as she twisted and braided the wild hair into a style rather becoming as of late.

"Perhaps tame isn't the best word, but I can't think of a better one. But you are strange. This profession of yours, a woman in medicine… It is odd."

"Yes, I know, women shouldn't work in professions such as medicine—"

"Ack, no. Just the opposite. There was a woman in my village, before I came to Glasgow," Mrs. Stevens said, as she pinned Grace's hair up. "She knew every plant and flower under the sun. She could make your insides turn or heal the worst of wounds, but she rarely ever left her little cottage in the woods." She shook her head. "I always thought her the cleverest of healers, but with modern medicine, there's nary a woman in sight. Yet that's who's been doing the healing forever." She paused and bent down, just over Grace's shoulder to see her work in the mirror. "But she was a bit wild too. Untamed. You remind me of her."

Grace smiled, unsure how to receive such a compliment that might insult someone with a more refined attitude.

"She sounds like a lady I know in Glencoe. Mrs. Fletcher. Locals call her a witch."

"Bah, country folk are always more skeptical than us refined city folk," Mrs. Stevens said, puffing out her chest, and Grace had to bite the inside of her cheek to refrain from giggling. "Come, breakfast is nearly ready. You too, Penguin," she whistled at the cat. "You're on kitchen duty this morning."

Grace slipped on her shoes and left her room, following Mrs. Stevens as she did. When she reached the dining room, however, she was surprised to see her aunt and Arabella, hunched toward one another like a pair of school children.

They were never up this early.

"Good morning," Grace said as she entered the room, causing the two to bounce back, each sitting straight up now that Grace was there. She paused. "Is everything all right?"

"Of course it is," Aunt Belle said, tapping her cane on the wooden floor twice. "Come, sit next to me and tell me everything about yesterday."

"Yes, you were up and gone before either of us were awake," Arabella started. "And then home after supper."

"Is this how it is to be your entire time studying with Dr. Hall?"

"I'm not sure," Grace answered honestly as a servant plated her food, a mix of cooked eggs, smoked fish, and a scone. "But I doubt it. I'll likely be in his office during his hours of operation. The Gallowgate visit was just a monthly visit."

"I should hope so," Aunt Belle said. "Either way, that is why Arabella and I have decided to be up early now, should it be the only time we get to see you during your apprenticeship days."

"It is very kind of the doctor to visit the poor," Arabella said, before leaning forward. "What was it like? Visiting a tenement house?"

Tenement housing had once sought to fix the issue of housing for the poor and working class, but as the industrial expansion exploded across the United Kingdom, those meager rooms had been overcrowded, leading to slums. The knowledge of tenement housing was often used to scare country folk from moving away from their farms to seek their fortunes elsewhere.

"It was not pleasant," Grace said honestly. "But I'm sure we did some good on our visit. Dr. Hall and I, that is."

Arabella leaned back and glanced at Aunt Belle.

"What a brave thing to do. Dr. Hall truly is one of the finest gentlemen ever to be known, I'm sure of it."

Grace smiled, although a small, insignificant part of her didn't quite agree. Yes, Dr. Hall was a fine doctor, and it was kind of him to volunteer his time to the less fortunate, but wasn't it expected of doctors to behave so?

"A better man I've not met," Aunt Belle said, a sound of reverence in her voice. "Don't you think so, Grace?"

She began buttering a piece of toast, without lifting her gaze.

"I suppose."

Silence.

"You suppose?" Arabella repeated. "Oh, but surely after working with him, you can attest to his kindness? Particularly with helping the poverty-stricken."

Grace's brows lifted.

"I saw no difference between Dr. Hall's handling of the sick than Dr. Barkley's. Efficient, compassionate, yes, but these are expected attributes of a doctor. He is no better or worse than any other in his profession."

Grace took a bite of her toast and only noticed that neither were speaking after a moment. Her jaw stopped chewing as she lifted her gaze and saw both women staring at her.

She swallowed.

"What? What is it?"

"Nothing, dear," Aunt Belle said, shaking her head as if to dispel the silence. "If you do not find the doctor interesting, far be it from us to try and tell you otherwise."

"I didn't say I didn't find him interesting."

"So, you do?"

"Do what?"

"Find the doctor interesting?" Arabella asked.

Grace frowned before applying a smear of jam to her half-eaten toast. These two were acting very peculiar this morning.

"I suppose."

Although she had answered, Grace knew neither were satisfied by her answer, but she couldn't begin to understand why not. Still, the moment passed and believing the topic of Dr. Hall behind them, Grace opened her mouth to speak when her aunt spoke.

"It's just, it truly is a wonder that the doctor has recovered so, after what happened to him last year."

Grace's toast paused midair as she looked at her aunt.

"What happened to him?"

"Hm? Oh, nothing, dear. It's not for you to worry about."

"Oh, but, Lady Belle, you must tell us now," Arabella said.

Aunt Belle took a deep breath and waited to exhale as both Arabella and Grace waited for her to speak. It was one of Belle's favorite things, to be the center of attention, but being the clever woman she was, she was always sure to make it clear that she loathed gossip, when in truth, nothing brought her more joy.

"Well, I suppose I should tell you, although I do not condone gossip," she said, nodding at each of them.

Grace's brow lifted in question, but a sharp glare from her aunt told her to remain quiet. Instead, Grace just smirked.

"I hope bad fortune hasn't befallen the doctor," Arabella said.

"Well, whether it was good or bad, is still to be determined. But it was rather devastating."

"What was?"

"The throw over."

Arabella's eyes went wide.

"Did someone throw over Dr. Hall?" she asked. "But how could someone do that? He is so clever and kind and handsome."

"Yes, I regret to say that Dr. Hall was once engaged."

"I—pardon me," Grace said, fixating on Arabella. "You think the doctor is handsome?"

Arabella's cheeks turned pink.

"Well, of course. Who doesn't? It's well-spoken of in Glencoe, that he's the most handsome man in the Highlands, although I'm not a fan of beards."

"Yes, the beard does hide a bit of his face," Aunt Belle said. "But we cannot fault him for it."

Grace wholeheartedly disagreed. Dr. Hall's neatly trimmed beard was rather distinguished. The sharp angle of it, especially beneath his chin seemed to accentuate a jawline that anyone might find attractive.

If they thought of the doctor in such a way, which thankfully, Grace did not. But it was surprising to hear that he had been engaged.

"Dr. Hall's aunt, Mrs. Fletcher, once told me that her nephew was incapable of being in a relationship," Grace said.

It was a fact that Grace had believed wholeheartedly. Heck, it was the entire reason why she had sought him out as a replacement to her tenure with Dr. Barkley, because he viewed the entire idea of romantic coupling as a symptom of society, a manifestation of pack living. Or at least, he was supposed to. He was supposed to be incapable of romantic relationships, like she was. It's what had solidified her decision to study beneath him.

This, however, changed everything.

"Well, now, why would Mrs. Fletcher say that?" Arabella asked.

Aunt Belle shrugged.

"I do not know. Perhaps she believed that being thrown over broke her nephew's heart."

Grace's brow creased. Dr. Hall had never once acted like a man with a broken heart, but that didn't matter. She wanted to know about this being thrown over business.

"Well?" she asked. "What happened?"

Aunt Belle, who always enjoyed a little flair, peeked to her left and then her right, as if a dozen or so gossip columnists were standing just behind her. Grace managed not to roll her eyes, and instead inched closer, interested to hear what she had to say.

"It was well known that Dr. Hall was engaged this time last year, to one Miss Catriona Ward, daughter of Douglas Ward. All of Glasgow had been invited to the wedding."

"Wait, *Sir* Douglas Ward?" Grace blurted out. "The surgeon?"

"Who is he?" Arabella piped up. "I've never heard of him."

"He's a brilliant man. Absolutely brilliant. You know, it was he who discovered the difference between sensory nerves and motor nerves in the spinal cord. There's even a condition named after him, when there's a unilateral idiopathic paralysis of facial muscles due to a lesion of the facial nerve."

Arabella blinked, then faced Belle.

"Who is he?" she asked again.

"A very well to do member of Glasgow society." Arabella bobbed her head up and down. "He was knighted for his advances in medicine and as he only had one child, a daughter, he made sure to have her educated far beyond your average subjects. To be sure, she was just as brilliant as her father. There was talk of sending her to Andersen's University because she supposedly possessed the same mind as her father and with his backing, it would have happened."

Grace frowned, unsure she wished to hear the rest of the story all of a sudden.

"What happened?"

"Well, she and Dr. Hall had been acquainted for several years, as Dr. Hall was once a student of Dr. Ward. They were engaged after a lengthy courtship and all seemed well and good, until…"

Arabella leaned forward.

"Until what?"

Aunt Belle's face scrunched to the side as she shook her head.

"It really is a bitter thing, but on the morning of the wedding, while everyone was waiting inside the church, including Dr. Hall, it was discovered that Miss Ward had disappeared."

"Disappeared?"

"Was she kidnapped?"

"Or run away?"

"The latter, I'm afraid. It turns out that she had been carrying on with an Englishman, a peer she had met while on holiday in Cornwall the year before. Supposedly he had shown up the night before the wedding and they ran away, never to be seen or heard from again."

"Oh, my, that's awful," Arabella said. "What a vicious thing to do."

But Grace could not think of anything to say. It truly was a vile thing to happen to someone, but then she remembered her own dalliance, two years prior, that had ruined a near marriage.

It wasn't as if she had ever intended to do what she did. Grace loathed Lord Bartley and had been quite vocal about her dislike after he had ridiculed her once for reading about sciences when the female brain was too delicate an organ for such a task. He had called her efforts to study Sisyphean, and what's worse, he had proposed to Grace's dearest friend, Lady Natalie Hawkins, who had been less than enthusiastic about the match, but had accepted due to pressures from her grandparents, the Duke and Duchess of Spotsmore.

"You cannot marry him. He is a toad," Grace recalled saying to Natalie only a week before that fateful night that had changed the course of her and her sisters' lives forever. "He's awful."

"I don't have much of a choice, Grace. Grandpapa has already decided it and my grandmama is picking out veils." Natalie had dabbed a kerchief to her eye. "Perhaps it will not be so terrible. He does prefer the country and we've discussed at length my love for the city. Perhaps we will simply live separately."

"There must be something that can be done."

"Short of publicly disparaging me, I don't see any way around it."

Grace shook her head, trying to dispel the memory from her mind. Yes. She knew the wreckage of a marriage undone and while she was sympathetic to Dr. Hall, a small part of her wondered if perhaps it had been for the best. If the lady didn't want to marry him, surely he was better off without her.

Wasn't he?

"Are you all right, my dear?" Aunt Belle asked, causing Grace to look up. Her aunt was watching her with a thoughtful expression.

"Yes, of course. I just… That's a very unfortunate thing to have happened to Dr. Hall."

"Isn't it?"

"Yes, but then there is the philosophy that everything happens for a reason," Belle continued. "Some things are better left unsaid and some things are better left undone. Isn't that right, my dear?"

Grace nodded, though she had the strangest feeling that Aunt Belle was trying to tell her something specific.

"Well, come, let's not discuss the misfortunes of a good man," Arabella said, changing the subject. "Let's instead talk about the ball being held by the Viscount of Collimore. I've heard they throw the most lavish of parties."

"That is true, although the viscountess can be rather dated in her dresses. I believe she found a particular style that complemented her form and has refused to change it for some thirty years," Belle said. "Now, I prefer these new styles. Wider skirts lend to the appearance of a smaller waist." She winked. "Even when that's not the case."

Grace smiled, allowing her spirits to lift as the topic changed from Dr. Hall to the opera that would be in town the following month. Musicals were one of Grace's most pleasing pleasures and while she wasn't at all talented at any instrument, she did enjoy listening to them. Thus, she was quite excited to learn that she would be attending the opera.

"In the meantime, Grace will start her formal training at the start of next week," Belle said, once more dictating the conversation. "And while I know it will take several months, I wanted to present you with something."

Belle raised one of her bejeweled wrists to signal for Andrews to come forward. Removing a small cream-colored velvet pouch from his pocket, he presented it to Belle.

"My lady."

"Thank you, Andrews," she said, picking it up. "Now my parents weren't very good at giving presents and so your grandmother and I were raised outside the idea. However, as I grew older, I've come to realize that giving gifts is one of my favorite activities. So, know that this is just as much a pleasure for me as it is for you."

Aunt Belle handed Grace the small bag. For a moment, she worried that it might be some sort of jewelry as Belle was known to have an extensive collection and Grace wouldn't be able to enjoy it as she had been told by Dr. Hall that she wasn't to wear any adornments. Turning the bag upside down, a small, golden tube fell into her hand. It was a pendant of sorts, though of what, Grace couldn't decipher. Thin, shallow marks had been carved into the sides, creating a delicate, cross stitch sort of pattern.

"It's lovely," she said, unsure.

"My dear, open it."

Grace glanced up, confused, before bringing her other hand toward it. Twisting and pulling, she was met with little resistance as the top popped off to reveal a pen.

"It's a propeller pencil. One I'm sure you'll need for your notes."

Grace's mouth fell open at the thoughtful gift. It was exactly what she needed and it would keep her from losing her pencils. Glancing up, she had to blink back the tears, as she was touched. Aunt Belle was truly supportive of her choice.

Standing, she moved around the corner of the table and bent down to hug her aunt.

"Thank you, so very much."

"Oh, well then." Belle patted her uncomfortably on the shoulder. "Come now, there's no need for that."

"There is though," Grace said, pulling back. "I'm so very grateful for you, Aunt Belle. I think I don't deserve you, but I'm so happy I have you."

The hint of a sparkle shone in the elderly woman's eyes as she blinked several times.

"Stop that, my dear. There's no need for such a display of emotion. You may keep it on that pretty chain Miss Fletcher gifted to you before you left Glencoe."

Grace blinked as her hand rose to her clavicle. The elegant, silver chain that Mrs. Fletcher had given her was not visible, for she wore it beneath the shirt of her dress, but she had not taken it off since she received it.

"You know about that?"

"My dear, I know everything. Now. When shall we go to the

modiste?"

Grace let out a watery laugh and sat back down, happy to discuss whatever trivial topics Belle had to speak of and she only let her mind wander back to Dr. Hall after a full ten minutes of discussing fabric. Surely she would not ask him about his previous relationship, but a part of her was suddenly very interested in his past.

Very interested indeed.

✦

Chapter Five

"FIVE DISAPPEARANCES IN this locale in the last month!"

A paperboy's voice called out, bouncing off the brick buildings that lined the cobblestone street that led to Dr. Hall's office. The rain from the night before had stopped sometime during breakfast and the cool autumn sky had cleared, revealing a rare pale blue that was often not visible from within the city. In recent years, the air in town had become heavier and James often noted the way his lungs seemed to feel weighed down whenever he returned from his visits in the Highlands.

It was rather humorous, he noted, even as he unlocked the black door of his office. To catch himself longing for the wide-open spaces and brutal landscape of his birth. As a child and young man, James had done little else but dream of the world at large, planning and plotting his escape from the unnerving calm and boredom that he had experienced as a child.

Not that he didn't appreciate growing up there. His aunt had never been cruel or unloving. Quite the opposite, in fact. James had never wondered about her affection for him, but she was an eccentric and with little money and no prospects, James had very nearly fallen into some menial job that would have him trapped in Glencoe all his life had it not been for Dr. Barkley.

A tiny bell above the door jingled as he closed it behind him and shrugged off his coat. He entered the spacious, long office and storefront with his usual vigor for work. At the front of the store, on either side of him as he walked through, were two glass display cases, under which a number of medicines and herbal remedies were meticulously marked with what they were for and tagged with the price. Behind the display cases were glossy black shelves, lined with medical books, glass cloches covering all sorts of things, and jars filled with dry herbs for James to work with. The ceiling above was covered with tin ceiling tiles that continued into the next space, an examining room, where James hung his coat on a metal hook.

A small wooden desk with a lamp on it sat in the corner of the room, in front of yet another bookcase that was stuffed completely with envelopes and papers. These were his patients' charts, of which he kept a record to judge which medicines worked for certain ailments, as well as the progress of his treatments. An examining table, that was really more of a cot on high metal legs, stood in the middle of the room, with a folded wool blanket on top. There was also a woodstove with a teakettle and a water basin stand.

It was a humble office, but one James took great pride in. Not only was it clean, but it was all his and of all the things in Glasgow that he loved, this office reigned above all else.

The small bell jingled once more and James was sure it was Virgil, his assistant and shopkeeper.

"Good morning, Virgil," James said loudly without peering out of his office as he bent over his desk to read the schedule. He had several patients coming today as well as a meeting with the Chief Constable of the Glasgow Police, Franklin Murphy, first thing that morning. "I'm in here."

"So you are," a familiar feminine voice spoke, sending a tingling sensation down his spine.

James immediately stood, forcing down whatever visceral reaction he seemed to have whenever Grace Sharpe was near him, and stalked out of the office.

"Miss Sharpe," James said, not at all pleased with how grave he sounded. He pulled out a small silver pocket watch he kept in his vest pocket. Glancing at it, he spoke. "You're not due here for another several hours."

"Yes, I know," she said as she began to peel off her kid gloves, before untying the silk ribbon that held her bonnet in place. She removed it, and James was appalled to be seized with another sensation.

Pleasure. Pleasure at seeing her shining eyes and pink cheeks, highlighted by the curls of her dark hair that were piled atop her head. But he couldn't fathom as to why he should find pleasure in the way she appeared?

He blinked. Then cleared his throat.

"You know and so you disregard our set appointment time?"

"Well, now, I was thinking about it last night, and it seemed rather silly of me to wait until noon to come to this office. I know that I'm to be here every other day bright and early, and honestly," she continued as she moved past him into the office. "I couldn't take yet another conversation about balls and soirées and the like over breakfast, so I decided to come early and provide whatever services I can. Goodness," she cooed, looking around the office. "This is lovely."

James had to exhale slowly, ignoring the flutter of pride he felt at her last statement. Not only was he far and away not interested in her services, but he had specifically requested she come at noon to avoid meeting with the constable. The last thing James needed was the Glasgow Police to undermine him because he had a female doctor shadowing him.

"Miss Sharpe, I don't need your assistance this morning, so if you would please."

He held his arm out straight toward the door, but Grace ignored him completely, instead tapping the schedule on his desk with her index finger.

"You've a number of patients coming in only a short time. Surely I can do something."

"Miss Sharpe—"

Ring-a-ling!

Both James and Grace turned to peer out of the office doorway and see a young man with a limp enter. Virgil.

"Good morning, doctor!" the young man called out. "I see you've beaten me here this morning. Very well, but you shan't win tomorrow! I've a plan, you see, foolproof to make sure that I… Oh," he said, as the young man's eyes widened to see Grace. "I didn't know you was seeing patients already."

"Miss Sharpe is not a patient," James said, annoyed. "She's the one I told you about."

Virgil's blue eyes shone with excitement.

"Oh! The lady doctor! How fascinating!" he said as he hobbled forward with an outstretched hand. Grace nearly shook it before he pulled back and with an expression of shock, bent his head. "Pardon me, my lady. I forgot that, well, it's just that, I don't meet many proper, society types."

James watched as Grace bent down slightly and reaching for Virgil's hand, she shook it as she pulled him back up.

"Please do not stand on any formalities with me, Mr.?"

"Virgil. Just Virgil."

"Oh, well, just Virgil, I promise I'm not at all like what you've heard about society ladies. Unless you've heard that we're all brilliant."

Virgil laughed at the teasing, as did Grace while James rolled his eyes. Wonderful, he thought sarcastically. These two were going to get on swimmingly.

"Miss Sharpe, like I was saying, I've a very busy morning—"

"Which is why I'm here," she said, with a firm nod at him, before turning back to Virgil. "Would you be so kind as to show me around so that Dr. Hall can ready himself for his first patient?"

"Yes, my lady!"

"You may call me Grace. After all, I know your first name and we are to be colleagues."

Virgil actually blushed at her statement and James couldn't help but roll his eyes at the flattery. She really could be rather manipulative when she wanted to be.

"Very well, Miss Grace!" Virgil said, turning as he limped

toward one of the display cabinets. "Come, come."

James's mouth was pressed into a hard line as he turned his back on the two, seething for reasons he didn't understand. Why should Virgil be able to say her first name? And didn't she realize how ridiculous it was to call him a colleague?

A sensible voice in the back of his mind called out, telling him not to behave so boorishly, but he seemed unable to stop himself. Grace was charming and bubbly, far more so than James had ever witnessed her to be during social situations. When they were within her aunt's home, Grace was reserved and somewhat quiet, but she would transform when the topic of medicine was brought up. He had noticed it immediately and had smugly enjoyed being one of only a few people who could cause her eyes to light up as they did when the topic was touched upon.

Of course, that wasn't the only time she was talkative. She had also been quite chatty when her brothers-in-law, Graham and Logan, were around. And even during their trip to the rookery, she had appeared far more attentive to their patients than with James.

He should like to ask her why she was so much more welcoming with others at some point, but as the tiny bell above the door sounded again, all his curiosities about Grace were pushed out of his mind.

Chief Constable Murphy was a stout, older man with a round face and very little hair, that encircled the bottom half of his skull. He was a serious man who rarely laughed, but one who was even tempered and dedicated to his job.

Removing his top hat as he entered, James waited, watching as the man noticed not only Virgil but Grace, who both came out from behind the display case.

"Virgil," Constable Murphy said, though he kept his curious gaze on Grace. "And who might this young lady be?"

"Miss Grace Sharpe, sir," she said with a curtsy, which seemed to chafe the constable. "I'm a student of Dr. Hall's."

James took a step forward, disliking the term.

"Ah, I'm afraid student is an unfair word. Miss Sharpe had been studying medicine for over a year now with my mentor, Dr. Barkley in Glencoe."

"I see," the constable said, though he appeared unsure. "A lady doctor?"

James gave him a tight smile, annoyed at how often he was likely to hear the term lady doctor over the next six months. Surely, people would eventually just call her Dr. Sharpe.

Wouldn't they?

"Chief constable, if you would," James said, heading toward his office. "We can speak in private in my office."

"Ah, yes," he said with a short bow to Grace.

James waited for him to enter and closed the door behind him. Walking around the room, he sat at his desk as Murphy studied the brim of his hat. Curious that, as the constable was always more chatty than despondent.

Ever since joining the force as a police surgeon, James and the constable would meet twice a week to discuss certain cases. There were a handful of other doctors who worked for the police, albeit part time, to keep their practices running, just as James was doing, but he was often the first to be called on when a murder had taken place, as the police were now attempting not to move evidence before notes were taken at the crime scene.

At present, the most pressing issue was the disappearance of several persons. It was happening all over the city, but more concentratedly in impoverished areas and unfortunately, the police seemed to believe that these missing people were out getting drunk or runaways, despite their families saying otherwise. But so was the attitude toward the disadvantaged these days. There was an unspoken belief that the poor were somehow morally bankrupt and more likely to become drunks or recluses who abandoned their families, but James had met more people across the classes than anyone he knew and he could state beyond a reasonable doubt that status had little to do with morality.

"So?" James said after a moment. "How goes the Chatterley case?"

"Hm? Oh, yes, we were able to garner a confession out of the sister-in-law. Evidently, the husband had taken to bedding not only his wife and his wife's sister, but another mistress. It seems the sister-in-law didn't wish to share him anymore, but when he told her that he intended to go on just as he had, she killed him."

James nodded, having investigated the scene himself. It had been rather gruesome, as the man had been stabbed several times, but it was important to note that multiple stab wounds usually indicated some sort of rage behind the incident. James had marked several similar cases, all people murdered by a close family member or friend.

"Case closed then."

The constable glanced back at the closed door. James was sure that he was wondering about Grace.

"I assure you, Chief Constable, that whatever you're worried about, you needn't be. Miss Sharpe will not be attending me on police matters. I plan to keep her plenty busy in this office." James added quickly, "By having her tend to my patients, you see."

The constable tilted his head.

"I'm glad to hear it, because we have a new case and…" He hesitated, visibly disturbed, which was a rarity for someone like the constable, who had seen his fair share of evil happenings within the city for at least ten years. "It's a grisly situation."

"What's happened?"

"Do you remember the Flannery case? Over on Leafy Hyndland?"

James remembered, having only worked on it eight months prior. Mr. Flannery had been a well-to-do merchant who lived with his wife and two sons in a rather distinguished residence in Glasgow's west end.

"Yes. Mr. Flannery was found frozen to death on his front doorstep after a particularly vicious snowstorm." James shook his head. "I believe the investigation was led by Dr. Stewart, was it not?"

"Aye, it was."

"I read his report. Supposedly, Mr. Flannery had been drinking, quite extensively, and walked home that evening from his club. He had barely made it home when he must have fallen asleep and eventually died."

"That was the extent of it."

James shook his head.

"I'm sorry, but what does a closed case have to do with us this morning?"

"Well, there have been rumors circulating, rumors about Mr. Flannery's offspring. Apparently, the old man had threatened to cut off his ne'er-do-well sons for racking up bills and debts all over Scotland." The constable leaned closer. "I'll tell ya, it doesn't do well to spoil children. But supposedly, the sons had the idea to inherit their father's fortune before they were removed from the will, so they poisoned him."

James frowned.

"Poison? But there wasn't any evidence for that. And word of mouth is circumstantial."

"Therein lies the gruesome part. A gentleman friend of the deceased heard of the rumors and came to the station to suggest a, well, something ungodly, really."

"What?"

"He suggested that we exhume the body, so that one of you lot might do some tests, or something." The constable shook his head. "I shouldn't have even entertained the idea, but being who he is and all, I felt rather conflicted, you see."

A hard stone seemed to settle in James's throat. He knew who the constable was talking about without even asking.

"I presume you mean Sir Douglas Ward has requested the inquisition."

The constable bobbed his head.

"Aye."

"Perhaps Dr. Stewart would want to take the lead on this then? It was his case after all."

"Begging your pardon, but Sir Ward has requested you to lead it."

James let out a long breath as he folded his arms across his chest and he leaned back in his chair. It was a strange case to be sure, but what was more pressing to James was the fact that his almost father-in-law wanted him involved. They hadn't spoken in over a year, not since Catriona ran away with some peer from England.

The pain and embarrassment of that day still haunted James, who had vowed never to allow himself to care for any other person like he had his former fiancée. The humiliation of that moment, when he realized that she wasn't coming, had sliced at him daily ever since.

"Why does he want me?"

"He said you were the best and the brightest and that if a murder, particularly a poisoning, had taken place, that you would be the one to solve it."

James refused to feel even slightly pleased that his former mentor had lavished such praise. More than likely, he was just trying to get James to come on to the job. Of course, a case like this, if led properly, could help lead the way for autopsies being more accepted. Many a crime had gone unpunished because of the lack of understanding about how the human body worked and if he could prove, beyond a reasonable doubt, that the old merchant had been poisoned, then he would help set a precedent for the medical community.

Besides, Sir Ward wasn't likely to show up. Catriona's running away had caused a certain amount of shame for the Wards, and James's former mentor wasn't the sort of man who enjoyed uncomfortable social situations.

"I'm surprised that this matter has been brought to the police," James said. "Aren't there fines and imprisonment punishments for body snatchers?"

"This is different. It's a matter of justice. We're not removing the body to be sold and carved up by a group of medical students." He paused. "No offense, of course."

The sentiment was the popular opinion among people who

didn't understand why working on real bodies was important to science. James successfully kept his expression blank.

"Very well, Chief Constable, I'll do it."

The constable's face was grim, but grateful.

"Thank you, Dr. Hall. I believe the body will be delivered to Sir Ward's theater at Andersen University this afternoon."

"I know it well, yes."

The constable turned as James stood to follow him out. Opening the door that led into the rest of the store, both men found Grace and Virgil suspiciously close to the office door. James glared at them as the constable replaced his hat to his head.

"Thank you, Dr. Hall," he said upon reaching the front door, before bowing his head to Grace. "A pleasure to meet you, Miss Sharpe."

"It was an honor, Chief Constable," she said.

"Er, begging your pardon, sir," Virgil said, stepping forward. "But have you heard of the missing peoples, down near Gallowgate?"

The older man shook his head.

"Not anything out of the ordinary. People disappear sometimes and it can be difficult to track them, particularly when they don't wish to be found. Good day."

And with that, the police officer was gone. James turned around to reenter his office, but stalled when Grace spoke.

"That's not terribly helpful, is it?"

"Aye, but it's true," Virgil replied. "Many a person has gone missing because they don't wish to be found. Be it because of the drink, or bill collectors, or because of other, more nefarious reasons."

"Such as?"

"Well—"

"Virgil, I'm sure there's a number of things that need your attention at the moment, more so than the scandalizing of Miss Sharpe. For instance, I've nearly run out of lime oil."

"Have you? That went quick. Well, I'll whip you up a new

batch this afternoon, I will."

Virgil bobbed his head and hobbled back behind one of the glass display cases, while Grace approached James.

"I'm not in danger of being scandalized, Dr. Hall. In fact, I'm more than aware of the realities of life and have not fainted once because of them."

Her knowing smirk both irritated and intrigued James, but he wouldn't give her the satisfaction of knowing it. Instead, he ignored her and returned to his office. Of course, she was close on his heels and when he sat down to start reviewing his first patient's last documented visit, he realized that she was standing in front of his desk, as if waiting for something. Tilting his head up, he squinted at her.

"Can I help you?"

"When are we going to examine the body?"

"What body?"

"The exhumed one."

"Ha," he barked and returned his attention to his papers. When she didn't move, however, he glanced back up to see that same, knowing hint of a smile on her face. "You can't be serious."

"I'm very serious."

He closed the folder on his desk.

"*We* are not doing anything. You'll not be attending me on that venture."

To his satisfaction and also his disappointment, her smile disappeared.

"Why not?"

"Because that is a case that does not require your presence."

"But I would be a great help. I've studied the human body excessively this past year as well as the reactions poisons can induce not only in the tissue, but hair and nail folic—"

"Miss Sharpe," he interrupted, standing up from the wooden chair and placing his fists on the desk before him in an effort to appear both irritated and imposing. "I would not take you to examine a dead man for a million pounds."

"But why not?"

"Because, it is neither the place, nor the circumstance to which I've agreed to let you shadow me. Your field of study will remain firmly with the living and how to treat them."

"But I can help—"

"And I will not be so cavalier as to have you involved with an active crime investigation. You may have bullied your way into studying medicine, but I refuse to allow you anywhere near the dangerous world of crime that runs rampant in this city. Not only would your aunt have issue with it, but Dr. Barkley would refuse it as well. The danger is too great."

"What danger?" Grace pressed, coming around the desk, seemingly oblivious to the fact that she was crowding him. For the daughter of an earl, she did not behave like one. Or perhaps, by insisting on having her way, she was acting exactly like the offspring of a peer. "I see nothing precarious about examining a body."

"If the man was poisoned and it's confirmed, don't you think that the ones who did so might be angry by the discovery?"

"A fact they should have considered beforehand, if they did poison him."

James let out an exasperated breath.

"Criminals rarely consider the consequences of their actions, do they?"

"I wouldn't know, Dr. Hall. I've never met a criminal."

"And you never shall, as long as I'm in charge."

"In charge?" she repeated, sounding surprised. "You didn't want me to shadow you in the first place."

"No, but now that you are, you will abide by my rules, or I will terminate your shadowing."

"But... That's not fair!"

Frustration and indignation flashed in her eyes as she gazed at him and James struggled with remembering what exactly he was talking about, because the crease in her brow, mixed with the challenge in her amber eyes made him feel out of sorts suddenly.

Clearing his throat, he was about to tell her exactly what was unfair when the bell over the front door rang out once more.

Glancing over her shoulder, he saw his first patient. He reached for the folder on his desk, handed it to Grace, careful not to touch her as he did, and stepped around her, although he paused. Unable to help himself, he leaned toward her and spoke softly, just above her ear.

"Get ready for a fight, Miss Sharpe. Mr. Williams hates doctors. And women."

He inhaled deeply then before walking away and regretted it instantly. She smelled like sunshine and, oddly enough, carline thistle, the same that grew all around his boyhood home in Glencoe.

For a moment, he was transported back to the Highlands, far away from the pungent city scents and wet brick buildings that surrounded him.

Shaking his head, he leaned out the office doorway.

"Mr. Williams? Right this way."

Chapter Six

GRACE WAITED A full minute after Dr. Hall had left the office before she quickly donned her cape and gloves. Virgil, however, was taking his time, putting away the last bits of dry herbs that had been out for weighing to distribute to the last patient, the elderly Mrs. Champs, who had come to get a pain reliever for her daughter, who was currently pregnant.

"Hurry," Grace said, leaning against the front window as she tried to spy the last of Dr. Hall before he turned the corner at the end of the street. "I can't see him anymore."

"Are you sure this is a good idea, my lady?" Virgil asked as he reached behind him, placing the small, white and blue porcelain jar on the second shelf behind him. "Dr. Hall didn't seem too keen on the idea of you seeing, well, whatever it is he plans on doing with poor Mr. Flannery."

Grace glanced over her shoulder. She knew it was wrong to have asked Virgil for his help, particularly because it went against his employer, but Dr. Hall was being unreasonable. If there was a chance for her to learn something, particularly about the human body and its demise, well, wasn't that the exact reason she had come to Glasgow in the first place? Surely, she should be able to, at the very least, see what an autopsy might look like. And who knows? She might even be helpful. If Mr. Flannery had been poisoned, it was likely with some sort of herb or plant and she had spent the last year gathering and learning about—every leaf, stem, and root in the country, as well as the signs that came along when said plants were consumed. Really, Dr. Hall was being shortsighted. She could help.

"If you've changed your mind, I understand." She tied the ribbons beneath her chin tightly. "Then I shall go alone."

"No! My lady, please," Virgil said, hobbling toward her as he reached for his coat hanging on the wooden coat rack. "Dr. Hall would never forgive me if he learned that I knew you meant to follow him without an escort."

"I am not so fragile as Dr. Hall believes."

"Still, I cannot allow you to travel alone."

She smiled at the young man, who puffed out his chest at his last statement. It was sweet of him to want to protect her, but with a damaged leg, Grace doubted he'd be able to do much. Still, she appreciated his concern.

"Very well. But we must make haste. I don't wish to lose sight of him."

"Fear not. I've been to Andersen University a dozen times."

"Have you?"

Virgil nodded as they exited the building. He locked the door behind them before turning around to face the late afternoon crowd. Men and women hurried home from work or the markets, trying to beat the setting sun as homes around the city began to stoke the kitchen fires for supper. Grace was certainly aware of the drop in temperature now that the days were becoming shorter. Thankfully, she had her aunt's own punch carriage that had been loaned to her and her alone for her time in Glasgow. Aunt Belle and Arabella would take the proper carriage around town while Grace was studying with Dr. Hall, and she had been loaned the smaller, three-walled punch coach, that was open in the front, separated by a bench where a driver sat. It wouldn't be practical when proper winter settled in, but for now, it was perfect and allotted Grace a fair amount of independence.

"Er, my lady—"

"My name is Grace, Virgil. I insist you use it."

The young man's pale cheeks turned bright red.

"Oh no, my lady. I couldn't."

"Well, I'm not going to answer to my lady anymore. So, you must call me something else."

It might be forward or unfair to insist upon, but if Grace was ever going to be seen as someone other than an earl's daughter or Lady Belle's niece, well, she needed to put her foot down.

"Er, perhaps I can call you Dr. Sharpe?" he offered, causing Grace's cheeks to warm in turn.

"Well, I'm not quite a doctor yet."

"Then, I shall call you Dr. Grace. As it's not quite correct, but not so informal. Agreed?"

She grinned.

"Very well. Now let's go."

Grace climbed into the carriage and sat, as she watched Virgil climb in without much issue and with a few words to the driver, they were off, riding down the road in the same direction Dr. Hall went.

"The university isn't too far. Really, it can be managed with a walk, but this will get us there faster."

"Is the constable's office close as well?"

Virgil shook his head.

"No, that's up in Maryhill. At least, for now. Rumor has it they'll be building a new police station over on Craigie Street." He sighed. "Of course, that'll be nearly twice as far from Dr. Hall's office, but luckily the doctor doesn't mind moving about the city."

"Tell me," she said after a few moments of watching the city go by. "How long have you worked for Dr. Hall?"

"Two years now, or, wait. No, just about three. My, the time does go by, doesn't it?"

"It does. And has he been a kind employer?"

"Oh, absolutely," Virgil said earnestly, his eyes downcast in the next moment. "It's why I'm sure he won't be pleased with me about this business. But if I know anything about the doctor, it's that he'd be even more upset if I let you go alone. At least now you've some protection."

Grace smiled, pushing off the guilt she felt.

"You're loyal to him."

"I am. It was because of him that I'm even alive."

Grace's brow lifted.

"Is it?"

"Aye. You see, my father's a butcher, a successful one too, best in the city. I've two other brothers." He smirked. "But I'm the youngest."

"I am too."

Virgil's smile faded, however, in the next moment.

"A sickness swept through the city some years ago. I was eleven at the time, and just about to start working for my father when it happened. Our whole family became ill, but I was hit the hardest. I couldn't get out of bed and when the fever and sickness finally subsided, after weeks, mind you, I couldn't walk."

"At all?"

He shook his head.

"Barely. But Dr. Hall had started doing his rounds in my neighborhood. A sort of charity he does, from time to time. You see, it's not only in poor areas. My family has done very well," he said proudly. "But it was a ravaging illness and the doctor was compelled to help as much as he could during that time."

"What happened?"

"I was in a great amount of pain, after the fever. My father was sure that if I only got out of bed, I'd regain my strength, but Dr. Hall insisted that I rest, for nearly two months, during which he gave me a number of medicines. When the pain was controlled, he turned to more medicinal herbs." He shook his head. "My mother called it witchcraft, but then she was from the Highlands and as a girl, had heard stories about miraculous recoveries at the hands of healers. Regardless though, Dr. Hall made it so that I could walk again, and while I never fully healed," he said, gently tapping his right knee with his fist. "I was able to walk. And when I couldn't help my father in the butchery, he offered me a job at his pharmacy."

Grace glanced down at her hands, clasped together in her lap. So, the doctor had used his aunt's teaching to help lessen Virgil's illness. It was telling, particularly from someone who appeared so severely attached to the idea that modern medicine was the only way to handle the sick. While there was always room for advancement, Grace was a firm believer in documented recoveries that utilized age-old practices. For instance, where bloodletting was falling out of fashion as something that could drain poison from the bloodstream, it was common knowledge that mugwort helped relieve inflammation, or mint was used to calm nausea. Things that were used in everyday households, but Grace had an idea that there was more to the ancient art of healing that modern medicine seemed to ignore.

"Do not feel sorry for me though," he said, interpreting her clasped hands and downcast gaze for pity. "I've learned a great deal from Dr. Hall and am grateful to him. I hope even one day that maybe I…"

Virgil's mouth snapped shut, seemingly aware that he might be oversharing.

"What is it?"

He shook his head.

"It's nothing. See," he said, gesturing with his hand out in front of them as Grace turned. "There's the university."

Curious about what Virgil had been leading to, but more so about the autopsy, Grace knocked on the roof of the carriage, causing the driver to come to a halt. Exiting the vehicle, Grace noted a building made of large gray stone, with a cattycorner entrance and stone figures carved into the exterior walls. Atop a large, rounded window was the image of a man, holding another man's arm out. They were surrounded by eight others, students, Grace guessed, seemingly learning from the first.

"Is this the university?"

"This building? No, but it is where the medical professors have their auditorium. Dr. Hall has performed several surgeries here."

"Surgeries?" Grace said, unable to keep the excitement out of her tone as they walked across the street to reach the building. "What sort of surgeries?"

"Well, there was this one, particularly gruesome one he was telling me about, involving a bread toaster that—"

"Virgil?" A man's voice sounded from their left as they reached the sidewalk. They both turned to see recognition flood the doctor's face. His nostrils flared. "Sharpe."

"Oh, bloody hell," Virgil said beneath his breath before taking a step in front of Grace, as if to protect her from Dr. Hall's visible wrath. "Now, see here, she was trying to come here alone."

"I should fire you," Dr. Hall said, his voice deep and furious as he came to stand before them as passersby hurried by, giving them curious stares. "The both of you."

"No, sir, you can't."

Grace moved around Virgil with her chin up.

"Do not be angry with him; it was my idea. And as I technically do not work for you, Dr. Hall, I think I should be allowed—"

"Do you have any idea where you are?" he snapped, causing her to shut her mouth. "How dangerous it is to go wandering about a city you've no business being in? A city you've never even been in before."

"I'm not going to get to know it cooped up in drawing rooms and offices, studying maps. Besides," she said, lifting her chin to her left. "Virgil was kind enough to escort me."

"Virgil can barely…" But Dr. Hall's mouth snapped shut, seemingly unwilling to disparage his employee.

His nostrils flared as he glared at the both of them, and though Grace was well aware that she was in trouble, she couldn't help but respect the doctor for keeping his temper in check in regards to Virgil, who, Grace noted, had the expression of a newborn fawn. It would break his heart if Dr. Hall was cruel to him, but that didn't seem like something the good doctor could do, for in the next instance, he exhaled, cursing as he did.

Grace glanced away, hoping to appear chastised.

"Virgil, you may go."

"I'm sorry, Dr. Hall."

He didn't speak as the youth dipped his head at Grace and hurried down the street. Grace watched as he disappeared in the crowd before turning back to the doctor.

"That was kind of you. Not to point out his disability."

Dr. Hall did not appear pleased.

"Virgil is still on the mend as far as I'm concerned. There's no reason why he can't gain back the full use of his leg eventually." He frowned at her. "But I won't have his progress ruined because of a need to protect a bull-headed fool who thinks that just because she knows all the right people, she can do whatever she wishes."

That was not the correct thing to say to Grace, as what little affection she had for the doctor disappeared.

"You think this is a joy for me?" she said boldly, taking a step toward him as her patience evaporated. "That I like being called ridiculous by every person I've ever known? That I somehow find pleasure in the constant sneers and snickers that go on in front of my face as well as behind my back? The idea of making a fool of myself and my family, you think that I'm not constantly aware and worried by that?" She lifted her hand and poked her index finger directly into his chest, annoyed that she would take note of the solid mass beneath his shirt and coat. "You, Dr. Hall, have no idea the pains it has taken me to come this close, to be this close to a dream realized, but I will not be half taught. I've come too far and am too clever for it. Now, I demand that you treat me like any other male student who would follow you and stop trying to protect me from my own choices."

The glare of the doctor's cool gray-blue eyes made Grace's mind somewhat dizzy, but she kept her eyes on him, unwavering. He moved forward a fraction, his mouth open as if to say some biting remark back to her, but instead, his gaze drifted down her face and she felt herself become warm.

"Very well." His voice came out a harsh whisper as she was

suddenly seized around the wrist by a large hand and pulled toward the building.

He opened the front door, releasing his grip on her as he met the chief constable in the foyer. The old man eyed Grace with rejection.

"Absolutely not—"

"Constable, I understand your opposition, believe me, but Miss Sharpe is my student and is required to attend me while under my tutelage."

The constable stepped forward, his voice dropping as he spoke, though Grace strained to hear him.

"The body is in an… advanced state of decomposing. The lady does not possess the stomach for such a scene."

"She will have to," Dr. Hall said, glancing back at her. "Because if she does not, I will no longer be required to instruct her."

Grace's eyes widened at his statement. He meant to be rid of her and there would be no ground for her to stand on if she fainted or became sick upon seeing the autopsy. With a calm firmness that she never summoned before, Grace made her face stoic, her back and shoulders rigid as if she were heading into battle.

Dr. Hall seemed to note the change in her stance, for he remained still, waiting for the constable to lead the way. The old man shook his head with disapproval, and moved down the hallway.

They descended two different spiral stone staircases that led to a cold, curious set of rooms. It reminded Grace of a sort of dungeon, as there was a pungent odor in the air that seemed to grow as they continued. At the farthest end of the hallway stood several men, each with their faces covered with white cloths. Grace immediately sized up their outfits, noting that the two were completely covered in dirt, while another two were dressed as police officers. Another, the last man, was wearing a tweed suit, although he was also wearing a white apron and a pair of spectacles. Grace swallowed as they came to a stop in front of this group, her nerves on edge as they all glared at her.

She remained completely and utterly stoic. Grace doubted that the devil himself would surprise her in that moment, for all her focus was on herself and remaining calm. If she faltered, if she showed an ounce of disgust or worry or weakness, they would all see it and dismiss her.

She couldn't let that happen.

"Dr. Hall," the man in the apron said. "I didn't know you were bringing a lady."

"She is no lady, she is a medical student," Dr. Hall said without emotion, reaching for two aprons that hung on the wall. He tossed one to Grace, who grabbed it immediately and began putting it on, as did he. "What are your notes on the body?"

But the man with the glasses resting on the end of his nose didn't seem to hear the question.

"A woman medical student?"

Dr. Hall sighed, visibly annoyed as one of the police officers handed him a face covering, before also offering one to Grace.

"Yes."

"But it's unheard of."

"On the contrary. Medical students often shadow mentors, particularly when said students do not have the opportunity to attend medical school."

"Because it's unheard of."

Grace remained perfectly still, sure that any words she might speak would be ineffective to pleading her point. Instead, she watched Dr. Hall, who turned to face the police just as he finished tying his face covering.

"Chief constable, is it illegal for a woman to practice medicine in Scotland?"

"Er, um, well, not that I know of."

"So, I am committing no crime at this moment?"

"Well, no."

Dr. Hall turned to face the doctor.

"There you have it. Now, Dr. Stewart, if you have some sort

of formal complaint about this, I'd suggest you take it up with the school. However, since Miss Sharpe is learning as an apprentice of mine, and she is protected to do so under the Apothecary Act of 1815, your only complaint would be to Parliament or myself, and as I do not care about your opinion, might I suggest you write to London. In the meantime, if you don't mind, open the damn door so we can see if Mr. Flannery was poisoned and keep your concerns regarding my student to yourself."

Confusion flashed in the man's eyes as Grace had to focus all her energy on not shaking, though her heart was likely visible beneath the apron she wore, for she was sure it was going to beat right out of her chest.

Never in her entire life had anyone spoken with such heat, such assurance when it came to her and her profession. She had support, of course, from family and friends, but at most they could only support with anxiety, fearing that she would flounder. But Dr. Hall was so confident, so serious and so respected that the other man didn't even argue. Instead, he opened the door and allowed them both to enter.

Grace was grateful to be present in a room with a decompos- ing corpse, for it was certainly the only sort of distraction she could manage to find that would pull her thoughts away from Dr. Hall.

The room was stark white, with small, rectangular windows set near the ceiling, allowing what little natural light to mingle with the brightness of several oil lamps that had been turned all the way up.

In the center of the room stood a wooden table, taller than any table Grace had ever seen, with a white sheet covering a mass of what she could only assume was the remains of Mr. Flannery. Setting her jaw, Grace followed Dr. Hall as he went immediately to the center of the room and, standing next to him, waited for instruction.

"Usually, an autopsy would take place in the medical thea- ter," he said quietly to her as he reached for a pair of thick brown gloves that lay on the edge of the table, next to where Grace assumed the head of the body was placed. "But because this body was exhumed so late after its demise, this room was chosen for the coolness to help alleviate the smell."

Grace gave him a single nod, having tried to avoid inhaling through her nose since entering.

Once the gloves were on his large hands, Dr. Hall pulled the white sheet down and revealed a truly nightmarish sight.

The translucent skin of Mr. Flannery's face was sunken in, almost as if a thin clay had been pressed over a skull. The man's hair was wiry and long, as if it had continued to grow even after death, and his neck had all but shrunk to the size of a billiards stick. Dr. Hall dragged the sheet down to his waist, revealing emaciated hands with long fingernails and a sunken in chest that was similar to the illustrations Grace had seen in medical journals.

Dr. Hall took up a long silver instrument from the side table. He searched the mouth, pulling the decaying skin back as gently as possible as he searched for something Grace did not know.

"Cyanosis," he said after a moment, standing up. "I'm sure of it."

Without thinking, Grace took a step forward and bent down to see the fingertips of the dead man. They were completely black, fading into an unnatural paleness up his hands. She frowned. Cyanosis was the condition having blue fingertips.

"How can you tell? The fingers are black."

"Do you know why?" She shook her head. "Blood begins to settle in the outermost part of a body's extremities after death. You wouldn't be able to tell by the fingers, but if you notice at the lips." He paused and stepped back, allowing Grace to move in front of him. Sure enough, there was a dull blue coloring around the entire mouth. "It will occur around the mouth as well."

She stared at him, wide eyed.

"So, it was poisoning?"

"That's not been confirmed," Dr. Stewart said, coming around the end of the table. "Blue around the mouth does not signify a poisoning. Cyanosis is just a discoloration, with which a dozen causes can be the culprit. He was half frozen when he was found, if you remember?"

"True, yet." Dr. Hall took the instrument up once more, and moving around Grace, opened the man's mouth once more. "Look at the teeth."

Both Dr. Stewart and Grace leaned over the body. Sure enough, the teeth were a bluish-purple color and instantly Grace knew the cause of death.

"This man ingested monkshood," she said, glancing at Dr. Hall, who appeared to be watching her with a semblance of surprise. "He was poisoned."

"Yes. Or he took it voluntarily."

She frowned.

"Suicide?"

He shrugged and placed the silver instrument on the side table before covering the body up with the sheet.

"Suicide or not, I cannot say. That is the police's job," he said. "But monkshood is without question the reason for his death."

"Now wait a moment," Dr. Stewart said, coming forward. "How can you be sure of this?"

Dr. Hall glanced at the older doctor.

"Who prepared the body for burial?"

"The family, of course."

"And you did not check the body beforehand?"

"He was frozen," Dr. Stewart said. "And Mrs. Flannery was inconsolable. She had him wrapped in blankets from the neck down trying to revive the poor bastard. I was practically thrown from the house before I was even able to confirm his death."

Dr. Hall began to peel his gloves off his hands.

"Then there you have it. If the body was frozen, you likely wouldn't have been able to open his mouth, and if it was the sons, I'm sure they had no issue removing you from the residence as soon as possible."

"But how did she know it was monkshood?"

All the men who had been in the hallway had followed them in and now they were staring at Grace as if she were some sort of miracle.

"I," she said, unsure how to address a room full of men. But with an affirmative nod from Dr. Hall, who stood taller than everyone, she found her voice. "Monkshood is a part of the *aconitum* genus and contains substantial amounts of aconitine. If ingested, it can cause respiratory paralysis and heart failure."

"I ain't never heard of monkshood," one of the policemen said.

"It's also known as wolf's bane."

The group glanced around at each other, silently stunned by Grace's knowledge on such a deadly herb.

"How do you treat someone who's ingested monkshood, Miss Sharpe?" Dr. Hall asked.

She shook her head.

"There is no antidote. Once ingested, depending on the amount, a person can begin to feel sharp pains in the abdomen, sweating, heart palpitations, and in some cases reported, they can see a bluish-purple haze in their vision, but if the amount is enough, death can be the result."

"Very good," Dr. Hall said, before calling the attention of the group back to him. "Any questions?" No one spoke. "Well, I believe our work here is done. Constable? I've given my opinion and I believe once Dr. Stewart finishes his investigation, he'll come to the same conclusion. Now if you will excuse us."

Grace removed the face covering and apron as soon as they exited the room and followed Dr. Hall back down the hallway and up the spiral stairs until they were back in the foyer of the building. To her surprise, Dr. Hall seemed to be walking with a bit of buoyancy in his step and when they were finally outside, he seemed almost jolly as she tried to keep pace with him as he headed toward her carriage. The driver had jumped down and was swift to help Grace up and to her surprise, she was followed by Dr. Hall.

"That was satisfying," he said, rather pleased as the carriage took off down the road. "Dr. Stewart is always so sure of himself, but I knew he missed something with that case."

"You did?"

"Oh yes. The report about Mr. Flannery freezing to death had always struck me as strange. He was a patient of mine, you see, and had never shown signs of any malaise or addiction to the drink. In fact, he seemed to loathe wines and whiskeys alike. The fact that he had frozen to death from supposedly overindulging always confused me. But I wasn't in Glasgow at the time and Dr. Stewart had taken inventory of the body. I always guessed he'd done a poor job and that confirmed it."

"Oh."

He glanced at her.

"You were rather impressive as well."

Grace had to concentrate very hard not to break into a silly smile.

"Thank you."

"I know Mrs. Fletcher likely taught you all she knows about medicinal plants. She's a fountain of information, that one."

"She taught you as well, didn't she?"

"She did," he said as the carriage turned north. "For as long as I can remember, she had me out in the woods and fields, picking plants and flowers, sketching them, identifying them, taking notes on their properties and the reactions they cause in the human body. I suspected that's why Dr. Barkley rented her one of his rooms above his practice in Glencoe. To keep his patients close if they didn't agree with his diagnosis and would turn to Mrs. Fletcher."

"She is your aunt, is she not?"

"Aye."

"Then why do you call her Mrs. Fletcher?"

Dr. Hall's dark brows lifted.

"I'm not sure. I've always called her that, ever since I was a boy."

"Because she asked you to?"

"No, it's just… What everyone else called her."

Grace was unsure how to feel about that information. She knew Dr. Hall had been orphaned as a child and that he had gone to live with his only living relative, but how his parents passed and what his childhood had been like were a mystery. One that seemed to grow more interesting to her by the day.

"She has always been very kind to me."

"That's because she likes you."

Grace smiled, her hand moving over her chest absently to where her necklace lay beneath her dress.

"Did she tell you that?"

"She did," he said, and for a moment Grace saw something in his eyes, something kind, not unlike Mrs. Fletcher.

It was the most striking thing, to see a flash of white in contrast to his well-kept beard as a sweeping, fluttering sort of feeling filled her insides. He blinked then and the moment was gone, but Grace couldn't seem to shake it the rest of the ride home.

Once they reached Aunt Belle's house, Dr. Hall exited the vehicle and turned to help Grace down. She hadn't even realized it until her feet touched the cobblestones and she tried to pull away, but he didn't let go.

Grace's entire being seemed to stall when she felt his fingers tighten slightly. She didn't peer up at him, or try to pull away, but instead glanced down at where their hands were joined together. Much too soon, however, Dr. Hall released her hand and with a short bow and a mumbled "good evening," he turned and walked away, leaving Grace to stare after him for a moment.

"My lady?" the driver said, waiting for her to climb the stairs to the front door.

"Hm? Oh yes," she said, hurrying up the steps.

But it would be some hours before she was able to think of something else other than Dr. Hall's fingers.

Chapter Seven

"I'VE NEVER BEEN so excited in my entire life!" Arabella exclaimed as she twirled in front of the large, antique cheval mirror that stood in the corner of Grace's room.

The pale blue gown had been embroidered with a silver thread at the hem and the neckline, creating an intricate pattern of swirls and circles. Arabella's blonde curls seemed to shine in comparison and her rosy cheeks and infectious smile almost made Grace excited for the evening.

Almost.

As she sat in front of the small vanity near the window, Grace's head was gently redirected by Mrs. Stevens so that she could see her own reflection in the mirror. Her wavy, dark hair was being pulled up and twisted in an elaborate style and though she rarely compared herself to others, Grace felt a twinge of inadequacy as she stared into her own amber colored eyes. Her brows were thicker and nearly black in comparison to Arabella, whose features almost seemed angelic in contrast. Grace's lips were thinner too and likely less appealing, although to whom she wished to be appealing, she did not know.

Well, perhaps she did.

She blinked slowly, as if trying to barricade her mind from letting it wander. She would not think about Dr. Hall tonight. Not after he had been at the forefront of every thought she had possessed for the last week, ever since she attended him with the Mr. Flannery case.

For five days straight, she had gone to his office and for five days she had done her due diligence at trying to be as accommodating and quiet as possible, because from the moment he squeezed her fingers when he helped her out of her carriage that evening a week prior, Grace had become acutely aware of him every time he was near.

It was embarrassing to say the least, for she had always prided herself on her ability to stop herself from feeling anything but cordial to most people. Particularly when she found that she had a small infatuation with someone, which had been rare indeed, but something about Dr. Hall had destroyed her ability to separate herself from her feelings and it was affecting her greatly.

Such as wondering if she might be more appealing if her nose was smaller, or her eyes a different shade.

"There we are," Mrs. Stevens said, stepping back as Penguin the cat meowed loudly from the bed. The housekeeper turned and smirked, addressing her new furry friend. "What do you think, Mr. Penguin? As pretty as a picture, innit she?" Grace gave a tight smile, causing the older woman to frown once she glanced back at her through the mirror. "What is it? Do you not like the style?"

"Oh no, it's very nice. Thank you."

"Nice? I am not satisfied by making ladies look nice. Tell me what you wish to change and I will do it."

"Oh, but you mustn't change a thing!" Arabella said, coming forward as she reached for Grace's hands. She pulled her up out of the chair she had been sitting in and directed her in front of the cheval mirror. "You're as pretty as I've ever seen you, Grace."

The wide, scoop neckline showed off her long neck and bare shoulders. The dress was a pale peach, with a sheer brown overlay that split down the skirt. Her sleeves were short and the fabric appeared pinched at the shoulders, in a Grecian sort of style.

It was really a very pretty gown and while it did complement her hair and eye color, Grace couldn't understand why she felt too exposed. She had worn fashionable dresses before, but this one in particular made her feel self-conscious.

She dipped her chin.

"That is kind of you to say, but I'm afraid I feel more confident in my work dresses than this."

"Nonsense," Mrs. Stevens said, coming forward. "You're quite striking, far more so now than when you're wearing one of those drab gowns. Now, give yourself a proper once over," she ordered. "With the pale peach of this gown and your dark hair, I daresay there isn't a gentleman alive who wouldn't take notice of you at the opera tonight."

Grace's insides twisted. She did not mean to gather compliments by self-deprecation; she was merely stating a fact. It wasn't as if she cared one way or the other how she appeared. And the last thing she wished was to garner any masculine attention. Honestly, to go unnoticed would be a boost of confidence while attending the opera, as she did not want to stand out in any way.

"Yes, thank you," she said quickly, hoping to satisfy Arabella and Mrs. Stevens, who seemed bent on making Grace feel self-assured.

"There we are." Mrs. Stevens nodded. "Now downstairs with the both of you. We wouldn't want Lady Belle to be caught waiting on you two."

Grace followed Arabella out of the room and down the stairs as she plotted to wear her black velvet mantle until she was seated at the opera. Perhaps then no one would find her too interesting a subject to study.

The unwelcome sight of Dr. Hall's steady gaze flashed in her mind as she descended the stairs, causing her to stall for a moment before regaining her steps. Why was it that nearly every time she dressed during the past week, did she wonder what he might think? It was ridiculous to care about any one person's opinion, particularly when it pertained to such a silly topic as fashion, but Grace couldn't seem to help herself.

Evidently, her inner turmoil was written all over her face, for when Aunt Belle spotted her, she frowned.

"What is it? What's wrong?" she asked, herself dressed in a full fur coat, over what appeared to be an emerald-green dress.

"Nothing is the matter."

Her aunt squinted her eyes.

"I do not believe you."

Grace sighed.

"I suppose I'm just a little uncomfortable," she said as a footman helped her with her mantle. "It seems a frivolous activity, going to the opera, when I could be studying."

"Too much studying will do more harm than good, my dear," Aunt Belle said with the tapping of her cane on the wooden floor beneath. "Besides, it will do your mind some good to relax and interact with someone other than that dreadful Dr. Hall."

Grace frowned, unsure what her aunt meant by that as all three women exited the house and were helped into the carriage. As the crack of the whip sounded, Grace leaned forward to speak.

"What do you mean by calling Dr. Hall dreadful?"

Aunt Belle's brow lifted.

"My dear, didn't you tell me that he has you washing utensils and answering his every beck and call? Surely you find it tiresome?"

Grace shrugged.

"It can be, but I enjoy it."

"I do not see how. Particularly when you can be doing a number of other things. It makes me worry about you."

"You needn't, really. I'm quite sure, more now than before, that this is what I wish to do with my life."

Aunt Belle bobbed her head, seemingly placated as Arabella chimed in.

"Yes, but it must be grating on your nerves, to have to do everything he says." She grimaced. "I don't know what I would do if I was forced to clean an open wound."

Grace smiled.

"Then it is a good thing I can do so without batting an eye."

"But is it not tedious? Being constantly working, particularly with the same person day in and day out?"

"No," she said softly. "Not at all."

It was actually terribly inconvenient, particularly now that she couldn't quite shake the feeling that there was some sort of feeling between them, but then her rational side was very much convinced that it was one-sided. Dr. Hall wasn't interested in her and she had made it a point to appear just as unaffected, however difficult that was coming to be. Whenever she was close to him, which of course was daily, she tried to be indifferent. If he asked her to perform a task, such as getting him more bandages to dress an injury, or to stabilize a child so that he might set a dislocated joint, she would do so without question and if she did have a question, she was sure to ask it in the most even tone, so that he couldn't guess at her mood one way or the other.

To be honest, tonight's opera would be the first time in over a week that Grace would be able to relax and realizing that, she leaned back against the plush bench cushions. She intended to enjoy her evening, despite the hollow feeling she felt in her heart.

Upon arrival to the Theatre Royal Dunlap Street, Grace was amazed to see that an honest to goodness crowd was gathered beneath the tall marble pillars that led into the opera house. Not since London had she attended such a social event and while she had always known that cities existed outside of London, to see and be a part of it elsewhere was rather jarring.

"I know," Aunt Belle said, leaning toward her after they exited the carriage. "It's funny the first time outside of London."

Grace turned to her.

"Am I that obvious?"

"Well, when one grows up in London society, it's practically indoctrinated that it's the center of the world and everything that happens outside of it is woefully unfashionable, but," she said, glancing around as her eyes twinkled. "It is a marvelous thing to be a part of society, wherever one is."

Grace nodded slowly as they were shepherded in through the

front doors into a massive entrance hall. The walls were painted gold and appeared to glow beneath the shining light of three massive chandeliers that hung above them. Once again, Grace was taken aback by the sheer decadence of it all, having long believed London to be the epicenter of culture.

With her head bent backwards, she didn't have time to see the man who spoke suddenly next to her.

"If the lady appreciates chandeliers this much, I should order a dozen for my new theater."

Whipping her head back, she saw a fair-looking man, with a white cravat, vest, and shirtsleeves beneath a pristine black coat. He had a mustache, as was the current fashion, and slightly wavy hair.

"Mr. Milton!" Aunt Belle said cheerfully, offering her hand as the gentleman took it. "It has been an age since I saw you last."

"Lady Belle. Always a pleasure," he said before turning back to face Grace and Arabella. "And who have you brought to town now? More dancers?"

"Ah, ha, no," Aunt Belle said quickly, her wrinkly cheeks turning crimson, Grace noted. "This is my niece, Miss Grace Sharpe and a family friend, Miss Arabella Scott."

The man's brow lifted.

"Is that so? I didn't know Lady Belle had any relatives," he said, bowing to both women.

"Do you not read the papers, Mr. Milton?" Arabella asked. "It was reported on nearly two years ago."

"Alas, I was not in Scotland this past year or the year prior. I've actually just returned from a tour on the Continent."

"Yes, I remember," Aunt Belle said. "You were going to study the architecture of the Austrian opera houses, were you not?" Before he could answer, however, Belle turned to Grace and Arabella. "Mr. Milton here is an architect."

"Ah, well, I wouldn't call myself that," he said quickly. "I'm an admirer of it, but my business is elsewhere."

"Yes, Mr. Milton built the Milton shopping arcade several

years ago. A very successful venture, I believe, is it not, Mr. Milton?"

"You flatter me, Lady Belle."

"Surely not. Mr. Milton is as modest as he is clever. Tell me, what new projects do you have on your plate?"

The man tilted his head, a satisfied grin creeping across his face.

"Well, I did go to Austria to study the opera houses for a reason. I'd very much like to open another theater, near my shopping arcade if possible."

"A smashing idea," Aunt Belle said, jabbing her walking stick on the ground. "The more theaters a city has, the better, I believe."

"Aye," he said, before leaning slightly toward Grace. "You see, Miss Sharpe, the Austrians have the very best theaters and I am eager to match their grandeur."

"They have the best medical theaters as well."

The man stared at Grace for a moment before Aunt Belle spoke.

"Ah, you'll have to forgive her, Mr. Milton. My niece is a student of medicine and can rarely speak on anything else," she added pointedly.

"A student of medicine? You mean to say you're studying to be a nurse? A noble pursuit, Miss Sharpe."

"Actually, I've plans on becoming a doctor."

"Oh, aye?"

"Yes."

For the briefest of moments, Grace felt herself and her company hold their collective breath. It was getting easier to discuss it, but it was still so uneven, the reactions she would get. But Mr. Milton only smirked and, to Grace's awareness, leaned ever so slightly toward her.

"I should think any sick person to have you as a doctor would be the luckiest patient in the world."

Stunned momentarily, Grace felt her cheeks warm at the

compliment.

"Thank you, Mr. Milton."

"Mr. Milton," Aunt Belle said suddenly, stepping between the two. "Be a dear and help an old woman to her seat. I cannot bear to walk up these steps alone. My leg, you see, it's acting up again."

"Is it?" Grace asked, concerned.

But her aunt shooed her away as Mr. Milton offered his arm, leaving Arabella and Grace to follow. Suspiciously enough, Aunt Belle seemed to make it up the stairs without issue, although she did appear to make a bit of a show of it whenever they reached the landing, where she saw an elderly gentleman whom she apparently wished to speak to. Waving to an usher, she spoke to Grace.

"Follow this man to the Smyth box, while Mr. Milton escorts me to speak with an old friend of mine, will you?"

"Yes," Grace said, just as Mr. Milton spoke.

"It was a pleasure to meet you, Miss Sharpe. You as well, Miss Scott."

"The pleasure was ours," Arabella said before quickly grabbing Grace's arm and turning to follow the usher. "My goodness, what a handsome gentleman!"

"Arabella, hush," Grace said, glancing around. "You mustn't speak so loudly."

"I cannot help it. I'm so excited. To finally be around so many people instead of being kept away in Glencoe. It's so refreshing to meet new people, isn't it?"

Grace nodded, unsure, as they were led to a heavy red curtain. The usher pulled it back and let them enter and Grace couldn't help but gasp. It was breathtakingly beautiful. With massive red curtains covering the stage, gold painted filigree walls, and rich, green velvet seats, it was the most decadent theater she had ever been to.

"Oh, my goodness, it's beautiful!" Arabella said excitedly.

"Yes, it really is."

Not moments later, Aunt Belle entered the suite and they each took their seats, just as the show was about to begin. It was an Italian opera called *Adelia*, in which the daughter of a duke's bodyguard is suspected of having relations with a nobleman. Arabella and Aunt Belle were very obviously enraptured by the tension of the play, showcased by Aunt Belle, whose opera glasses were unmoving from her eyes, although she did turn around a few times, as if searching for someone in the audience below. But even that couldn't hold Grace's interest. As much as she tried to pay attention, she couldn't seem to care enough about it, as her mind continued to wonder about things she didn't want to wonder about.

Such as the exact color of Dr. Hall's eyes.

It was mortifying, to be sat in a dark theater, ignoring all the hard work of the singers and actors, and only being able to concentrate on trying to figure out if the doctor had gray eyes with a bluish hue or blue eyes with gray streaks.

"My dear," Aunt Belle said suddenly, shaking Grace from her thoughts.

"Yes?"

"I need you to, um, go fetch my medicine from the carriage."

"Medicine? What medicine?"

"My pain relievers. Dr. Barkley gave them to me and I feel the draft in this building is causing my leg to ache."

"Pain relievers? Aunt Belle, why didn't you tell me you were taking such things?"

"Do not argue with me, my dear, just go get them."

Grace frowned as Arabella leaned toward them.

"Surely one of the ushers can do so?"

"No, no," Aunt Belle said. "I want Grace to do it."

"Why?"

"Because. If you are going to be a doctor, you must learn to be called away from whatever it is you are doing at any given moment to perform your duties," she said. "Now, go on."

Grace sighed, unsure what sort of lesson Aunt Belle was

trying to teach her at that moment, but as she wasn't much interested in the opera, she left without arguing.

Walking down the hallway that led to the staircase, Grace noted the quiet peace of being in such a large space alone.

Well, almost alone.

There, in the middle of the staircase, halfway from the landing on both sides, was Mr. Milton, staring up at the chandeliers. Tilting her head, Grace stilled as she reached him.

"Mr. Milton?" she asked, as he turned. "What are you doing out here?"

"Studying. I'm afraid I can't ever seem to pull myself away from it," he said, glancing up one last time before focusing on Grace. "Tell me, why were you so interested in the chandeliers when you first came into the theater?"

Grace shook her head.

"I'm not sure. I suppose it was because they seem so grand and I wasn't expecting it. Why do you ask?"

"I'm planning on breaking ground on a new theater, over near Cowcaddens Cross, and I want it to be just as spectacular and grand, if not more so, than this theater." He glanced at her. "And I should feel very blessed indeed if I could see the reaction I saw on your face tonight on the faces of my guests when it opens."

Grace felt her cheeks warm once more.

"That's very kind of you to say, Mr. Milton."

He bobbed his head, but spoke no more of it.

"Are you enjoying the opera this evening? Or perhaps not, considering you're out here."

"I've been sent on a task for my aunt, who is trying to teach me a lesson."

"Oh? What lesson is that?"

"Likely something about choices, I presume, but I won't read too far into it."

Mr. Milton chuckled and Grace felt a little bolstered by the noise, only to be distracted in the next moment. The faint aroma of lime swirled around her when a grave, familiar voice sounded behind them.

"Ahem."

Turning around, not three steps above her and Mr. Milton, was Dr. Hall.

Chapter Eight

JAMES STILLED AS he glanced down the staircase to find Grace and a broad-shouldered gentleman, speaking with one another. Oddly, for a night that had been merely irritating, he was surprised to feel the muscles in his back tense and his heart rate increase, more so than his current aggravation seemed to warrant.

He hadn't wanted to come to the opera tonight, but he had done so at the behest of Lady Belle, who had sent him a letter, requesting that he escort the elderly Baroness of Glengirth as a personal favor. Why he had agreed to it, when he had already done enough for that woman he did not know, but a deep, instinctual part of him couldn't seem to ignore her. He blamed his own aunt, for having instilled in him a need to help those who requested it and his good deed had not gone unpunished. For the last two hours, his aging companion had complained about the noise of the crowd, the lack of vocal ranges of the entertainers, disparaged James's upbringing as well as asked in an endless number of questions regarding the phantom pains the baroness was convinced she was suffering. Usually, James was more patient when someone was describing pains, but when the baroness revealed that they were actually the old riding injury suffered by her deceased husband, and how she believed they had been transferred to her by his ghost, well, that had been enough. He had very nearly told her that her imagination was the only illness she had when the old woman ordered him to find her a cool refreshment, right in the middle of the second act.

So, he had sighed and thanked whatever being above for the opportunity to escape for a few minutes. It was annoying, and yet, his irritation seemed to expand into a proper rage at the sight before him.

Grace was dressed in a gown of pale peach, covered in a sheer chocolate overlay, and James fought to swallow. He had seen her in practical dresses, but this was different. She had been styled with purpose. Dark brown curls were piled on top of her head, with one errant strand falling down at the side, just behind her left ear. Her long neck was exposed and the wide, scooping neckline displayed the roundedness of the top of her breasts.

James swallowed again.

Grace was wearing her usual smirk, the one that seemed perpetually on her lips, particularly whenever she was about to say something clever. He had come to expect it in the days since Grace had started coming to his office for work, yet to see her now, smiling at a man he did not know, well, if he didn't know any better he might have guessed that the emotion he was experiencing at the moment was jealousy, but…

No. James was not jealous. Why should he be? Because Grace was smirking that same infuriating little grin that had seemed exclusively for him?

He took a step down, wanting very much to ignore the pair, but then stopped when her gaze met his and that irksome smile disappeared.

There was only a brief moment then, before the man noticed that he had lost Grace's attention, where she stared at James, but he felt a deep, thunderous beat in his chest suddenly. It was singular yet profound, and for all his days to come, he knew it to be a pivotal moment in his life. But at that moment, all he could comprehend was that they saw each other and even that was almost too much.

The wide-shouldered gentleman turned then and to James's surprise, he knew him.

"Dr. Hall!" Mr. Milton said, turning as he climbed the several steps that separated them. "I didn't know you were in attendance tonight."

"I…" He tried, his focus still on Grace, who appeared suddenly anxious. He blinked and turned to Milton. "I'm afraid I've been summoned tonight."

"A better man I know not," Mr. Milton said cheerfully as he turned back to Grace. "There was never a man more willing to toil in the muck and mire as Dr. Hall. Oh, forgive me, I haven't introduced you. Dr. Hall, this is—"

"Grace Sharpe, yes," he said as Grace slowly climbed the steps to meet them. "We know each other."

"Do you?"

"Yes," Grace said finally, her voice slightly breathless, causing a part of James to wonder why. "Dr. Hall and I have the same mentor. I've come to Glasgow to study under him."

"Oh," Mr. Milton said, his brow lifted. "So, you are her teacher?"

"No."

James silently cursed at himself for his blunt response. The hurt that flashed in Grace's eyes was enough to bother him, but there was something about being called her teacher that felt wrong. He was, in every sense of the word, teaching her medicine, but the power balance seemed inexcusably skewed. If she were a man, he'd likely have no trouble being introduced as a teacher, but there were other things at play. Her rank in society, her cleverness and determination. The way she became still whenever anyone spoke, as if she were not only taking in every word, but every detail. It was heartening and yet, it couldn't be because he didn't want to think of her as someone that had any effect on his heart.

No, God forbid she did that.

"I mean, yes," he said, remembering himself. This was not a situation that he wished to have any part in and he wanted nothing to do with Grace Sharpe, or any of her personal relationships. It would be best to remove himself from this little tête-à-tête. He needed to walk away that instant, or he might do or say something that would ruin whatever reservation he had left. "If you'll excuse me."

Moving past the two, he was already down the steps when he heard Grace speak.

"If you'll excuse me, Mr. Milton, I believe Dr. Hall might be able to help with my task."

"Of course. Until next time, Miss Sharpe."

James felt trapped. Whatever he was meant to be doing out here, he had forgotten and suddenly he wished to leave the opera house altogether. But then the gentle graze of fingertips on his sleeve stalled him. He turned around to see Grace's amber eyes watching him.

"I'm sorry to have interrupted you. Please, do not let me hinder you."

She frowned and glanced back toward the stairs where Mr. Milton was no longer.

"You mean Mr. Milton? I've only just met him."

"Is that so?"

"Yes."

"It certainly seemed you and your new acquaintance are on friendly terms. I would have guessed you met before."

"I'm afraid not. I was only just introduced to him this evening by my aunt."

The mention of Lady Belle set a bitter taste in James's mouth.

"Yes, your aunt. Tell me, is it her fault that you're out of the opera box, wandering the halls unaccompanied?"

Grace tilted her head.

"Yes, actually. She requested some sort of medicine she had left in the carriage."

That got his attention.

"Medicine? What medicine?"

"My reaction exactly."

"An usher couldn't handle the task?"

Grace sighed and her chest rose. James had to avert his eyes, lest he appear to be staring at her.

"She insisted that I do it."

There was no possible way for Lady Belle to know that the Baroness Glengirth would have requested a refreshment at the same time Grace was sent to gather medicine, yet James couldn't help but feel as if the entire meeting had been orchestrated.

But really, that was likely his imagination running away with him. Good Lord, he sounded like the baroness. So instead, he held out his arm to her.

"Come. I shan't let you go out into the Glasgow night to search carriages without at least an escort."

The familiar, warm grin appeared on Grace's face and James had to mentally beat down the pleasure that shattered in his chest at the sight of it. He repeated his mantra silently as she stepped toward him and gently placed her hand in the crook of his arm. But the moment she touched him, all ability to control his inner dialogue was lost.

"You know, Dr. Hall, if you continue to be so agreeable, I'm going to have to take back the things I said to my sisters about you."

They stepped out into the chilly night air, which felt more welcoming than he imagined it might.

"You've spoken about me to your sisters?"

"Oh yes. Particularly after Aunt Belle's birthday ball."

Ah, the night he told her he wouldn't allow her to shadow him. He had often replayed their conversation from that night in his mind, particularly the first part, when she wished to speak with him alone. It would be too embarrassing to reveal to her now that he had first assumed she wished to speak to him as well… It didn't matter now.

"I suspect it wasn't at all pleasant." James waved to a footman. "Lady Belle Smyth's carriage?"

The man leaned back, glancing down the street.

"It's about eight carriages down, sir. I can get it for you?"

"That won't be necessary, thank you," James said as he and Grace turned down the road. He glanced down at her. "Your silence is telling."

"I will not lie. I didn't speak very generously about you, but I'm afraid my own pride is the reason for that."

"How so?"

"Well, I hadn't considered what my request might mean for you. That is to say, I understand the weight of having a female student. The issues it could cause between you and your other responsibilities, including colleagues and the like—"

"Miss Sharpe, I do not care what my colleagues think."

"You don't?"

"No."

"Then why were you so against the idea of my shadowing you? Dr. Barkley made it sound as if you were against the whole situation."

James counted, six, seven, eight until they reached the carriage, trying very hard to ignore her questioning as well as the scent of her. Why was she so intoxicatingly sweet smelling? The truth was too embarrassing to tell and yet, to refuse her an answer felt equally as damning.

He opened the carriage door and climbed in.

"What does the medicine look like?" he asked as he began smoothing his hand over the velvet cushioned seats.

"She didn't say," Grace said, climbing in after him. "Perhaps it's in the liquor compartment."

He turned around, sitting down as he watched Grace sit opposite, her hands going to a small rectangular door that unlatched from the interior wall, revealing a small crystal bottle of reddish liquid and two sherry glasses.

"Your aunt has a liquor compartment?"

"Of course. She gets sick from the swaying of the carriage on long journeys. She takes a dram or two of sherry to fall asleep."

James shook his head, as a humorous breath escaped his lips.

"That woman is an enigma," he said, leaning forward to trace his hands along the carriage floor. "Is it a vial of liquid? Perhaps powder or pill form?"

"She didn't say."

"Well, what's it for?"

Grace shook her head.

"She said it was for pain, but I'm not sure I believe her. She seemed secretive," she said, leaning forward until their faces were quite close. "A trait you and she share, evidently."

James had stilled, noting the miniscule space between them. It was exactly the sort of situation that would usually make him wary, but there was a comfort in Grace's amber eyes that steadied him and he exhaled.

"What do you wish to know, Miss Sharpe?"

"Why were you so against me shadowing you when I first asked?"

James felt his nerves fray at the question, but he would answer it, because despite what he had thought that night, it wasn't as if he was in an embarrassing position.

"In truth, I was caught off guard that night and perhaps my ego was bruised a little," he said steadily, staring at her. "It is not a very professional thing to admit."

The slight bounce between her brow caught his attention.

"But I don't understand. Why would your ego be bruised? Unless you... Oh..." Her face suddenly smoothed with recognition. "Oh."

Oh indeed. Was there ever a more pathetic *Oh* spoken before?

"Yes, well, I wouldn't worry about it."

"Oh dear," she said, her eyes unfocused as she leaned back away from him. "I can't believe I didn't realize it."

"It's quite all right."

"No, it isn't. You thought..." Her gaze fell to the ground. "But, your aunt."

Now it was James's turn to frown.

"My aunt?"

"It's just... She told me that, well, that you were, um... how should I say this?"

"In her own words. I'm used to them, believe me."

Grace hesitated before continuing.

"Well, she said that you were outside the idea of companionship ever since, um… Well, you know."

He let out a sigh.

"Since Catriona." Grace nodded. "Yes, well, that was a situation." A silent pause followed and when he glanced at Grace, she appeared far more interested than he cared for her to be. He sensed her curiosity building, questions hovering on her lips as was her usual response to learning a new topic. He leaned back himself. "What do you wish to know?"

"Everything."

A laugh escaped him.

"Everything?"

"Yes. How did you meet? Were you in love with her? Was she in love with you? Why did she leave? Were you able to forgive her?"

Although it was a series of incredibly private questions, James seemed almost eager to unload the answers, as he had never been able to speak freely about it. Not with his friends or family. It was just something that he was expected to bear by himself, silently and stoically as he always behaved. Not to mention, no one had ever asked him point blank any of these questions.

Taking a deep breath, he leaned forward again, resting his elbows on his knees as he clasped his hands together.

"We met three years ago, during one of her father's lectures. I had known Sir Ward for a few years, since the end of my studies at the university, but never knew he had a daughter. She was the Wards' only child and so they raised her to have a proper education and she was brilliant." He peered up. "She wanted to be a doctor too."

Grace's eyes widened at the confession.

"Did she?"

"Yes, and she was quite capable. She was studying under her father as an apprentice since she wasn't admitted to any of the universities due to her sex. Even with her father, who is re-nowned in the medical field, they still wouldn't permit her.

"We were fast friends and soon our relationship turned ro-mantic, except that, from my point of view now, I daresay that it was one-sided."

"How so?"

He hesitated for a moment, but the weight of relieving him-self of it all was too tempting.

"Catriona was rarely affectionate. I had told myself that it was because she was an educated woman, too refined in that her mind was preoccupied to be distracted with basic human instincts. But the idea of her, of us together, was too tempting for me. I was in awe of her mind and mistook it for love, or at least that's what I have to believe." He smirked, bitterly. "I think she accepted my proposal at the behest of her father. It wasn't until the day before the wedding last autumn that I was made aware of her relation-ship with an English peer that she had met during some lecture. They had been writing to one another ever since, but her father didn't approve of him for reasons unknown to me. But it seems she couldn't bear the thought of marrying me, because she ran away to be with him and I never heard from her again." His mouth quirked to the side as the memory of their last meeting engulfed him. "I was not completely unaware of her feelings, although I must admit now that I wasn't as attentive as I should have been. I should have listened more to what she wasn't saying."

Grace's brow flinched.

"How could you listen to what she wasn't saying?"

He sighed, amazed that he was revealing so much of the things he had gone over and over in his mind since being left by Catriona. But the darkness of the carriage that engulfed them made him feel comforted. Perhaps it was the company too.

He shook his head.

"When I asked her if she was happy and she said yes, but the expression on her face said otherwise. When I asked her if there was something I should know about when she started acting sad, she told me not to worry. I should have recognized the anxiety she was displaying. I should have been able to see it, to identify it."

"You wanted to diagnose the problem between you." A long pause followed his confession. "And did you forgive her?"

"Forgive her for what? Loving someone else? It's hardly a thing to forgive. Besides, she doesn't require it of me."

"But you might."

James's gaze lifted and he saw Grace staring at him.

"Yes, I forgave her. I hold no ill will toward Catriona and what's more, I'm grateful that she left. It would have been a miserable life to be married to someone who didn't love me."

"And you loved her?"

"I thought I did."

Another pause followed and James felt a creeping sensation crawl up his spine, as if Grace might begin to pity him. Wanting to suddenly be out of her presence, he moved to leave the carriage.

"It seems your aunt's medicine has vanished, if there ever was some to begin with. Let's return—"

But Grace's hand touched his forearm and he stopped as a wave of heat wafted over him.

"Your aunt told me you were outside the idea of companionship."

James's brow crinkled.

"Yes, you said as much."

But Grace was shaking her head.

"No, I mean… It was why I wanted to study with you. Because you were supposed to be incapable of amorous feelings."

James frowned.

"I'm sorry to say that I'm not. I'm only human, Grace."

The use of her name seemed to reverberate around them as she stared at him; she appeared almost in a panic.

"You must though."

Confused, he slowly sank back down to the velvet seat.

"Why must I?"

"Because… Because I can't… You can't. We can't—"

He reached for her hand to try and help steady her. He had never seen Grace in a panic before and yet, she seemed to be having an issue all of a sudden.

"Grace, it's all right. We've been able to work together these last few weeks without issue. I'm not a worry to you, believe me."

But she was shaking her head.

"It's not you I'm worried about. It's me."

He frowned, confused.

"You?"

"Yes." She paused. "You see, I-I've been too aware of you, I suppose, for lack of a better way of explaining it. That is, there are things about you that I often find myself thinking about and while harmless, I do tend to, well, that's not to say that I often do, but I have done so in the past—"

"What have you done?"

Grace closed her eyes and sighed.

"This is going to sound mad, but I… I didn't ever believe that I was capable of amorous feelings."

James tilted his head.

"Oh?"

She opened one eye, as if to peek at his reaction.

"But I've tried."

His brow lifted, unsure what she was telling him.

"Have you?"

"That is to say, I tried once, to see if I might have the ability to feel such things. It was when we were in London. Actually, it's the entire reason we left London," she began. "You see, my friend was set to marry a man who was very smart, but also very dull. He spoke endlessly on mathematics and bored everyone around him, and when someone would try to interject or even add to the conversation, he refused to allow it."

James nodded, unsure where this was going.

"All right…"

"Well, my friend, she was set to marry him, an arrangement with her parents had been made, and she was sure that his brilliance was the reason she couldn't feel anything for him. That he was too clever and that only other clever people found him interesting. Well, I am a clever person and seeing how upset she was at the match as well as being consistently curious, I decided to try something."

"What did you try?"

"I kissed him."

James had heard that one of the Sharpes had caused a scandal in London, which had been the reason they had come to Scotland in the first place, but he had always assumed it was one of Grace's sisters, either Hope or Faith who had been rather cavalier with themselves. Not smart, steadfast Grace.

"Why?"

"I wanted to see if it was true. If perhaps clever people were attracted to other clever people, not to mention that it would help my friend get out of what most certainly was going to be a loveless marriage. So, I kissed him and… And there was nothing."

"Nothing?"

"Not a feeling, not an idea, not an epiphany, not anything. It was rather boring actually, and from that moment on, I always assumed that there were people who were outside of the world of companionship." She glanced at him. "When your aunt mentioned that you were similar, I thought this might be a practical partnership."

"And now?"

"I'm not so sure."

"Because you believe that I'm incapable of helping myself?" he asked. "I assure you; I can control myself."

"No, no," she said quickly. "It is because I am no longer sure of myself."

It took a moment for her words to sink in.

"Pardon?"

"I'm saying, I've noticed certain reactions that I have whenever you are near and I can't help it," she said, glancing down quickly. "I'm mortified to admit this, but for the sake of my apprenticeship, I feel that I must tell you." Her gaze lifted and James felt the air go out of him. "I believe I'm attracted to you."

The honesty, however small and seemingly insignificant, affected James in more ways than he'd like to admit. She was attracted to him. Outside of their work together and their differences in social standings, here was a woman, whose very image had haunted him for months, admitting that she felt a certain way about him.

James had always prided himself on his practicality. Even in dire situations, his mantra to "trust the journey" had always managed to bring peace and stillness to any circumstances he found himself in.

But this was something he had never experienced. With Catriona, it had been mostly one-sided and even when she did finally admit to having some feelings for him, it had taken nearly a year and he knew now that said feelings were likely more platonic than romantic.

Yet Grace Sharpe didn't seem to be hindered by shyness or even social decorum. She was straightforward and rather blunt in her confession and it was... Stunning.

She looked away once more.

"I'm sure you understand why then, that I would like to end my apprenticeship."

And that was the last thing he had expected to hear. James felt a knot form in the pit of his stomach at her suggestion.

"No," he said, leaning forward still. "Grace, you don't have to stop your studies because of this."

"It will hinder me."

"It won't. I won't allow it."

"How can it not?"

"Well, because. We are two practical, well-behaved people

who can be aware of a symptom without provoking it. We'll just take the extra caution to not be affected by it."

"Do you really believe that we can?"

"Absolutely. Besides, it's not as though we cannot control ourselves. Right?"

He held out his hand, in a gesture of good faith and with a slight smile, Grace took it.

"Right."

With a single shake of their hands, they agreed to continue their professional relationship while ignoring whatever silly feelings might be between them. Yet in the next moment, her smile vanished and a force beyond both her and James seemed to settle around them.

His thumb glided over hers and the air began to thicken with tension. Grace's gaze was transfixed on their hands when she suddenly pulled his hand back toward her. It was not enough to command him anything and yet he went toward her, as if she possessed the strength of ten men.

Grace's other hand came up and she stroked the edge of his jaw.

"I like your beard."

What a silly thing to make a man's heart beat, but beat it did.

"Do you?" he asked gruffly.

"Yes," she said, her voice soft as her gaze moved over his face. "Perhaps, in the name of science, you might oblige me just this once. So that I might make a decision possessing all the facts."

"And what facts are you hoping to acquire?"

"Basic ones. Facts based in human nature and instinct."

"I see," he said. "And how might I be of service to this inquiry?"

"Well, Dr. Hall, I'd like it very much if you would kiss me."

Thunder sounded in his ears at the request and he went to shake his head, but then that same pang he felt on the steps of the opera house reverberated within his chest and he bent his head down and kissed her.

Chapter Nine

A SERIES OF starbursts flashed behind Grace's eyelids as a rush of fire coursed through her veins the moment James's lips touched hers. Her fingers reach up, curling into the dark hair at the back of his skull, and holding him close as his tongue swept against hers as every one of her senses filled with him. She felt the short-clipped hairs at the back of his head against her fingertips, tasted the faint hint of port on his lips. The familiar scent of lime wafted around her as she listened to the way his hands ruffled against the fabric of her dress while her eyes remained only half open, so taken with the moment was she.

When she had kissed Lord Bartley, she had kept her eyes wide open, noting how foolish the man appeared mere inches away from her, with his eyes closed. But now, her eyelids felt heavy and her need to observe faded away as his large, warm hands wrapped around her back, holding her in such a way that he was trying to keep her.

It was rather romantic, she mused vaguely as his kiss deepened. This was wildly different too. Where Lord Bartley had merely opened and closed his mouth, like a fish out of water, making it rather awkward as Grace had been kissed *at*, instead of partaking in as a partner, James's kiss felt organic and seeking, as if she might hold some sort of answer or reaction. Like he wished to discover something about her and for the life of her, she wanted to give him answers she did not have.

What would happen if she put her hands on him? With a hazy

determination, Grace lifted her hands and pressed them against his chest. A slight intake in his breath made her aware of her effect on him. So, he was provoked by her touch? A detail to remember, she noted as his hand drifted up along her ribcage to her breast—

Oh.

It was Grace's turn to gasp as the warmth of his hand sank into the fabric to the sensitive skin beneath. Suddenly, her body felt as though it were being slowly set on fire as a heat spread across her skin. She needed to feel his bare hand against her skin. It was a wild, intrusive thought, but one of pure animalistic desire. One she had never experienced before.

Pressing against him, leaning into their shared kiss, Grace followed her own urgent need, but was pulled sharply out of her own mind when James's hand came to her shoulders and pulled away from her. He settled her back down on the seat behind her before sitting back himself.

Blinking, confused, Grace stared at him slack-jawed, while they both breathed heavily. His eyes seemed alight with an emotion Grace couldn't name and his mouth was open slightly, his breath labored for some reason, as if trying to control himself. She wanted to feel his beard against her cheek again, and leaned once more toward him, but he held her in place.

"Someone's coming."

Grace frowned, unsure or rather unable to comprehend what he was saying. But just as she was about to open her mouth, the carriage door swung open. The driver had done so, only to reveal Aunt Belle, who appeared both pleased and suspicious.

"Ah, there you are, my dear. And Dr. Hall, how curious to see you here. I suspect my niece required your help in retrieving my medicine?"

"I, I mean, we couldn't find it," Grace stuttered softly. Why did she sound so breathless? "That is to say, I don't believe you took it from the house."

"Really? My mistake then," she replied, her attention fixated on James. "Are you all right, doctor? You look a bit unwell."

Grace stole a glance at James whose mouth opened before shutting as he climbed out of the carriage. She leaned forward to watch him leave.

"I'm curious, Lady Belle, what medication were you so desperately in need of that you sent your niece out into the night alone to retrieve for you?"

"But she isn't alone, Dr. Hall. She's with you. Which is rather fortunate, as I saw the Baroness Glengirth asking about you in the anterior of the opera hall." Belle shook her head. "She did not appear very pleased to be abandoned, but I reminded her that professional men have responsibilities and a duty to the public, which seemed to satisfy her for a moment, but I would not keep her much longer. She can be prickly when provoked, I'm afraid."

He seemed to stare at her for a moment before giving her a single nod.

"I see."

"I doubt it," Aunt Belle said beneath her breath as she climbed into the carriage, followed by Arabella, who curtsied.

"Good night, Dr. Hall," she said before she entered the carriage.

With a final, heated glance, James closed the door rather soundly and walked away, leaving Grace in the presence of her aunt and Arabella, both of whom were watching her with open curiosity.

She swallowed.

"H-how was the rest of the opera?"

"Very interesting," Aunt Belle said. "You wouldn't believe who the hero actually turned out to be."

"Wasn't it the soldier?" Grace offered as the carriage took off. Although her mind was still reeling from what had just transpired between her and the doctor, she forced herself to remember some detail so as to appear undistracted. "The lowly one whom the duke kept calling a fool?"

"It was the soldier!" Arabella said happily, turning to Aunt

Belle. "And you said she wouldn't remember a thing about the opera."

Grace gazed at her aunt.

"You said that?"

"Only because it was a very dull and obvious opera," Aunt Belle said quickly, though a slight blush rose in her wrinkled cheeks. "So much so that we decided to leave a little early. I loathe when plays and musicales have such apparent plots."

"I like it," Arabella chimed in. "Especially when it's a romance. Tragedies, however, can be as unpredictable as possible."

"I don't know about that."

Grace was only partially listening to the two discuss what made for a good story, while her thoughts lingered back to the way she had reacted to James's kiss. Never in her life had she believed that she could respond to anyone the way she had to him. Of course, her only comparison was Lord Bartley, but she had been so utterly uncharmed by the man, not to mention the fact that she hadn't ever felt strongly about anyone her entire life. For the better part of her adult life, Grace had felt different from her sisters and the majority of society. She had never entertained the idea of companionship because she had never been able to form the sort of feelings that other people seemed to be able to do. Her aunt and sisters had all loved and loved deeply, to the point where Grace had felt a fragmented sort of jealousy, for how could she be envious of something she didn't understand? And she still wasn't quite sure what she was supposed to feel, but that kiss had awakened something she had never realized was within her.

Desire.

It was the oddest feeling when she realized exactly what she was feeling. She desired James. She wanted to be near him, to graze his beard with her fingertips, to press her body against his and feel—

Goodness. No, she couldn't do that. She was incompatible. Wasn't she? And surely, there might be a logical way to understand why her pulse increased whenever he was close, or why her skin would tingle if he should accidentally brush against her arm or hand.

Perhaps I might take notes on when and why I react the way I do. Yes. That seemed a practical thing to do. She would document her reactions and see if there was a way to map it out somehow, so that she might learn to understand it better.

Later that night, as she got ready for bed, Grace wondered if she might attempt a sort of experiment, to see if she would always respond the same way, or maybe if it was a temporary phenomenon.

For the rest of the evening, Grace lay awake in bed, unable to think of anything else and she wondered if perhaps she might settle her growing desires by tackling the entire event as a scientific experiment. By definition, a scientific experiment was a series of steps within a controlled environment that would lead to a hypothesis. What exactly she was hoping to learn, she wasn't sure, but there was obviously some sort of physical reaction shared by the two of them and ever being the curious mind, Grace wanted to test it further. Perhaps she would only enjoy kissing and nothing more. Or maybe, it was that she was only attracted to men of a certain height? But then that didn't quite make sense to her. Mr. Milton was just as tall as Dr. Hall. Maybe she only liked men with facial hair? But that couldn't be true either, as Lord Bartley also had a mustache.

No, there was something about James in particular that caused Grace to react in a chemical way and she intended to find out why.

By the time she arrived at the pharmacy office the following morning, Grace had decided to explain her planned experiment to the doctor, having rehearsed what she was going to say in her mind all morning, but upon stepping out of the carriage, a paperboy on the far corner of the street shouted and distracted her.

"Three more missing in Gallowgate! Gates go up around

Glasgow Necropolis to fend off grave robbers! Hear all about it!"

Grace frowned as a voice spoke behind her.

"G'morning, Dr. Grace," Virgil said, causing her to jump. "Oh, I didn't mean to frighten you."

"Oh, no, you didn't," she lied, peering over her shoulder. "I was just listening to that paperboy. It seems more people have gone missing in Gallowgate."

"Aye, someone is always missing in Gallowgate," Virgil said as he opened the front door, allowing Grace to enter before him. He followed her inside. "It's where a lot of people go to be forgotten as it were."

"Forgotten? But why?"

He shrugged as he hobbled around the glass display case.

"A number of reasons, really. Debt, crimes, the drink." Virgil shook his head. "It's not quite where respectable people live, you know."

"That's nonsense. Any place people live can be respectable, regardless of their means."

"Were that it was true, Dr. Grace. But the people in Gallowgate aren't exactly shining members of society."

"A lot of them are factory workers and their families. The very people who produce products for our consumption, Virgil. It is a mark against the company if they cannot provide decent housing and wages for the people who make the owners rich."

"Ah, well, now you're sounding like a Reformist, Dr. Grace. None too many would be pleased to hear you speak like that."

"They are simply facts."

"Aye, but some aren't too keen on hearing truths."

"And I'm to worry about that because?"

"Well, begging your pardon, but in your line of work, wouldn't it be smarter to keep on people's good side? I can't think it will be easy persuading people to see a lady doctor, and a reformist to boot."

Grace made a face, aware of what Virgil was trying to say, but not liking it at all because it was true. She would have a far harder time in her field if she went around spouting off her feelings about workers' rights and sanitary living conditions. But it didn't mean she had to be quiet, which she was just about to say when a voice cut through the air.

"Miss Sharpe? A word, if you will."

Grace spun around to see James standing in the doorway of his office at the back of the pharmacy. He nodded briefly once their eyes met before reentering his office, leaving her heart pounding and her head somewhat dizzy.

When had he gotten here?

Evidently, her stunned expression was painted all over her face, for Virgil glanced at her as he hobbled toward the opposite wall, carrying a glass jar full of dried herbs.

"Startled you, did he? My, you're jumpy today."

"I thought he hadn't arrived, is all," she said lowly, hoping the doctor didn't hear her.

"He can be incredibly quiet, when he wants to be."

"Miss Sharpe?" James called again.

Virgil jerked his head.

"Best go see what he wants. He sounds a bit miffed, doesn't he?"

Did he? Grace hadn't heard any difference in his tone, except perhaps a bit of urgency and deciding not to keep the doctor waiting any longer, went to the office.

James was standing in front of his desk, with his back facing her and upon hearing her enter, turned.

"Please close the door."

She did so, unsure why she felt as though she were suddenly in trouble. When she faced him again, however, she was startled to see that he had stepped closer, effectively eliminating any and all space between them. He opened his mouth to speak, but Grace spoke first.

"Dr. Hall, er, I would like to speak first, if I may?"

He stared at her a moment, before speaking. And then—

"James."

"Beg pardon?"

"You can call me James, if you'd like."

"Oh, yes, of course," she said, before exhaling. "I just want to thank you for last night."

James blinked.

"Thank me?"

"Yes. You see, I've decided to test a theory. One that has been on my mind for some years now and I think, because you are as practical a person as I, that it would do well to test this theory. Only if you're willing to, of course, I wouldn't want you to feel obligated in any way, it's just… I'm terribly curious and trying to discover something about myself."

"That discovery being?"

She paused, unsure how to tell him. It was rather embarrassing and yet, there was something trustworthy in him that she felt enabled to be honest. Taking a deep breath, she spoke.

"For as long as I could remember, I've felt outside of society. As a child, I was never one to run around wildly, or play tricks on family or friends. I've always been rather even tempered. Although, my sisters have done their best at provoking me." She smirked for a moment before it disappeared. "After my parents passed away, I was expectedly sad, but I also became obsessed with how they died. I thought if modern medicine had been more advanced, had a cure been discovered, they might not have needed to pass away so young. It became my obsession. Learning how the human body worked, the cause and effect of one's surroundings, their environment, food, disposition. I wanted to learn everything I could and so I read and read and read. I was sure if I could find enough texts, I might be able to start to puzzle together not only the human body, but also the human mind." Her gaze drifted, unfocused, around the room. "Emotions have always been a secondary situation for me. I know how I should react to things, how I'm expected to perform, but I've never felt anything on a deeper level, at my core. That's not to say I haven't experienced things such as love, but it's always been familiar at most. I've never fancied anyone, nor have I found anyone particularly attractive. For years, the only true emotions I felt were worry at my abnormality and disappointment in my failures, but then, last night…" She shook her head, unable to find the words to describe how she had felt. "It was almost other-worldly, I suppose." She glanced at him only to find him watching her intently with his bright gray-blue eyes. She swallowed. "I fear I'm not explaining it very well, but being who I am, I would like to investigate it further. With your permission, of course."

For a long moment, James did not speak and Grace began to worry that she had said the wrong thing. Finally, he inhaled deeply and folded his arms across his wide chest, exhaling before he spoke.

"Grace, it's not a practical thing to study, nor is it very wise for a lady to even entertain."

"But I'm not a lady. I'm going to be a doctor."

"Even so, there are certainly standards of society that we, you, me, everyone must comply with, particularly if you're seeking to fulfill a place in the public eye. Doctors are supposed to be pillars of their communities and something like this would tarnish a reputation, more so for you because you are a woman."

She nodded, grateful that he had refused her based on realities and not superfluous things, such as her looks.

"I understand," she said, just as an idea struck her. Well, not so much suddenly as what she had planned to do if he had said no. "If you are not willing to participate, I will not force you."

A huff of laughter escaped him.

"Believe me, Grace, you would not have to force me. But for the reasons stated, as well as our working relationship, I cannot agree to it."

"Absolutely," she said as he began to turn. "I suppose I'll have to resort to my secondary choice."

James stared at her, then blinked.

"Secondary choice?"

"Yes. I suppose Mr. Milton will do, although I doubt I will

have the same results. Still, it is something that needs investigating and I intend to do just that."

James's body froze in its spot and the air between them turned curious.

"Excuse me?"

His tone was suddenly different and by the jump in her pulse, Grace felt very much like she was suddenly in a locked room with an animal. Not something voracious, like a tiger or a bear, but something more cunning. Still, the expression on his face gave her pause.

"Are you feeling all right?" she asked.

"Mr. Milton?" James repeated, his voice rough, before clearing his throat. He gazed at her, though really it might be more of a glare. "What does Mr. Milton have to do with this?"

Grace's brow lifted.

"Well, like I said, I've been curious about this lacking part of myself for some time and I intend to learn about it one way or the other. I had hoped that you would be willing, considering how very alike we are in regards to our methods of learning, and as I believe we would be able to stay fairly level-headed. But, as you have decided not to participate, I will have to look elsewhere."

His dark brows drew together as he faced her once more and Grace was surprised to see such a quick change in his mood.

"So, Mr. Milton is to replace me?"

She tilted her head.

"How could Mr. Milton replace you if you were not in the experiment to begin with? I shall start with Mr. Milton, detail my findings, and try my best to learn what exactly is wrong with me."

"There's nothing the matter with you," he said hotly. "And you cannot simply replace me with the likes of Mr. Milton."

"Well, I refuse to abandon my research. And Mr. Milton is a fine candidate. He's just about your height, has all his teeth, which I will vainly admit I am partial to, and seems a smart man with an independent view on life."

"Teeth? That's one of your requirements?"

Sensing the sarcasm in his tone, Grace squared her shoulders.

"I'm afraid this is a topic I shan't discuss anymore with you. It is a private matter now and I would rather not hear you disparage it."

He stepped toward her.

"I cannot condone this, Grace. It's beyond foolish. It's dangerous. Your very reputation will be at stake."

Grace opened her mouth to argue, but shut it when she realized he was right. She lifted her chin.

"Possibly. But I am determined to sort out this part of me."

"And you're certain Mr. Milton will remain silent? That he will not blackmail you? Or threaten to expose you?"

Grace frowned.

"Why would he wish to do that?"

"Good God, Grace, have you no idea of the inner workings of a man? They can become possessive, insistent, downright evil when they want something."

"Rather harsh on your sex, aren't you?"

"It's facts. What if Mr. Milton falls in love with you? Asks you to marry him?" She laughed, but stopped suddenly when she saw the expression on his face. "What's so humorous?"

"I'm never getting married."

"How do you know?"

"Because I've decided not to, a long time ago."

He frowned and cocked his head.

"Why not?"

"Why would I? If I married, I would undoubtedly have to stop my work as a doctor. There is no man in the world worth such a sacrifice and I refuse to be in a position where I would have to get married."

The refined lines of James's face seemed to sharpen.

"How far do you plan on taking this experiment of yours, then?"

"How do you mean?"

"I mean, are you just going to write a few notes about kissing, or are you going to…" The last words seemed to die on his lips and Grace gave him a pitying look.

"I will go as far as I intend to on any given day."

"Bloody hell," he cursed, turning around as he began to pace the floor of his office. "This is an asinine thing to do."

"I do not remember asking your opinion on it."

"As your teacher, I forbid it." She made a face at him, as if she couldn't quite understand his ire, but then he stopped. "I mean it. If you go through with this and are discovered, it will be not only a mark on your family and friends, but your professional acquaintances. I cannot allow it."

Just then, a knock came to the door. Grace turned to open it and saw Virgil holding her coat, as well as James's.

"Yes?"

"It's ten to ten, Dr. Hall. You have an appointment at Andersen University. You mentioned it yesterday?"

"Gads. Yes, all right," James said, pulling out his pocket watch. "Two minutes and we'll be on our way."

"Yes, sir."

Virgil disappeared.

"An appointment at the university?" Grace repeated. "I didn't know you were going to be out of the office today."

"We're going out of the office. There's a lecture on the heart and the vascular system today and the lead professor asked that I attend him during the dissection."

"Dissection?" she repeated. "You mean, there will be a cadaver being used?"

"Yes. Sourced ethically, if you're worried. That newsboy at the end of the road certainly enjoys riling up the neighborhood, but I assure you, there hasn't been any sort of bodysnatching concerning Andersen University."

"I would hope not," Grace said, though she was hesitant. "Because I believe any university using unethical cadavers would be in violation of the law, correct?"

James pulled his coat on, one sleeve at a time.

"Correct." When Grace didn't answer, he glanced at her and all the irritability that had been in his gaze moments ago had vanished. "You're not opposed to cadavers, are you?"

"Not at all."

"Shall we then?" she said as she pulled on her own coat, only to be stilled by the touch of James's hand on her hip.

"We're not finished discussing your experiment, Grace," he breathed into her ear, causing her to take a deep breath. "Not by far."

And though Grace exited his office demonstrating a composure of complete indifference, a world of turmoil rolled within her.

Chapter Ten

THE OPERATING THEATER of Andersen University was on the top floor of the building, in a room known as the sun garret. Several large windows had been installed in the ceiling to allow the natural light of the day to shine down on the surgical table that was surrounded by ten circular rows of terraced bench seating and wooden railing.

The room was surprisingly cool, considering how warm the rest of the school was, having climbed the six stories to reach the surgical theater, and while the entire autopsy had been going on for nearly an hour, Grace felt as though she were the cadaver.

As the only woman in an audience of about twenty other young men, she had been sat on the far side of the room, on the top of the tenth row, where the curtain that had been drawn to highlight the operation for the other students partially blocked her view. It was disadvantageous to say the least, but it was the only place the lead physician, a Dr. Cameron, allowed Grace to sit, as he was outraged that she was in attendance.

James had argued on her behalf, but only just as she had instantly climbed the stairs to take the seat Dr. Cameron had offered. She wasn't interested in arguing, particularly when she could be removed from the theater completely and so took what was offered without hesitating, ignoring the discontentment displayed on James's face as he gazed up at her from the side of the operating table.

He and Dr. Cameron were dressed in white robes by an assistant. And his wasn't the only displeased glare she had to suffer. When the other medical students arrived, they had all glared at her. They pointed in her direction and whispered to one another, appearing agitated, if not downright hostile at her presence, but then the autopsy had begun and their ire turned to curiosity.

Still, every minute or so, one would sneer at her, as if it was unbelievable that she was there and in truth, it was.

But she couldn't keep allowing her focus to be drawn away from the task at hand, so she straightened her shoulders and leaned to her left, hoping to get a better view.

"And here we finally have the heart," Dr. Cameron said. His aged, narrow face appeared almost bored. "As you can see, there is a slight discoloration, indicating that it was damaged in its final moments. The organ itself is enlarged, which according to our medical records of Mr. Ferguson, indicates what, Mr. Jones?"

A short, round man with long sideburns stood up.

"Heart disease, doctor."

"Correct, and what other evidence might we discover that would lead to a diagnosis of heart disease? Mr. Collins?"

"A build-up of plaques in the arteries."

"Correct," Dr. Cameron said, pleasing the red-headed Mr. Collins. "However, if we examine the lungs, there is some fluid in the air sacs. What is this an indication of, Mr. Roberts?"

A dark-haired man sitting next to Mr. Collins frowned.

"Pulmonary embolism?"

"Incorrect, Mr. Roberts. Anyone have an idea?"

Grace went to raise her hand, but remembering that she wasn't readily in view of the attending doctors, as well as the glares she received from across the room, she lowered her hand.

"Miss Sharpe?" James's voice spoke, loud and clear.

Grace's cheeks warmed as she stared down at the center of the theater. James was watching her, the smallest of nods sent in her direction as if to buoy her confidence, while twenty young men above him stared daggers at her.

"Dr. Hall, there is no need to involve the lady," Dr. Cameron said.

"It's evidence of pneumonia," she answered loudly. "If Mr. Ferguson was ill with pneumonia at the time of his death, which is indicated by the state of his lungs, then it is likely what brought on the heart attack."

"How so?" James asked.

"The body's inflammatory response to pneumonia likely caused the plaque to break away from the artery, causing clots to form."

"But he died of a heart attack," Mr. Collins. "Not pneumonia."

"If the embolus is overlapping the bifurcation of the pulmonary trunk, then that's indicative of a blood clot," Grace said. "The cause of death may be a heart attack, but it was due to the complications suffered from pneumonia."

"Are you saying that if Mr. Ferguson didn't have pneumonia, he'd still be alive?" One of the other men scoffed. "He had a history of heart issues. Long documented."

"I'm not contesting that," Grace said calmly. "All I'm saying is that there isn't a single answer to Mr. Ferguson's demise, or at least, there is a secondary cause."

Several students glanced at one another and then down at Dr. Cameron, who, for all intents and purposes, appeared equal parts annoyed and satisfied. James was standing at the head of the table, his face covered with a cloth, so it wasn't possible to see his face, but Grace noted the slight crinkle at the corners of his eyes. He was pleased.

Dr. Cameron rolled his eyes and sighed out loud, making sure his frustration was noted by the entire class. Including Grace.

"Which is precisely what we set out to learn at the beginning of this lesson," Dr. Cameron said, as he turned to the assistant, who began removing his leather gloves and robe. "Do not let the most obvious answer be the only answer, gentlemen, or you will find yourself outsmarted by a woman."

Though the class seemed irritated at this, the distinct sound of a single laugh came from James's direction, causing Grace's cheeks to burn. Thankfully, it seemed that the class was over as the students began to stand up and shuffle out of the room. Grace stood and with a jerk of his head, James directed her to follow the others, which she did, only to be met by Mr. Collins and Mr. Roberts.

She gave them a small smile, hoping to go around them, but Mr. Roberts was quick to put himself in front of her, causing her to stop abruptly.

"Miss Sharpe, was it?" he asked, extending a hand. "I'm Mr. John Roberts. This is Mr. William Collins."

Unable to avoid it, Grace took his hand, surprised by the rough shake that he gave her.

"A pleasure to meet you, Mr. Roberts. Mr. Collins. I'm Miss Grace Sharpe," she said, pulling her hand back with a good amount of force before being released. "Are you students of Dr. Cameron?"

"Yes, we are."

"Two years now," Mr. Collins said. "We're just about to start our apprenticeships, but er, you've already begun yours, it would seem?"

"Yes," she said. "I wasn't permitted to any universities unfortunately and have been apprenticing for the past year and a half."

"Not with Dr. Hall. I've not seen you here before and he's a bit of a reputation for keeping his apprentices close."

"No, I've only just started with Dr. Hall. My mentor, Dr. Barkley, has been overseeing my studies."

"Dr. Barkley?" Mr. Collins said, his brow pinched. "The country doctor from Glencoe?"

"Yes, the very same."

"Er, not to discount what I'm sure are shining credentials, but Andersen University is on the cutting edge of modern medicine. This isn't a school for common country folk."

Grace tilted her head.

"Are country folk not susceptible to all the maladies of people who live in the city?"

"What Mr. Collins means is, we're not herbalists here. This is a school for surgery, for the progress of medical sciences. There's no bloodletting or potions done in this facility and I'm not sure a lady, particularly one who's studied beneath someone like Dr. Barkley, quite fits in here."

"Yes, it would probably be best for you to try nursing or something less complicated," Mr. Collins said, a smug appearance in his eyes.

To diminish the profession of nursing was inexcusable to Grace, particularly when it was nurses who did the majority of patient care. But Grace was used to being underestimated and rarely cared about the opinions of others when it came to herself. Still, to her surprise, her heart began to beat irregularly and the back of her neck prickled with hostility.

"Say what you will about me, sirs, but Dr. Barkley is a brilliant man, one of whom either one of you would be lucky to study under, although I can say with certainty that he would have neither of you."

Mr. Roberts glowered.

"Oh? And why's that?"

"Because medicine, according to Dr. Barkley, requires patience, perseverance, and possibility. It is why they call what we do a practice and not a perfect."

"What we do?" Mr. Roberts scoffed. "Be aware, my lady, that we do not do the same things. Mr. Collins and I are to be surgeons and you will likely be some sort of children's nurse. As you should, considering the delicate nature of the fairer sex."

Her pride somewhat hurt, she should have allowed them to turn away with the last word, but Grace was behaving quite out of character in that moment.

"Dr. Hall is no country physician and rather respected, is he not?" she called out, causing the two to pause at the top of the stairs. "I wonder what your thoughts are about him, having taken me on as an apprentice."

Mr. Collins and Mr. Roberts stared at one another for a moment before a satisfying smirk spread across Mr. Roberts's face. He glanced back at Grace.

"I'm sure whatever reasons Dr. Hall has for taking you on as an apprentice have everything to do with your family's position."

She laughed.

"Really? You think I've somehow bought my way into an apprenticeship?"

"Yes. Your aunt is Lady Belle Smyth, is she not?"

Grace frowned.

"Yes, she is."

Mr. Roberts pointed up at the doorway behind Grace, causing her to turn around. There, above the doorway was a brass plaque that read:

In honor of her esteemed donation to the betterment and progress of medical studies, Lady Belle Smyth, 1850.

The snickers that disappeared behind her were like stones being tossed into a well, the well being her stomach. How had she not known about her aunt's donation to this school? Surely, it should have come up in conversation, particularly since she had known that Grace was going to attend a class here?

Why hadn't Aunt Belle told her?

Confused and deflated, Grace wished to return to the pharmacy. Reentering the theater to find James, she was momentarily lost in thought when she heard raised voices from behind the curtains.

"It's not only ridiculous, but dangerous!" Dr. Cameron's voice echoed in the cavernous room. "A woman shouldn't be anywhere near an operating table."

Grace froze.

"I think you're overexaggerating," James's voice countered.

"Really? Would you let her operate on you?"

"Inconsequential. I wouldn't let any of your students operate on me. They've never even cleaned a wound. At least Miss Sharpe has removed boils."

"Because they need to learn the basics before they can begin to attend a lead physician in a surgery. Miss Sharpe hasn't studied nearly enough—"

"She's quite well read—"

"Not beneath an instructor."

"Because she is not permitted to attend university."

"Exactly! Because women cannot be doctors. That mentor of yours should have his license revoked for even considering this madness. Just because Barkley couldn't find another pupil to teach does not mean he can just pick a woman up out of a briar patch and instruct her on medicine."

James's tone turned frosty.

"Disparage me all you like, but I will not hear anything against Dr. Barkley."

A beat. And then.

"I understand your position, Dr. Hall. Really, I do and I sympathize. If it weren't for Dr. Barkley, you'd not be where you are today and you are a fine doctor." He paused. "But if you insist on this, allowing a woman to apprentice for you, I fear I will not be able to quell the growing outrage at this decision. You saw my students today. They will not tolerate a woman in this space."

Grace strained to hear James's response. A defeated sigh escaped him and Grace was certain she would not like his next words.

"Perhaps you are right," he said, as Grace's heart sank into her stomach. "Perhaps there is no place for a woman in your school."

Although she had become used to the remarks that people made about her once they discovered her intention to become a doctor, this lack of faith hurt for some reason. Quickly, she exited the room once more and waited for James. Once Dr. Cameron and his assistant departed, James followed and he and Grace left the building in silence. Although he couldn't know how she was feeling, Grace was aware of him watching her. When they were finally in the carriage, he spoke.

"I'm sorry if you were met with some resistance by the others. Dr. Cameron and his students can be particular about who shares their surgical theater."

Grace remained perfectly still.

"It was an informative lesson. Thank you for including me."

Though she tried to speak with a stiff coldness, her heart was racing. James frowned.

"Are you well?"

"Yes."

A pregnant pause.

"You don't seem to be."

"Would you like to check my forehead?" she asked sarcastically. "I am fine."

"Very well," he replied. "Then perhaps we should return to our previous discussion."

"What discussion?"

"Your experiment."

Shame suddenly reached up and wrapped around her, like a drowning hand searching for leverage. Why she had ever even considered speaking to him about that, she couldn't comprehend. It was just that, for a moment during their night at the opera, Grace had felt sure and safe with him. As if she could tell him anything and yet, in the miserable aftermath of hearing him agree with Dr. Cameron, Grace couldn't help but feel betrayed.

"I don't wish to discuss that with you."

He stared at her as the carriage rocked back and forth across the cobblestone streets. His cool blue-gray eyes bore into her and she had to look down.

"Why not?"

"Because."

"I think I'm entitled to it."

Her gaze snapped up to meet his.

"How so, are you entitled to it?"

"If you're planning on carrying out some sort of affair while under my tutelage, I should like to be aware of it, so that I might take some precautions in protecting my reputation as well as yours."

She stared at him and blinked.

"You would try to protect me? Even if I did something so foolish?"

"At least you are aware that it is foolish, although if you intend to go through with it, I may question your sanity. But yes. I would try to protect your reputation."

"So that I might experiment with another man?"

There was a small twitch just below his right cheekbone. Though she couldn't see if he was clenching his jaw through his beard, the heat in his stare seemed to confirm it.

"Yes."

"Augh!" She let out, unable to control her frustration. Her hands curled into fists as she pounded the seat on either side of her. "Arrogant man."

He blinked.

"Excuse me?"

"I do not wish to experiment with Mr. Milton and I will not stand to be pushed out of this profession. I will be a doctor one day, James. Mark my words. If I have to shadow Dr. Barkley for ten years, I'll do it and no amount of cutting remarks or people's opinions will deter me."

He stared at her for a moment before finding his voice.

"I believe you will succeed."

"Then say it."

"Say what?"

"Say that I will be a doctor."

"I don't see how—"

"Say it."

His brow furrowed as if he were confused.

"You will be a doctor, Grace."

"Now believe it."

"I do—"

"Then don't shrink when others tell you that I don't belong," she said as the carriage rolled to a stop. The driver was quick to scrabble down from his seat and open the door. "Good night, Dr. Hall."

But James reached for her forearm before she could reach the door. They stared at one another, challenging and yearning, in a swell of confusion. Slowly, he unfurled his fingers, but she didn't move. She wanted him to pull her toward him, to hold her against him and press his mouth to hers and kiss her just as he had the night before.

The small cough of the driver seemed to break the spell they were both under and Grace slid across her seat and exited the vehicle. The door shut behind her and she jumped, her nerves having finally reached the end of their limits.

As she climbed the stone steps and entered into the foyer of her terrace home, Grace removed her coat and slowly began her ascent up the stairs, only to be stopped by her aunt's voice.

"Grace? How did your day go?"

"It was fine," she said halfheartedly over her shoulder, as she continued her climb, eager to bathe and get into bed. "Just fine."

Chapter Eleven

JAMES JABBED TWICE with his left hand, then hooked with his right as his gloved fist connected with his opponent's jaw, sending the heavy man back a few steps.

"Gaw, Hall! You've a right wickedness about you today!" the burly man yelled.

"Did he hurt you, Perry?" The familiar masculine voice of Graham McKinnon called out from the bench seat, causing James to drop his guard.

"Graham?" he asked, before a meaty fist slammed into the corner of his jaw, causing him to fall back.

"Bad form, Perry!" Graham called out, though the sound of his voice was muffled as James rubbed his gloved hands over his head.

"You shouldn't have distracted him!"

James rolled to his side, knees bent up in the fetal position before he rocked himself into a crawling situation. Graham, who had climbed through the ropes of the pugilist ring, was on all fours next to him. "Are you all right?"

James nodded, though he was far from all right. His head was pounding and his body was achy and sore from being in the ring for hours, but it was the only thing he could do that would distract him from obsessing about Grace and their last conversation.

It had been telling how much her perceived lack of faith had affected him, as she had apparently been listening in to his conversation with Dr. Cameron. What was worse, however, was the fact that she had stopped listening before he had said his peace.

"Perhaps there is no place for a woman in your school," James had said as Dr. Cameron came around to pat him on the back.

"There you are," his colleague had replied.

"But then it is at the loss of this school, these students and the doctors that teach them. Because Grace Sharpe is a brilliant mind and the world will be a better place when she becomes a practicing physician."

The betrayed wonder that had shown on Dr. Cameron's face wasn't at all unlike the expression Grace had given James when she left the carriage. His ego had been to blame when he reached for her, eager to tell her everything he had said, but a wee modest part of his heart told him to let her go. If she wanted to believe that he was a man without conviction, what did he care?

Pushing himself up to his knees, he took a step up on one wobbly leg, then another. He intended to finish this round.

"Out of the way," he said, waving his friend to the side.

"Are you mad?" Graham asked, standing in front of him. "You've just been rocked."

"I don't care."

"Would you allow one of your patients to continue?"

"I'm not a bloody patient. Now move."

Graham was hesitant as he finally sighed, shaking his head as he left the ring to watch from the floor. James signaled to his opponent and put his hands back up.

"Ye're a bit muddled, ain't ya, doctor?" Perry asked.

"Try it."

Perry obliged.

"All right. It's your funeral."

The large man came bounding forward, but James was ready. He sidestepped his opponent's charge and turned around, just as Perry did, only James was faster. With a jab to the jaw and a double shot to his ribs, James stepped back to allow the stunned Perry to sway.

"Bloody hell. Where'd that come from?"

But James didn't answer. Instead, he stepped forward again, faked right before uppercutting from the left. Perry stumbled back, but James wouldn't let up and charged, hitting him in the ribs repeatedly until Perry fell on the ropes and began waving his hands.

"All right! All right!" He spat, droplets of blood spraying James in the face, causing him to jump back. "What the bloody hell is wrong with you?"

James rolled out of the ring as Graham came forward to help remove the tightly laced leather gloves. Although gloves were often used in sparring, Perry had once been a bareknuckle fighter. He was talented too, but James himself had tended to Perry at the end of his career and convinced him to teach with gloves, as it was far safer than scarring his students.

Of course, James didn't have to worry about that.

"Where did that come from?" Graham asked as James toweled himself dry from the sweat that glistened all over him.

"What?"

"That. You never attack to the end like that. You've always been, well, rather annoying when you fight, actually. Always trying to teach your opponent what they did wrong, or where to try and strike. But that," Graham said, bobbing his head at the ring from where Perry was glaring. "That was brilliant."

"It wasn't brilliant," James spat. "It was stupid and irresponsible." He threw his towel to the bench and walked over. "I'm sorry, Perry. That wasn't right of me."

Perry made a face and shook his head before letting out a laugh.

"Aye, it wasn't. But it's fine," he said with a laugh, showing that he wasn't bothered. "You're just full of fire and piss today, is all."

"Yes," James said before heading toward the corner of the room.

St. Mungo's Pugilist Club was something of a social club for professional men that had been set up in an old stone building, across the street from the cathedral in the center of Glasgow. It had once been a place where church members could go to discuss charity, particularly what to do about donations and where to allot certain monies. Of course, several times arguments would erupt and the men would start physical altercations and soon it seemed that fighting with one another in a sequestered spot gave them a better attitude in their private lives, as well as a time and space to settle their disagreements. Thus, the natural progression of things turned it into a pugilist club.

Graham had followed him to the area in the back of the room, where a wall of open, wooden cupboards had been fitted, where each individual section was fitted with a hook and a stool. An employee known as Roger met James there with a bucket of clean water and a length of white cloth. James was quick to dip the fabric in the water and wash his face, neck, and hair, before he ran it over his body. He was shirtless, and fitted in a loose pair of pantaloons that had been specifically made for this sport.

Graham folded his arms across his chest as he watched James, seemingly searching for something.

"What?" James snapped finally, as he finished washing himself.

Graham shook his head.

"You seem out of sorts, Hall. What's the matter?"

"Nothing's the matter, and I wish to God everyone would stop asking me what's wrong."

One of Graham's brows lifted.

"Forgive me, but that's the exact response someone who is in a foul mood would say and being as you're, one, never in poor spirits, and two, always fairly even tempered even when you're three sheets to the wind, you must excuse everyone for trying to learn why you're in such a contrary way."

"If it is my prerogative to be contrary, that I shall be," he said, flinging the cloth into the bucket. "I'm damn tired of trying to please everyone around me."

Graham nodded.

"Fair. But this wouldn't have anything to do with Lady Belle, would it?"

James paused as his gaze snapped to Graham's.

"What would make you say that?"

He shrugged.

"Belle's always been a thorn in my side, and more recently to the people she's convinced to do her bidding."

"I've not consented to any bidding."

"Oh no? Haven't you allowed Grace to shadow you these past few weeks since she's left Glencoe?" Something must have shone on his face, or perhaps he took too long to respond, because as he pulled his shirtsleeves over his head, he saw a telling expression form on Graham's face. "Ah. So, this has to do with Grace."

James undid the ties of his pantaloons as he turned away. There would be no use denying it to someone like Graham, who had been a close personal friend and somewhat an enemy of Lady Belle and therefore knew all the Sharpe sisters fairly well, having married the eldest, Hope.

"First, Dr. Barkley asks that I let the woman shadow me," James began as he took up the washcloth again and began wiping the sweat from his legs and buttocks. As a physician, and someone who grew up swimming in the nude in the lochs of the Highlands, James hadn't any reservations about his body. "Which, I refuse, considering what it would look like to my colleagues. Then, Lady Belle requests that I allow it, as a personal favor. Again, I refuse, only to have my own aunt threaten to come to Glasgow and shadow me herself if I do not consent to Miss Sharpe's apprenticeship. So, I oblige them, all of them, and do you know what I found?"

Graham shook his head as James dropped the cloth and grabbed his pants.

"No. What?"

"A capable, clever apprentice. She's smart and hardworking. She doesn't react to open wounds or broken bones in the way that so many believe women would. She's determined."

"She is that," Graham said, having lived with her for a period. "She knows a great deal about the human body and the maladies that affect it. For as long as she lived in Lismore Hall, she had her head buried in a book."

"Yes. And she knows she's clever, which unfortunately is construed as arrogance, particularly to these men who don't believe a woman can become a doctor."

"That's good, though, isn't it? She's a perfect demonstration of what women are capable of."

James shook his head as he pulled on one pant leg, then the other.

"It wouldn't matter if she was Asclepius himself. They don't care if she's capable; they only care that she is a woman. And thus, I'm in the very position I knew I was going to be in."

"Which is?"

"Arguing with nearly everyone in my profession on her behalf, and not because she's lacking, but the very opposite. I did not want to be some sort of champion, Graham. I have a practice, patients, not to mention these stints at university and the police with their ever-growing list of victims. They want to give every bloody person who dies in this city an autopsy."

"It sounds like you have a lot on your plate."

"I do. And through all of it, there's Grace. Just steadfast in her work and by my side through all of it and…"

He closed his eyes, his body stilling as he dressed. He would not betray her confidence about her experiment, but from the moment she had explained her intent in his office, he hadn't been able to think of anything else. And when he had refused her and she had told him that she would simply ask Mr. Milton to replace him, well, he had thought of little else since.

James's jaw tensed. That thought and that thought alone had given him the energy to battle ten rounds with Perry in the ring.

James had been incensed when she had told him her plan and what was worse, he hadn't refused because he didn't find her attractive.

It was because he was so very drawn to every bit of her, that he refused. Grace was everything a man could ask for. She was beautiful, yes, but it was secondary to her brilliance. Her patience and her fortitude. She was so sure of things, that her confidence buoyed him. He wanted her with him always, at work, at the university, at home…

That was the worst of it. Every evening when they closed the office, he set out on his way home, following her carriage until he reached her street. Then, he would continue up one block and enter his own empty home. He ate dinner alone, then he would retire to his bedroom, which just so happened to have a perfect view of her bedroom.

James had noticed it one of the first days after she had arrived in Glasgow. He had been undressing for bed and saw her move across the window, dressed in a conservative nightgown, staring down at a book in her hands as she paced, back and forth, for nearly two hours. He had tried not to watch, knowing that it was a great invasion of privacy, but as the night settled down around the city, the warm glow from her room seemed to call to him, like a moth to a flame. Since that first night, it had become something of a ritual, one that he was ashamed of, but he couldn't help it. Every once in a while she would stop her pacing and gaze up, as if she were making a point to remember something. A few times, she had even gone to her window and stared up at the night sky and for those few moments, James wondered what it might be like if she saw him.

"James?" Graham said, as if he had already tried to get his attention.

He opened his eyes, sighed deeply, and began to finish dressing.

"It's not anything," James said finally, deciding not to confide in his friend. His relationship with Grace, whatever it was, was something he'd rather keep to himself. Not to mention, Graham was her brother-in-law and had become something of a surrogate guardian to the Sharpes. James couldn't tell him about his feelings regarding Grace. "Tell me. What are you doing in Glasgow?"

Graham watched him for a moment longer, as if he was contemplating to press his friend about Grace, but then Graham nodded, and James was grateful.

"Actually, I've only come to do a walkthrough of the candy factory before Hope gives birth. I likely won't be in town for several months after the bairn is born."

"I'm surprised you left her," James said as he sat to put his boots on. "You've barely left her side since she told you of her condition."

"Yes, well, Hope threatened to climb Ben Nevis if I didn't leave to take care of the factory. She seems to think I've become unbearable," he said, with an expression of disbelief. "Dr. Barkley assured me that she is still a few weeks away from her due date, so I am here to finish whatever business I can before then."

"Well, it's good to see you. Are you staying in town then?"

"No, but I do have to stop by to see Belle. Would you come? I prefer not being outnumbered by her household."

"Understood," James said, pulling on his jacket. He reached into his pocket to check his watch. Although logically, he knew he should keep his distance from Grace, he couldn't help but want to see her. It was Sunday, the only day he kept for himself, but as it was already past noon, and he had done what he wanted for the day, he nodded. "I suppose I can lend you some support."

Graham gave him a knowing smirk and patted him on the back.

"I'll owe you," he said as the men left the club.

As both men had taken their own horses, the cobblestone road appeared busier than usual for a Sunday, although, the pugilist club was directly across the street from a church. Small cart vendors, eager to take advantage of the crowds, set up along the way and a number of people were walking and stopping, enjoying the clear, crisp day.

A flower seller handed a bouquet of dried blooms to a fashionable lady, while a small fishmonger appeared to be closing up.

"Break in at the Glasgow Necropolis!" the voice of a paperboy called out from the corner as James climbed up onto his horse's back. "Two shillings per paper! Read it all here!"

"Two shillings for a paper?" Graham asked, seemingly surprised. "The cost of living in a city."

Soon they were off, riding through the city at an advanced pace and they were able to reach the royal crescent in a short time. As Graham had visited his factory that morning, he had gone on and on about the production lines that had been installed that summer. By the time they reached Lady Belle's house, James had learned more than he ever expected to about turning honey into candy and Graham was still talking when the footmen took their horses, only for the front door to open.

James's entire demeanor soured instantly at the sight of Mr. Milton placing his top hat on his head, bowing to Grace and Arabella.

"Graham!" Grace said as she brushed past Mr. Milton to hug her brother-in-law.

Graham twirled her around once before placing her squarely in front of James, who was trying hard not to breathe in the scent of her.

Mr. Milton's brow raised.

"Mr. Milton, this is my brother-in-law, Mr. Graham McKinnon."

"A pleasure," Milton said as the two men shook hands. "Ah, and Dr. Hall. A pleasure."

"Milton," James said tautly as Milton turned his attention back to Grace.

"Well, I look forward to seeing the both of you. It will be a pleasure to host such ladies," Mr. Milton was saying as Graham and James came forward.

"Mr. Milton here was gracious enough to invite us to a ball

he'll be hosting in a few weeks' time."

"You are also invited, the both of you," Milton said, gesturing to James and Graham. "It should be a rather large affair."

"I'm afraid I will not be in Glasgow," Graham said, as he patted James on the back. "But I'm sure the good doctor would be thrilled to attend."

James glared at Graham who was smirking, pleased with himself for some reason.

"Of course," James said, his entire manner stiff. "Good day, Mr. Milton."

"Hm? Oh yes, I was leaving," he said, turning back to Grace and Arabella. He bowed. "It was a pleasure, ladies."

Arabella blushed, covering her smile with her face while Grace curtsied. For some reason, the simple curtsy was enough to tip James back into bad spirits, when suddenly Grace's hand was on his cheekbone, pressing the tender skin ever so slightly, in front of Graham and Arabella.

"Dr. Hall, what's happened?" she asked, worried. "Your face is swollen. And there seems to be broken blood vessels all along your eye."

"Ah, don't worry about that," Graham said, as James stared down into Grace's concerned eyes. "He just went a couple of rounds at the club."

"You were fighting?"

"Boxing," he said, as he raised his hand to gently pull hers away.

"That's a dangerous activity."

"I am aware of it," he said as he forced himself to release her hand. "But one I unfortunately find invigorating."

"You should put a poultice on that."

"I will."

"Soon," she insisted.

James glanced at the others, who each seemed to be watching them with varying levels of interest. Nodding, he took a step back.

"I believe you are correct, Miss Sharpe. I shall do so now. Graham?" he said, shaking his hand. "It was good to see you."

"Are you leaving?"

"Yes. Good day, Miss Scott," he paused. "Miss Sharpe."

"Good day," she said softly, almost sorry as he left.

James had decided that being in her home was not a smart move. If he was to think clearly, he needed to be out of her presence and in the short time it took him to reach his own house, he had decided to leave Grace alone.

Exhausted from the day, James took a bath once he returned home and fell asleep in his bed, having no energy or desire to eat or stay awake. After a short, fitful sleep, he woke up in the dark, wide awake. It was his own fault, he knew, but as he lay on his back, staring up into the darkness, he questioned the very restless feeling that seemed his constant companion these last few days.

There was one thing he thought of that he could do that would send him back to sleep and though social constructs might label him a vagrant for such behavior, he was a man of science. That, and the way the memory of Grace's kiss haunted him was too much.

Eyes closed, her image appeared instantly, honey-colored eyes wide and eager, mouth barely open, just as it had been in the carriage. James's hand moved down his abdomen, gripping the length of himself in his large hand. He squeezed tight at first, almost as a penance, before the picture in his mind shifted. He imagined Grace in a short-sleeve muslin nightgown, one that was oversized so that it could be removed with ease. His breath hitched as the illusion of her lifted her shoulder, pulling her one arm up over the collar, followed by the other as it slipped low, revealing what he had only felt.

His brow pinched, the fantasy lacking, but he was too desperate, too in need. God, what he wouldn't do to have her in his bed. He flexed his other hand, wanting to run his fingers through her hair, to smell the mint that seemed to linger in every room after she left. He hadn't been able to drink mint tea in weeks now, having become semi-hard at only the scent of it.

His hand pumped, up and down, faster, squeezing just so every few seconds as he edged his pleasure as his breath became ragged. He imagined that it was her hand on him, sat next to him in bed, and when his mind dared to picture her lowering herself over his lap, he tensed as the image of her in his mind blurred and he spent himself with a final moan, gasping as he did.

Once James's heart rate finally subsided, a wave of guilt washed over him as he rolled off the bed to clean himself up. Man of science he might be, but he was only a man. As he walked to the water table that was near the window, he glanced up to see Grace, in her own window, staring in his direction.

James froze, momentarily worried that he was visible, but as his room was pitch black and the night was dark, he realized she couldn't see him, even though she was staring right in his direction. In the next moment, she turned away and soon after the warm glow dimmed and James was left wondering what had possessed her to gaze in his direction.

It was many minutes later that he finally turned away and continued a restless night's sleep.

⟫✦⟪

Chapter Twelve

"Aɴᴅ ᴛʜᴇɴ Mʀ. Clayton said why is the devil riding a mouse like one and the same thing? Because it is synonymous!" Arabella said with a chuckle, while Aunt Belle let out a hearty laugh. "Did you hear that, Grace? Sin-on-a-mouse? Isn't Mr. Clayton humorous?"

"Hm?" Grace asked, glancing up from the paper she was reading.

It was early, far earlier than when the house usually took breakfast, but as it was the day Grace was to take her monthly visit to Gallowgate with James, she had to be up and ready before the sun. Aunt Belle and Arabella, who had felt that Grace was working too hard, had decided to wake up so that they could share breakfast with her.

Unfortunately, Grace wasn't very good company, as she had become used to having a simple breakfast of fruit slices, whether it be damson, apple, or gooseberries, toast, and tea while she read the paper alone. The morning headline was particularly interesting too, as it said there were two more disappearances that were reported on the past week, bringing the total to fourteen missing persons in the course of two months.

"My dear," Aunt Belle began, having to cover her mouth with her bejeweled hand as she yawned. "It isn't very polite to read the paper while you're in company."

Grace dropped the paper and gave her aunt and Arabella an apologetic smile.

"I'm sorry, truly. I've just become rather used to taking my breakfast alone."

"Which is exactly why we've decided to wake up with you now, although," Arabella said, covering her own yawn. "This cannot be a sustainable way to live, waking so early. The sun is barely up."

"I agree," Aunt Belle said, taking a sip of tea as she stared deliberately at her niece. "Too much work and too little sleep will lead to an early grave."

"Yes, but there is an argument that oversleeping can do just as much harm. There was a German doctor who wrote a book about the topic of sleep. I believe it was Dr. Ackermann," Grace countered, finishing her own tea. "He said that one cannot sleep peacefully without expending a certain amount of energy throughout the day. If I didn't work, I'd likely never sleep, and that would be worse than waking up a little early."

Aunt Belle shook her head.

"You are my least favorite of your sisters to argue with, you know. Always so practical and precise with your list of facts and footnotes. It's a bore, really."

Grace smirked as the grandfather clock chimed from the hallway. Six o'clock. She stood up while wiping the corner of her mouth with the napkin as she smoothed out her skirts as Penguin came sauntering into the dining room. She bent down to scratch him behind his ear as he purred loudly, but she didn't have time to waste today. James's carriage would be pulling up in exactly two minutes, as he left his own residence at exactly this time.

"Enjoy your time at the Milton arcade today, and do take details of everything. I wish to be well informed before attending Mr. Milton's ball next week."

"We should do no such thing," Aunt Belle said, her chin up high. "You should come with us and see for yourself."

"I cannot abandon Dr. Hall in Gallowgate."

"Did he not venture to Gallowgate alone before you arrived in Glasgow?"

"Actually, he took Virgil to assist him, but Virgil's leg bothers him when it rains and," a crack of thunder boomed around them, highlighting Grace's point. "I'm afraid duty calls."

"Well, do not feel envious when you return home and find that we are not here," Belle said pointedly. "Because after the Milton Arcade, I plan on taking Arabella to visit the Baroness Glengirth. It's a few miles outside of the city and we shan't be home until late in the evening, if we come home at all."

Grace brought her hand to her forehead in a faux salute.

"I promise, I will not sulk."

"And Mrs. Stevens is coming with us, so I gave an extra day off to the rest of the staff." She paused, as if to let her words sink in. "I hope that will not be too troublesome for you? But considering how independent you are, I doubt it will cause you any issue."

Grace's brow scrunched, confused as to why her aunt seemed so intent with this information.

"I promise, Aunt Belle, I will be perfectly fine alone."

"We will come back, I'm sure," Arabella offered, seemingly worried as she glanced at Belle. "We cannot let her spend the entire night alone in an empty house."

"Nonsense," the elder woman said, waving her hand in the air. "Grace is perfectly capable. Now go."

Belle turned her cheek up, so that Grace could kiss it and once she did, Grace hurried out of the dining room, shaking her head at her aunt's strange behavior. Mrs. Stevens had her coat open and ready. Grace quickly donned the garment and tied her bonnet under her chin as a footman hastened to follow her out of the house while keeping an umbrella above her head until she reached the open door of James's carriage. She was quick to climb in and sit across from him and glanced up to see him, stoic and silent, dressed in his usual black suit and sat slightly off center, as he was too tall to sit straight.

It was a wild, bracing sensation she felt in her chest, every time she looked into the doctor's eyes. After her last biting words, she half expected that he might go to Gallowgate without her, or that he might be angry with her, but as she gazed back at him, all she saw was something that didn't make any sense.

Yearning.

It was instant, and disappeared in a flash, but for an entire second, Grace could have sworn that she saw a longing in his eyes that matched exactly how she had felt the night before, when she had stared out the window of her room. After her brother-in-law had left, she had retired to her room and spent the better part of the evening trying to read, although every few minutes she had stopped to gaze out at his dark house. Had he gone home after he left her house yesterday? It didn't seem so. No one appeared to be home which had caused her a great deal of curiosity. If he hadn't gone home, where had he gone?

Perhaps to a friend's house, or maybe somewhere else. Maybe he had plans. Possibly with another doctor, or maybe there was a female acquaintance that Grace hadn't learned about yet.

She hated how desperate she had become to know if there was another woman in his life.

"The weather is not in our favor today," he said suddenly, his face angled to peer out of the carriage window. "I fear rain can make our work more difficult."

"How so?"

"The lodgings can become damp, particularly those housed on the first floors of these buildings. It's harder for patients to keep dressings dry and uninfected." He sighed. "Hopefully it will not last."

"Winter is not far off. This will be snow in a few weeks."

"Which can be worse. The winter is forever wet in this part of the city. There is no escaping it."

Grace nodded, taking in the gravity of his words as they rode the rest of the way in silence. It seemed today was not the day for them to discuss any sort of situation that might be budding between them, and for that, Grace was somewhat grateful. At the very least, the work they had in front of them would keep her plenty busy so that her thoughts wouldn't wander.

Upon reaching Gallowgate, Grace smelled the familiar pungent smell of rotting vegetables and human waste. James pulled the small vial of lime oil out of the breast pocket of his jacket, dabbed some on his forefinger, and wiped it beneath his nostrils. He handed it to Grace, who did the same and as the carriage came to a stop, she handed it back to him before climbing out.

They were quick to enter the same factory lodging building as they had a month ago. This time, however, they went to the top floor of the building and started their visit with the last patient they had seen a month ago.

"Why?" Grace asked as they made their way down the hallway to the last room.

"It's a way for me to keep my practice even." He knocked on the door. "After seeing eighty-two patients, I tend to become tired and so if I switch it, I'm giving my best to this family, the Walshes, at least every other month."

"Oh." Grace nodded as a young girl opened the door and she followed him into the room.

For the next nine hours, Grace and James worked their way through the building, visiting room after room to either spend a few moments just checking on patients or upward of twenty minutes where they would clean wounds, monitor fevers, or distribute medicines to the ill.

James had been correct about the weather. The rain had somehow made most of the interior walls damp, and the smell of mildew and mold seemed to permeate off them, effectively making the lime oil above their top lips useless.

Although Grace knew that this was how factory workers lived in cities across the United Kingdom, she couldn't help wanting to do something about it. The very building they lived in seemed to be choking them. These people deserved to live with dignity and not in squalor.

After finishing with the Harrison family, Grace and James exited their room, just as several raised voices echoed down the hallway. There were two sets of men, each carrying a third man through the door. It appeared that both men were injured. The first was wearing a bloody bandage wrapped around his one eye, moaning in pain, while the man in the middle seemed to be choking as his head slouched back as the others tried to hoist him up. An older woman came out of one of the apartments, just as James hurried forward.

"Get Mrs. Muller!" one of the men yelled. "And Cassie Mac-Intosh!"

"What's happened?" James asked.

"Ah, Dr. Hall, thank God," the same man said. "There was an accident at the factory."

"A gauge broke on one of the power looms. Snapped right off and the entire operation went haywire. Heddles and shuttles flew everywhere." He motioned to the bandaged man he was carrying. "Got poor Lonnie in the eye."

James gave him a tight nod before facing the other man.

"What about him?"

"Daft thing. He tried to help Lonnie, but the reed snapped up and the way he was angled, he caught the blasted thing in the throat. He can't breathe correctly."

Grace came to stand next to James as they moved the men into one of the apartments. It was Mrs. Muller's room. They brought the man with the eye injury to a straw cot while seating the man struggling to breathe on a wooden chair.

"Right. I'll take the eye, you see what you can do about him," James said to Grace. "He likely just has a swollen pharynx."

Grace split from him instantly to tend to her patient, but knew almost instantly that something wasn't right. The man's body started to tense and the soft gurgling that she had heard in the hallway had stopped.

"He isn't breathing," she said, coming to her knees. "Bring him here, lie him down on the floor."

The men were quick to follow her instruction, kicking away the chair as they laid him flat on his back as she leaned over him, her ear to his mouth. The gentle, scoffing of air being laboriously pushed in and out could just barely be heard. He was choking.

Just then, a young lady entered the room. Terror on her face, she saw the man lying on the floor and came around, trying to push Grace away.

"What has happened to my Michael?" she asked, tears welling up in her eyes.

Grace shouldered her away.

"He can't breathe."

"Can't breathe? Oh, Michael."

"Please, I need to see if there's something obstructing his airway."

Bending back up, she aligned his head, tilting his chin up and tried to see down his throat as she heard James calmly ordering someone to hand him one of the tools from his bag. They were working in tandem but separately and while the situation at hand was serious, Grace felt a spark of kinship with him.

Trying to gaze down her patient's throat, she couldn't see anything, but using her fingers, she felt an unnatural dip against his throat and when she pressed on it, his arms flailed up, striking her against the cheek.

"Grace!" James called, but she ignored him.

"You're hurting him!" the woman yelled, trying once more to push Grace out of the way.

"Hold him!" she barked at the men, putting the sting she felt out of her mind. Once he was secure, she spoke to the woman on her left. "If you do not get out of my way, this man, whoever he is to you, will suffocate and you'll be helping him along to his final reward. Now stand against the wall and let me work."

The watery-eyed young woman's mouth dropped. Seemingly believing Grace, she shuffled to her feet and hurried to the wall, while Grace leaned over the man once again. "I'm sorry, I know you are in pain, but I believe your throat has collapsed." The man's frightened blue eyes stared up at her. "Can you speak?"

He shook his head.

"I thought so. That means the damage has occurred in the larynx." She bit her lip and shook her head. "I know what needs to be done, but I'm afraid it's rather dangerous and painful. However, if this isn't tended to..." She hesitated for only a moment before continuing. "You will choke to death."

A chilling silence fell over the room. Grace glanced up at James who was watching her, when the woman against the wall interrupted.

"Please, Miss Lady Doctor," she said, catching Grace's attention. She glanced up to see the young person, hands clasped in front of her chest as if she were praying. "If you can, please. Save my Michael."

Grace gave one last look at James; she focused on the patient. Touching his head gently, she saw his eyes flutter as a terrible, gurgling came from his throat. He started to shake and the men held him down tightly.

"I need a scalpel. Now."

"Here, Miss MacIntosh," James called out to the woman who crossed the room in Grace's peripheral vision. "Give this to her."

Grace waited with an outstretched hand until the cool metal was placed gently in her palm. With her other hand, she felt along the front of the man's neck for the cricoid cartilage, or the ridged rings that could be felt beneath the skin on the throat. With a steady, but firm hand, Grace pressed the tip of the scalpel into the skin, and cut vertically.

"You're slitting his throat?" the woman cried.

"I'm saving his life."

Through the platysma muscle, exposing the strap muscles, she was able to see the thyroid gland. Breathing steadily through her nose, Grace cut a small portion of the thyroid, only enough to see and nick the trachea with the tip of her blade.

Instantly, a gasp of air pulled into the hole as the man's chest lifted, now fully able to breathe. Grace needed a needle to suture the muscles when one appeared right before her eyes. Turning, she saw James, kneeling next to her.

"I'll dab the incision with laudanum while you stitch. Hopefully, it'll numb the pain."

Grace took the silk thread and needle, bent low, and worked as though she were a lady working on a needlepoint. This was where she was her calmest, her most focused. Working to save a man's life.

Within minutes, he was cleaned up and set up to a sitting position.

"Now, you must keep this area clean," James was saying as Miss MacIntosh gripped Michael's arm. "Miss Sharpe was able to stitch you up, and it seems as though there might be a chance at recovering from your initial injury. I want you to visit my office in a few days. Do not speak until then. Miss MacIntosh? Might you be able to communicate for this man?"

"Aye, Doctor." Miss MacIntosh reached for Grace's hand. "And thank you, Doctor."

Grace's heart swelled, but she remained still.

"Of course," she said, a little breathless as she and James left the room.

Grace let out a long breath as the door closed, and to her sudden surprise, James instantly grabbed her around the waist and lifted her up, twirling her around right in the middle of the hallway. When he set her down, he was beaming down at her, pride and amazement shining in his eyes.

"God above, Grace, that was brilliant. Brilliant!"

"I, no," she stuttered, shaking her head. "It was just what needed to be done."

"How did you learn to do it?"

"Dr. Barkley had me practice. On pigs."

"At the butchers?"

Grace tilted her head.

"How did you know?"

"It's where I learned how to suture myself. But a tracheotomy. That incision was clean, and done with a near diabolical speed." He shook his head. "You've really an amazing talent for this sort of work."

Grace swallowed, trying not to let his praise affect her, but she had to admit that she felt several stories tall as they made their way to the last room on their list. But as Grace went to follow James inside, Mrs. Monty stopped her.

"Oh, no, you don't. You're not allowed in, what with your loose tongue."

Grace bobbed her head.

"I'll wait in the carriage."

"Miss Sharpe is assisting me," James tried, but Grace held up her hand.

"Really, I wouldn't want to make Mrs. Monty uncomfortable."

After giving her a concerned expression, James nodded.

"All right. I shouldn't be long. I'll meet you in the carriage."

Grace turned to walk the short distance to the front door and exited. The streets were unsurprisingly empty as the rain had been steady in its downfall. With a small bounce in her step, she hurried toward the carriage as she glanced around at her surroundings and just before she reached the door, she saw him.

Mr. Roberts.

At least, she thought it was him. He was wearing a rounded top hat, a coke hat, she believed it was called, and the collar of his great overcoat was turned up, hiding his chin, but she could have sworn it was him.

What was he doing in Gallowgate?

She paused, unaware of the rain that fell as she watched him hand two poorly dressed, rather rough looking men several paper notes as he glanced around them. He saw Grace, or at least, she thought he did when he froze, staring in her direction.

"Mr. Roberts?" she called out, only for the man to spin around promptly as he stalked down the street.

The other two men glared at her before turning back to enter the building behind them. Unsure why she was provoked to investigate or what she even planned on doing, Grace glanced both ways along the street before hurrying across, where she saw a sign hanging above the door that had just been slammed. Rabbit House Boarding. She glanced up the road, but couldn't see Mr. Roberts anymore, and so, facing the door once again, she knocked.

But no one answered.

"Hello?" she yelled, knocking harder. "Hello!" She stepped back, to gaze up at the structure. She cupped her hands around her mouth. "Hello!"

Instantly, a hand wrapped around her arm and whipped her around. James's intense, wide eyes were watching her as if she had lost her mind.

"What are you doing?" he asked loudly through the sound of the storm.

"I saw Mr. Roberts," she answered, pointing down the road with her free hand. "Just now. He was paying two men who went into this building."

"This is a boarding house for the poor," James said. "And who is Mr. Roberts?"

"One of the students from Andersen University. One of Dr. Cameron's men."

James frowned, his expression doubtful.

"I don't think so, Grace. This isn't the sort of neighborhood one of Dr. Cameron's students would frequent."

"It was him. I saw him."

"Come." He pulled lightly at her arm. "Let's go out of the rain."

Grace allowed him to escort her back to the carriage where the previously missing driver was, holding the door open. She hurried inside, followed by James as they sat and within moments, the vehicle was moving.

James removed his hat to shake off the rain.

"Now, who do you think you saw? A Mr. Roberts?"

"I don't think I saw him; I did see him. Right outside that building, Rabbit House Boarding. There were two men, one was bald with a beard and the other was long in the face, with sunken in cheeks and both were dressed in dirty old suits, more rag-like than proper clothing. Mr. Roberts was handing them banknotes, or what appeared to be banknotes. He was mouthing numbers as he counted them into one of their hands."

James shook his head.

"Why would one of Dr. Cameron's students be in Gallowgate?"

"I'm not sure. He recognized me, however, and so I called out to him, but the moment I did, he turned and left. The other two men went straight into Rabbit House and closed the door. I tried knocking, but well, you saw. They didn't answer."

For a long moment, James's face was scrunched up, as if trying to figure out a math problem. But after a while, he shook his head again.

"There must be some sort of mistake. I know the majority of Dr. Cameron's students are from well to do families, and almost all of them are English. There wouldn't be any reason for them to be in Gallowgate except for administering medicine, but without a license it would be unethical."

"He wasn't giving them medicine, though. He was paying them."

"For what?"

Grace sat back, surprised that James couldn't figure it out.

"Isn't it obvious?"

"No, I'm afraid not."

"I think that there's a possibility that Mr. Roberts was paying them to, well, *you know*."

He frowned.

"I'm afraid I don't."

"Do you not read the papers? This morning's paper in particular?" He stared at her, obviously unaware, and she sighed. "There was a break in at the Glasgow Necropolis last night. Two graves have been dug up; the bodies removed."

The realization dawned on him at the exact same time injustice shone in his eyes.

"Grave robbing?" he spoke, his tone harsh. "Have you lost your mind?"

Grace blinked, confused.

"Excuse me?"

"Do you have any idea the stigma that the medical community has had to deal with when it comes to such accusations? The absolute panic that would set in if it was said in public?"

"I don't think it's an accusation. I think it's what's happened."

"What evidence do you have to accuse someone like that?" he asked, visibly annoyed. "That is a tremendous allegation."

"And not one that I make lightly, but what else could it be?"

"Even still, what was your plan if it were true? Confront him on the spot?" he asked, his hand going through his short hair, as if trying to calm himself.

"I wanted to see where he was going."

"You can't go gallivanting around Glasgow, particularly Gallowgate. It's dangerous. Filled with ruthless thugs, murderers, women of ill repute—"

"Your patients," she interrupted, cutting him off. "And I was not gallivanting. I was merely trying to discover why Mr. Roberts was paying two men who happen to be covered in dirt."

"It was irresponsible."

"It was fine."

James's nostrils flared as he glared at her as the carriage swayed from left to right before turning one last time before coming to a stop. Grace was quick to exit the vehicle without so much as a "good day" as the rain came down in sheets, heavier than before, as she trudged up the stone steps to the front door. To her surprise, however, James's form cut in front of her, and upon opening the door for her, all but pushed her inside.

"What are you doing?"

"I'm not finished speaking with you," he snapped, before glaring up at the ceiling above. "Lady Belle! Where are you?"

"What are you going to do? Tell on me?"

"Exactly that. It seems no one can get through to you except that woman and if I must use her as a speaking point to get it through to you just how grievous your accusations are, then I will." He stalked about the foyer. "Belle!"

"She isn't here," Grace said with a great amount of satisfaction.

"Where is she?"

"Visiting the baroness with Arabella."

He turned.

"And your staff?"

"She gave them the day off, as no one was here and they had plans not to return tonight."

"She left you all alone? In this city without even a skeleton staff?"

"I'm perfectly capable of—"

"For the love of Christ, what is wrong with you women?" he bellowed suddenly, causing Grace to close her mouth. He took a step toward her and instinctively, Grace stepped back. "Are you all mad? Is it some inheritable trait?"

"Now see here—"

"I will not. You are stubborn and capable and brilliant, Grace Sharpe, but you are also willfully ignorant and double foolish," he snapped, glowering down at her. "Thank whatever deity you'd like that I saw you in front of that building before something happened. You could have been snatched up in a moment and no one would have seen you."

"I'm not a child, James. There's no use in trying to frighten me with tales of bad men in dark alleys—"

But in the next moment she found herself locked in his strong arms.

"I'm not trying to scare you; I'm trying to make you see the facts. Have you any idea what one of those men might have done to you if they decided to take you?"

Grace's eyes were wide, frozen partially by the fact that his mouth was mere inches away from hers. His gaze dropped for a moment; his lips parted as he watched her. The beating of her heart was so loud that she was sure he could hear it as she waited for what, she did not know.

She barely shook her head.

"No."

"No," he repeated, his forceful tone now raspy. "No, you don't. How can you? You barely understand your own urges, let alone those of men."

Insulted, she tried to pull away from him.

"Let me go."

"This," he said softly, coming closer still, his mouth once more finding her ear, which caused her eyelids to flutter shut. "They'd take you, against your will, ignoring all your pleas."

"James, please."

He brushed his face against the side of her cheeks, his beard sending all sorts of sparks against her skin. She let out a pathetic sigh as her wrists twisted, but not out of his grasp. Instead, her fingers found the fabric of his overcoat, and she moved her hands to his sides, gripping the wet wool as tightly as she could.

Everything stilled in that moment as they held one another in a half urgent, half desperate embrace. Even the thunderous storm outside seemed to quiet as all the world seemed to become immobile, save their shared erratic breathing. Her eyes searched his and in an instant, she knew what was going to happen and silently, she urged him on.

For what felt like ages, James seemed to weigh his next move, but Grace knew what would happen if he thought too much, and so she leaned forward, just enough so that her mouth pressed against his chin and kissed him in the most chaste way possible.

Days might have passed before he spoke, and fearing his rejection, Grace tried to steel her emotions when he did.

"Do you," he began, tone rough and raw. He cleared his throat. "Do you know the consequence of this, Grace? What would happen if—"

"I understand."

"But—"

"Please, James. Please," she whispered. "Kiss me."

The good doctor's resolve finally broke and with one last moment of hesitation, he did just that.

Chapter Thirteen

S HE TASTED LIKE water mint and the Highlands and a dozen other things that James had forgotten, yet a dozen things he had never known. What was this feeling? Every time her touched her, kissed her, dreamed about her, his mind was wiped clean of everything he had ever learned, yet if he asked himself in that moment what was the meaning to all of it, he would only be able to breathe her name as the answer to all life's mysteries. For at that moment, he knew in his bones that his only reason for being on this earth was to be near her. To hold her, feel her. Kiss her until the end of days.

His one hand went into the mass of her hair, just like he had imagined before, and the other went to her ribcage, feeling the warmth of her, yet still hesitant. To his surprise and immense satisfaction, Grace's hand found his and pulled it to her breast. She moaned into his kiss when she did so and James was close to spending then and there.

Her hands went to the silk buttons at the front of her dress. It was a split gown, as James soon found out, one where the top was able to be removed apart from the skirt. The camisole beneath was somewhat bunched up, over a restrictive corset that disappeared beneath her skirt. He spotted a silver chain around her neck that he hadn't seen before. She had been wearing it beneath her dress.

"What's this?" he asked, reaching for it.

"Oh, it's a pen from my aunt and a locket from, well, yours."

He shot her a look.

"My aunt? She gave you a locket?" Grace nodded. "What's in it?"

"Herbs." She shrugged. "She said it was for protection."

James lifted it and breathed it in. Water mint. That's why she reminded him of home. He gently dropped it, bemused by it.

"They really know how to insert themselves into situations, don't they?"

Grace removed the necklace and tossed it onto the chaise in the parlor, a few feet away before reaching for his collar and she pulled him close, kissing him hard, and he was breathless. Then, like a page ripping from a book, she tore away from him and turned.

"Untie me."

Not needing any further instructions, his hands went to the fine strings of her corset as he undid the double bow. Once pulled apart, she breathed deeply and a wild desire to banish all fabrics from her body consumed him. She twisted at the waist, untying her skirt and stepping out of it, along with her petticoat before she turned and melted into him once more.

This was madness. They were half in the foyer, half in the parlor and yet James couldn't stop himself. Grace was insistent, desperate to be with him and while a miniscule warning tried to sound in his mind, he couldn't bring himself to deny her anything.

His only purpose in life was to please her. But for the briefest of moments his eyes opened and he saw a painting in the foyer of Grace and her sisters and that tiny warning grew. He tried to pull back, but kissed her again, closing his eyes. This is what she wanted, but did she know what she wanted? Did she know what this would mean?

He pulled back.

"Grace, wait…"

"No."

"Grace, yes. Wait," he said, bringing his hands to her shoulders. She finally paused. "I want this too, I do, but the repercussions of us doing this—"

"I don't care what the repercussions are."

James shook his head.

"Then you don't understand it."

Grace pulled away from him, folding her arms across her chest as she did, stopping only a few steps away from him. Confused, James waited for her to speak. Thankfully, he didn't have to wait long.

"I am not... Equipped like other people," she said after a moment of silence. "I never..." She shook her head, seemingly unsure of her own words. "That is to say, I didn't think that I could feel these things."

"These things?"

She twisted around to face him, looking like a frustrated angel.

"This. Desire. Want." She swallowed, her gaze dropping. "I had accepted that I wasn't the sort to experience the sort of things my sisters did. The thought of being with someone never inspired anything in me. When I kissed Lord Bartley, it was as if I was kissing a stone and I thought, well, perhaps there was something I lacked."

"Grace, there is nothing lacking in you."

"I don't mean to garner kind words. I mean to say that, before you, the idea of laying with someone, in that sense, was less appealing than cold porridge."

James blinked. Then, he stepped toward her, reaching for her elbow to turn her back to face him. Thankfully, she did.

"What are you saying?"

"Just that, I didn't think that any of this was possible." Her gaze lifted to meet his and his heart missed a beat. "And if I seem eager, I am. Because I'm afraid that it's fleeting."

So that was it. She was afraid that this feeling between them was a flash in the pan, an anomaly to her reality. While to him, it felt more permanent than anything he had ever experienced.

James's fingers trailed down her forearm, gripping her hands in a light squeeze.

"I understand. But speaking as someone who has some experience here, I must tell you that this, whatever this is between us, is not how it usually feels."

"It isn't?" He shook his head. "What's different?"

James let out a breathy laugh, uncomfortable with exposing so much of himself. Yet, here Grace was, honest to a fault and still standing. If she could be honest with him, then he could do it too.

"With Catriona, there was an attraction, yes. But it was containable."

"Containable? I don't understand."

He shook his head again.

"I mean that we liked each other, were always pleasant and never confrontational. We never argued, or even disagreed. And while we found each other attractive, it wasn't like this."

"It wasn't?"

"No. This is something I've never experienced before. But if I was a betting man, I'd place a fortune on the notion that this isn't a common occurrence."

It was Grace's turn to shake her head.

"It must be."

"Why?"

"Because these feelings make me want to do things I've sworn never to do." *Yes.* James felt the same way, but worried that he might frighten her, he only nodded. "And I cannot, James. I promised myself never to marry anyone."

Although he wasn't considering proposing, her staunch stance on the topic of marriage irritated him. The finality of her tone made him want to argue, but to do so would only push her away and he didn't even want to marry her.

Did he?

"Grace, while this is probably the most unconventional, stupidest thing I've ever even considered doing in my life... I promise, I wouldn't do or say anything that might pressure you."

She shook her head. "Nor would I cast you aside if that was your fear."

"I'm not worried about that. I just… I would like to explore whatever this is, from a scientific point of view, without the constraints of social pressure to do something that I, or you, might regret. Like marriage." She swallowed. "Which is why I'm probably so eager to continue. So that you don't stop to think and realize what an outrageous experiment this is."

An experiment? Is that how she honestly saw this? James nearly laughed at the absurdity of the word while also disliking it. This was not some sort of research to be conducted for the benefit of a thesis. But she seemed so uneasy at the idea of being married that he couldn't resist asking about it.

"What is it about marriage that frightens you?" She immediately tried to pull away, but he held her. "No, Grace, please. Tell me."

For a moment, he didn't believe that she would speak, but after a moment, she exhaled.

"I know what my life would be if I married. All my studying, all my work would be lost. And it would be no fault to anyone. I'm sure my husband would try to be supportive at first and I would believe it, but there's a reason there aren't married professional women. Eventually something would turn. My work would become too bothersome, or there would be arguments and one day my husband would forbid my work and he would have the power to do so." She shook her head. "I would try and convince myself that it was for the best, and for a while we might live in harmony, but eventually I would resent him and I don't want to resent you, James. But I also don't want to live a life only half fulfilled."

She was asking for something James had never considered before. A relationship that was separate from their professional one, one based entirely on their primal instincts, without consequences.

"So, you'd like to sleep together, but for it not to lead any-where? Is that right?"

"Yes."

"Grace, I don't even know what to call that."

"It doesn't need a name," she said softly, her hand reaching for his jaw, dislodging all his practical reasoning to stop this. "Perhaps it can be a mutual experiment?"

There was that word again and once more, James found a dislike for it. Yet, if this was the only way to have her, then he couldn't very well say no. Instead, he gave her a single nod.

"Very well. Let whatever this is be on your terms."

Grace's chest expanded, her eyes awash in joy as she smiled at him, melting every bit of resolve he had.

"Truly?" she breathed, leaning toward him.

James couldn't help but kiss her, deeply. Then, he pulled back.

"Yes. Whatever you wish."

Grace's hand reached behind his head and pulled him close, kissing him with equal enthusiasm. While the gentleman in him wanted to argue some very obvious points, such as what were to happen if their tryst was discovered, the baser version of him only wanted to make her happy. Her beaming smile was reward enough for agreeing to her terms.

"James," she spoke into his mouth, her fingers coming up to move against the edge of his chin.

His name on her lips was an intoxication in and of itself.

"Yes?"

"Undress me."

The blood in his veins surged with fire. Without another practical thought, James spun her around and pulled the edges of her corset loose, until it fell over her hips to the floor. Her camisole was pulled up and overhead and when he turned her back to face him, she was left wearing only her chemise.

Just like he had imagined a hundred times.

A playful grin hovered on her lips as she watched him.

"I admit, I'm new to this, but, am I the only one to undress?"

James chuckled as he reached for her hand and pulled her

from the doorway of the parlor.

"Come."

Bending down to gather her gown and under dressings, James led her up the stairs and down the hallway to her room. When they reached it, he closed the door behind him.

"How did you know where my room was?"

He motioned toward the window.

"I've seen you here."

Grace's mouth fell open slightly as she glanced out the window before turning back to him.

"You've spied on me."

"I wouldn't say that."

"What would you say?" she asked as he came forward, peeling off his jacket.

"I'd say you've haunted me, day and night for weeks. That I've had no peace from you." He leaned down, brushing her left ear with his lips, causing her to tremble. "Even when in my own home, I can't escape you."

Grace sighed as he kissed her ear, then her neck, down to the hollow of her throat, and back up again to her other ear. She shivered in his arms. Pulling gently at the sleeve of her chemise so that her shoulder showed, James was mad with yearning. She pulled her one arm up and out of the confines of her garment, and then the next, just like in his fantasy.

Unbuttoning his vest as quickly as possible, tearing off his shirtsleeves, then his pants, James was nude by the time she tugged her chemise down, exposing a pair of perfect petite breasts, far more satisfying than anything he could have ever imagined.

Pushing the fabric down around her waist, Grace stood in front of him completely nude and not nearly as self-conscious as he would have expected. She appeared pleased, happy, and sensual and her confidence was almost as equally beautiful as the curve of her hips and the slight swell of her stomach. She was a brunette Botticelli, a vision beyond comprehension or comparison and he knew he was lost to her. Whatever she would want from him, for the rest of his days, he would procure it for her.

"You're perfect," he said softly, almost more to himself than to her.

A faint blush swept over her body and he was at her mercy. The pull of a grin teased the corner of her mouth as her eyes swept over him.

"You're everything," she whispered back and in the next moment, she was in his arms.

Skin against skin, all the worries James had ever known or would know vanished as he kissed her. This was his life's purpose, making love to this woman. His hand held her breast up, and he suckled at her, causing a jolt to shoot through her as her arms came up and held him close to her, while his other hand moved around her backside. Gripping her, he picked her up and swung her around the room as she gasped. Placing her gently back on her feet in front of the bed, he pulled back and, with his eyes on hers, he bent his head to kiss her as his fingers cascaded down to find the hot center between her legs. She gasped when he pressed a finger into her, leaning slightly back onto the bed to give him better access and he growled, grateful for such an appeasing lover.

His mouth moving down her neck, across her breasts, down her abdomen. Her hands tried to stay him as he knelt, kissing lower.

"James, no—"

He reached for her wrists and held them at each side of her hips.

"This is your experiment, Grace," he breathed into her stomach, kissing it. "Stay still and experience it."

Without waiting for a response, James's mouth dropped to where his fingers were, moving inside her as he found the heady scent of her. He licked her, deep and slow, which caused her feet to slip beneath her.

"James!" she breathed, her fingers going to his hair.

Yes. Her response only fed into his own desires. Using his fingers and tongue in a rhythm, he felt her fingers curl tighter, almost painfully at his short hair.

"James, wait."

"Lean into it," he said, aware of what was happening as her thighs began to shake.

Determined and impassioned with lust, James continued, lapping and kissing her center as his fingers moved in and out, drawing out an orgasm that went on for nearly a full minute. Once the tremors subsided, he stood, standing over a limp Grace. Her arm lifted, as if to reach for him and that was summoning enough.

Coming over her, he kissed her breasts once more, up her neck and her ear as he lined his shaft up to enter her.

"Grace," he whispered in her ear. "Do you know what I'm going to do?" She bobbed her head, eagerly. "Are you sure you want this?"

"Oh, yes, James. *Yes.*"

The crack in her voice pulled at his heart for some reason and even now, on the edge of his own pleasure, he paused.

"Are you sure?"

"Please, James," she begged, her hands touching his shoulders and pulling at him, as if to bring him closer.

And closer he came.

"Hold on to me," he whispered as he entered her, hating every painful whimper that came from her lips as he pushed into her.

The tension in her arms emanated from her, as so he was slow to move deeper. She let out a ragged breath as he pressed farther until he was completely surrounded by her. If he had been at her beck and call before, now he was her servant, for all that mattered was this moment, this connection between them.

After a moment, Grace's hips lifted and he began to pull out, before pushing back in, settling in a rhythm that would surely kill him.

"James," she begged, her eyes closed. "Yes, more."

He would remember those words until his last breath, he decided as he began to pump into her, faster, deeper, until his own body began to tense as she clutched around his shaft. Before he could finish, he pulled out of her, releasing himself on the sheet beneath them.

It was almost as painful as it was pleasurable. James fell to the bed by her side and pressed his face into the bed, only vaguely aware of the scent of mint as she rolled over.

For a long moment, neither spoke, but only watched one another. As their breathing evened out, James couldn't help but smile, his hand reaching to touch her cheek. Reaching for her, he pulled her close to his chest and they both fell asleep.

Some hours later, when it was dark, James opened his eyes. Grace was still there, pressed against him, but by the stilted breathing, he guessed she was awake, so he hugged her.

"I can't believe that happened."

"Me neither," she replied. "Thank you."

He chuckled.

"Love, you never need to thank me. The pleasure was all mine."

But at the word *love*, Grace sat up.

"There's no need to call me that."

He frowned as he came up onto his elbow.

"It was only an endearment."

"I know, but I'd prefer it if you didn't use it."

"Very well."

A moment of silence.

"It's just that—"

"I don't see how—"

They both started and stopped. After a moment, Grace gave him a smirk.

"It's just that, I don't wish anything more to develop between us."

"Anything more?"

"Yes. Besides physical relations."

James nodded, though a hole felt as if it had just developed in his chest and a strain in his throat. He had not expected her to say that and rolled onto his back, staring up at the canopy. Perhaps this wasn't as clever an idea as he first thought.

Sitting up, he climbed out of bed and went to her water table. Picking up a washcloth, he dipped it in water and went back to Grace. He attempted to clean her, but she was quick to take it from him.

"Thank you."

He watched, feeling muddled. This was not what he had expected and yet, it was exactly what he had agreed to. A situation without attachments.

"I suppose I should dress then?" She shrugged. "And be on my way?"

"If you think so."

Well, that wasn't exactly encouraging. Deciding not to further embarrass himself, he began to dress, as did she, although she dressed in a night gown. It was night, but what the exact time was, James didn't know. He didn't like the idea of leaving her alone, but he wasn't likely to get any sleep here and she would refuse letting him stay, should her aunt come back in the middle of the night.

"Thank you," she said, and for some reason James felt a small little stab in the heart at her words, but he had agreed to her terms and therefore had no room to speak.

"Of course," he said and with a final nod, he left.

Walking through the house and out the back kitchen, across the street, James felt wholly empty. Like a discarded rag. When he reached his front door, he turned back to gaze up to see if she was maybe looking out of her window, but to his own misery, he found that she wasn't and so he opened the door to his house and tried not to think about how painful an encounter it had actually been.

✦

Chapter Fourteen

THE BALLROOM AT Mr. Milton's estate house, aptly named Milton House, that had been built on the very edge of Glasgow proper, was one of the most extravagant rooms that Grace had ever laid eyes on. In all her years in London, even during her presentation to the queen during her coming out, never had Grace beheld such magnificence.

The gold filigree walls were taller than any she had ever seen and the glass window panes that allowed the evening sky to shine down on them was a wonder in and of itself, save for the four massive crystal chandeliers, each identical to the last and positioned in between the large skylights. It was not only a modern marvel, but a glowing display of status and fortune. Nearly every guest there, and there were hundreds of people, all kept their heads bent backwards to gaze up at the pitched roof and the stars above, amazed at the craftsmanship, if not the expense.

"Goodness," Belle said as she, Arabella, and Grace reached the refreshment table after having been introduced by the footman. "This is as grand as any palace I've been to, and I've been to my fair share."

"Mr. Milton must be the wealthiest man in Scotland, if not one of the richest in the entire world," Arabella said, her gaze heavenward.

"It is very nice," Grace said, taking a glass of lemonade from a servant to take a sip. To her embarrassment, the citrusy taste reminded her of James.

Grace had lain in bed for hours after he left that night, staring up at the canopy above her bed, stunned that she should feel so desperate for him. She hadn't wanted to be so affected and she forced herself to stay in bed instead of running to the window to watch him. She needed to remain impartial, even though every inch of her wanted to demand that he stay with her.

It had sent her into a spiraling sort of depression, containing her feelings the way she had. But what could she do? She didn't want her feelings to get in the way and yet, her heart ached every time she saw him.

It was miserable.

"Nice is an understatement," Arabella muttered.

It *was* an understatement, yes, but Grace couldn't help it. Mrs. Stevens had tied her corset too tight and it was pinching her skin, directly in the center of her back. While the result had been stunning, as the pale green gown that had been embroidered with dainty white lilies that Grace wore had caused several people to stare openly, it wasn't enough to sate her. She'd rather be comfortable than breathtaking.

She glanced at her companions, who were staring at her blankly. "What's wrong?"

"Nice?" Belle repeated. "My dear, daisies are nice. This is extravagance. Vulgar even in its décor. Certainly, a telltale sign of new money."

"I think it's elegance incarnate."

"It's very… posh," Grace tried again, but failed to do so.

While Milton House was certainly an impressive bit of architecture, and she had never seen such grandness before, it mattered little as her entire being was preoccupied with thoughts of James.

No. Dr. Hall. She would cease being so familiar with him if he was to behave so boorish, which is exactly how he had been behaving the entire past week. Every day, he barely spoke to her unless it was absolutely necessary, and even then his attitude was singular and his speech monotone, except for when she made the foolish attempt to speak with him about possibly meeting in secret. He had practically barked at her, telling her that her experiment was deranged and that he hoped she had a fine time at Mr. Milton's ball and not to expect seeing him as he would not be going. It was a vast difference from all the praise he had bestowed on her when they were—

She took another bracing gulp of her lemonade, forcing the memory out of her mind. She couldn't, wouldn't think about that here. Not in front of so many people, particularly her aunt and friend, who were watching her with such blatant curiosity that she was becoming annoyed. Her aunt and Arabella exchanged looks.

"What is it?" she asked, placing her glass down on the table.

"Well, dear, it's just that you've been rather quiet lately, and well, we had hoped that coming to Mr. Milton's ball might cheer you up a bit."

"Yes, you've possessed a—melancholy, I suppose—as of late and we had thought that maybe your spirits might be lifted coming here."

Grace made her face blank, hoping not to convey any sort of emotion.

"Well, I'm sorry to disappoint."

"It's not that dear, it's just—"

"Ah, Lady Smyth, Miss Scott," Mr. Milton said with a bow, before giving Grace his full attention. "Miss Sharpe. I'm so glad to have you here."

"The pleasure is ours," Grace said with a curtsy.

"Mr. Milton, I must say, you have an impressive home," Belle said with a strike of her cane.

"Oh, there's no need to flatter me, Lady Smyth. I built this house with a motive."

Grace tilted her head, curious.

"What sort of motive?"

"Aye, well, when I was a lad growing up in Glasgow, I may

have once or twice tried to get into a party or two of one of the well to do families. Of course, I was immediately removed, but not without first seeing the style in which those great houses were decorated. If you remember, Miss Sharpe, I've a fondness for architecture."

"I do remember," Grace said, ignoring the curious expression of Arabella and the suspicious glare of Belle.

"Well, it was my memory of that first house that inspired me to build this. It's grand, excessive, even gauche, if you ask the right people." He winked, causing Grace to smile. "But it was built in reverence and in response to my dreams as a youth."

His sparkling eyes seemed to be trying to draw her in and while there were a number of qualities that Mr. Milton possessed, none seemed to speak to Grace's soul and for that, she was grateful.

"Then I take back my comment about it being nice and now see it as a wonderful testament."

"Nice?" he repeated, obviously tickled by the word. "I don't think anyone's ever called it nice. Over the top, uncouth, tasteless, beyond self-awareness, but never nice. That is a first."

Grace laughed at his self-deprecating honesty.

"Well, you'll have to forgive me. And I no longer think it is nice. I think it is wonderful, as I just said."

"Aye, you did," he said, his tone warm as the waltz came to an end. "Miss Sharpe, I know I'm to see to my other guests, but might I steal you away for a dance instead?"

A troublesome pain pinched the center of her heart at his question, but she refused to acknowledge it. Instead, she held out her hand.

"Of course, Mr. Milton."

He reached for her fingers and lightly drew her toward him. However, with a backward glance at Arabella and Belle, Grace saw a taut expression of concern. Why, she did not know, as they had both been particularly excited to come to Mr. Milton's ball and had talked of little else all week. Confused, Grace moved into position for a quadrille as the musicians plucked their instruments.

"Is there something amiss?" Mr. Milton asked, evidently noting her expression.

She instantly made the muscles in her face relax as she smiled at him.

"Not at all."

With her left foot, Grace stepped forward and brought her right foot forward in a circular motion before falling on both feet as she straightened her knees. As someone who struggled with dancing before her coming out, Grace had spent many months reading and practicing her footwork, but she had to focus, otherwise she would miss a count.

Coming together with another gentleman, before twirling around to the back of the line, she was met with Mr. Milton, who appeared charmed.

"You're quite a natural, Miss Sharpe."

"Ha," she said as she twisted to face the opposite way, as their hands joined together. "I assure you, nothing is natural about dancing."

Mr. Milton chuckled at the bemused quip and Grace felt pleased. This was just the sort of companionship that she should be seeking. There was nothing about Mr. Milton that made her insides turn and twist. It was rather pleasant, knowing that her body wouldn't react so when their hands touched, or that her pulse would remain completely unfettered when he glanced in her direction.

As they continued their dance, Grace noted a number of reasonable, perfectly agreeable attributes about him. He was obviously a progressive sort of man who had a passion for architecture and travel. He was agreeable, and kind, not to mention the fact that he was extremely well off. If he became the patron of a hospital, his wealth could truly make a difference and while Grace refused to marry, they could form a rather powerful partnership.

Passion-wise, well, she had yet to discover if there was any-thing between them. Of course, with the lack of heart racing, temperature rising, entire body shivering reaction, Grace doubted there was much, but even that was more welcoming than how she felt around James. At least with Mr. Milton, she would be able to focus on her experiment with an unaffected mind and she wouldn't have to experience this constant ache in her heart.

With a final step, the music ended and each of the dancers bowed or curtsied and when Grace gazed up, Mr. Milton was there, offering his arm to her to escort her back to her aunt.

"You really are quite the dancer, Miss Sharpe."

"Mr. Milton, if you insist on teasing me, I should refrain from continuing to seek out your company."

The man put his free hand to his heart as they reached Aunt Belle and Arabella at the refreshments table.

"With that threat, I promise I will never tease you again."

Grace couldn't help but be mildly pleased at his sincerity.

"You may tease me, Mr. Milton. I am not so rigid."

"Then perhaps you might join me for a picnic sometime next week?"

"A picnic?" Arabella spoke, confused. "Sir, it is November."

"Yes, surely you do not intend to freeze my poor niece to death."

"Not at all, my lady. I've a project I'm partially heading near Kelvingrove Park," he stated, turning to Grace. "We're building a wrought iron glass house, but one of enormous size. I'd like to show it to you, if you are interested."

"How enormous?" Grace asked.

"Grace," Aunt Belle hissed, as Arabella appeared dumbfound-ed.

Mr. Milton smiled.

"Quite. Of course, I would expect the company of your aunt and companion to join us. It really is an impressive feat of ingenuity, if I do say so myself."

"I don't see why not then."

"Er, my dear, would it not interfere with your work with Dr. Hall?"

Grace's smile fell.

"No. It would not, I'm sure."

Aunt Belle, whose expression had gone from mildly hopeful to downright irritated, shook her head.

"Very well, Mr. Milton, we will join you. But I should change my mind if you don't behave like a proper host and start paying attention to your other guests," Aunt Belle snapped, tapping her cane on the parquet wooden floor. "It is not becoming of a gentleman to invite so many guests that he cannot speak to each and every one of them."

"Aunt Belle," Grace tried, but Mr. Milton only laughed.

"Of course, my lady. I'll send word to your house in the next day or so to confirm our plans. Until then." He bowed and disappeared into the crowd behind him.

"Rather forward that one," Belle said, and to Grace's surprise, Arabella nodded in agreement.

"What is that matter with you two? I thought you liked Mr. Milton."

"We do, er, well, we did," Arabella said. "It's just, well. Lady Belle is right. He shouldn't be ignoring all his other guests. It isn't polite, is it?"

"No, it is not," Belle retorted.

Grace frowned at the two, unsure what to make of their sudden aversion to Mr. Milton, who again, had been the main topic of discussion for that past week.

"I don't understand. The both of you were quite complimentary whenever you spoke of him—"

"Oh look!" Belle said loudly, interrupting Grace as she strained to peer over her shoulder. "Dr. Hall has arrived."

Grace spun around and cursed her foolish heart that had jumped into her throat. In a sea of clean-faced gentlemen and pastel-dressed women, James appeared nearly a head taller than everyone else, dressed in a moss-green plaid kilt, black jacket, and matching vest over a stark white shirt. He wore hose up to below his knees, black shoes, and a large fur sporran with three black tassels that bounced against his thighs as he walked toward them.

Mouth open, Grace was paralyzed where she stood as he approached, rather like a magpie entranced by a shiny object. Never had she seen the doctor dressed in formal Highland wear and she was amazed at how very handsome one person could be. Every inch of him seemed to reveal something new and magnificent that she barely recovered herself by the time he reached them.

"Hello," he said to her and her alone, his gray-blue eyes, two warm pools of want as they gazed over her. Grace fought off the urge to shiver.

"Hello," she said softly. "I thought you said you weren't coming."

"I wasn't, but I…" He hesitated, before glancing over Grace's shoulder. "Lady Belle. Miss Scott."

"Dr. Hall, what a pleasant surprise," Belle said, scooting around Grace to get in front of her. She certainly seemed to be able to move quickly when she wanted to, despite the cane. "Grace said you weren't coming?"

"Yes, well, my previous engagement was canceled and I found myself rather bored, to be honest, when I remembered that tonight was Mr. Milton's ball."

"How fortunate for us then. Grace was in want of a new dance partner, after her charming cotillion with Mr. Milton just now," Belle said, adding in a faux whisper, "You know, Mr. Milton was very eager to dance with our Grace. He made it a point to interrupt his duty hosting, just to do so."

"Aunt Belle," Grace breathed, embarrassed. Hadn't her aunt just criticized the man for doing so? And now she sounded as if she were bragging about it. "Please."

"I cannot fault him for doing so," James spoke, seemingly unaffected. "Indeed, I should follow his lead. Miss Sharpe?"

He held out his hand and whatever animosity that had been

between the two for the past week melted away. Her fingers were gripped gently.

"Do remember to tell Dr. Hall about our upcoming visit to Kelvingrove Park," Belle added loudly as James led Grace out onto the dancefloor.

Grace stared daggers at her aunt over her shoulder before she gave James a tight smile, just as a waltz began.

For several moments, neither spoke, as the music began. Instead, they just stared at one another, moving with an amount of grace she had never experienced before. He was a proficient dancer, of course, and led the way with such ease that she barely had to count her steps.

"Your aunt is trying to make me jealous."

"Oh, no," Grace countered, worried. "I don't think that was her meaning in telling you about Mr. Milton."

"I think it's exactly her meaning and I do not fault her."

"You don't?"

"No. I'm beginning to think that Lady Belle believes that something might transpire between us." He leaned down, close enough to lower his voice, but not quite close enough to be considered indecent. "And while I do not completely understand the rhyme or reason for your experiment, Grace, I have come to the conclusion that I'd rather be at your disposal than be your opposition."

The words sank into Grace's heart and once more, a pulsating need coursed through her. Every time she was sure she knew what James was thinking, he surprised her and what's more, it was always something that made her like him more. Still, she tried not to appear so taken with him.

"You called my experiment deranged."

"Oh, I still believe it's deranged and I'm convinced you're playing with fire, but at least with me, I might be able to protect you from getting burned."

Grace felt her insides melt as an overwhelming sense of something came over her. She wasn't sure what it was, having never felt it before, but it was intense. Her affection for this man had grown exponentially since her arrival to Glasgow and she wished she could kiss him at this very moment, to demonstrate her fondness for him.

Of course, she could do no such thing, not in a ballroom full of people. Instead, she squeezed his hand with her fingers. He smirked down at her, eyes alight with pleasure at the small gesture.

"So, tell me about this trip to Kelvingrove Park."

Grace's smile vanished.

"Oh, yes. Well, just before you arrived, Mr. Milton invited me, I mean, us. That is, Aunt Belle, Arabella, and I to Kelvingrove Park. A glass house is being constructed and he wishes to show us."

James's eyebrow gave a slight twinge.

"I see," he said, and then after a long pause added, "I should think that with your experiment, you might refrain from giving a man like Mr. Milton false hope."

"False hope?"

"Yes."

"How is visiting his structure giving him false hope?"

"Grace, you cannot be so naive as to the happenings of the world," he said. "Mr. Milton fancies you."

She let out a laugh.

"I doubt it."

James frowned.

"How could you?"

"He is merely a friendly acquaintance. One that has proven to be quite pleasant whenever we meet, but I don't believe he has any sort of affection for me. And even if he did, it wouldn't amount to anything. Or at least, I'm very close to being certain that it wouldn't."

"Why wouldn't it amount to anything?"

"Because I'm not... That is to say, I don't feel..." Her brow creased as she tried to find the appropriate words. With a lowered voice, she spoke. "Mr. Milton is a fine man, but I do not react the same way with him the way I do with you."

Though the words came out quiet and quick, a flash of yearning crossed James's face and even that made Grace's heart race. He cleared his throat.

"I don't think you know what you do to me when you say such things, Grace." She ducked her head, feeling suddenly overwhelmed by the moment. "But Mr. Milton is undoubtedly under the impression that you may fancy him as well."

She frowned as she gazed up.

"I don't think so. I haven't given him any sort of hope that might lead him to believe that."

"Men do not need nearly as much coaxing as one might think. You've already said yes to his invitations twice."

She shook her head.

"And?"

"And if it were me, I'd believe that you were feeling a particular way."

Grace couldn't believe that Mr. Milton believed there was anything more than friendship between them. They had just danced after all, and while she had considered replacing James with him in her experiment, internally she knew that it wasn't a possibility because there wasn't any inkling of desire between them.

"You are mistaken. There isn't any feeling between me and Mr. Milton."

"There may be on his behalf though. You cannot know his thoughts on the matter. And if you go with him to Kelvingrove Park, whatever his feelings are now, they're liable to grow."

"Are you suggesting that I renege on my intention to go?" James didn't answer, though his expression seemed to speak volumes. "I cannot. I already promised to go."

The dance concluded then and though their conversation was far from over, James appeared contrite and remained silent as they removed themselves from the dancefloor. Surely he understood that she was expected to go, and in the company of her aunt and Arabella, it was hardly a romantic sort of venture.

He had to know that. Didn't he?

"James, I—" she began just as the Baroness Glengirth and Aunt Belle came into view.

The baroness was a short woman, dressed in a black velvet gown with lace trim that was covered in what appeared to be hundreds of bows. Her square, wrinkled face sneered at James.

"Ah, my former escort," she said, her voice sour. "Come to abandon my dear Lady Belle and her companions as you did me the other night?"

James gave her a nod.

"Baroness, it is a pleasure to see you again."

"Do not try to flatter me in front of my acquaintances, doctor. I will not be fooled again." She leaned toward Aunt Belle, though her eyes remained on James. "You know, he left me alone for a good hour during the opera and when he returned, he had completely forgotten to retrieve for me a beverage."

"The insolence," Belle said, though she winked, obviously used to the complaints of her elderly friend. "I should never again refer such a ruffian to escort you to the opera."

Grace tilted her head.

"You did?" she asked, the cogs of her mind turning slowly.

There was something suspicious about that, but Grace couldn't seem to recall what.

"Ah, yes, but that is neither here nor there. Tell me, Dr. Hall, did Grace mention our trip to Kelvingrove Park with Mr. Milton?"

"Aye, she did. I hope you all have a pleasant time," he said.

Belle frowned.

"Will it not interfere with Grace's apprenticeship? I should think you would have a bit more to say on the matter."

"I do not. If Miss Sharpe wishes to attend a picnic," he said evenly, "I cannot stop her. Now, if you ladies will excuse me."

"Where are you going?" Grace asked.

"Goodness, child, never ask a man such a thing, unless you wish to be made a fool," the baroness said. She lifted her hand and shooed him away. "Leave us, if you must."

James did not hesitate and so with a final nod, he turned and left, moving into the crowd with surprising ease. And it wasn't lost on Grace that while she had practically confessed to her feelings for him, he seemed disheartened by her upcoming visit with Mr. Milton. But why? She had already expressed that she viewed the man as a friend and nothing more, and even if Mr. Milton expressed something different, well, she would simply explain to him that she didn't have any sort of affection for him. That her heart was otherwise engaged, because wasn't it?

"Hm," Belle mused. "That did not go as I expected it to. Well, this just will not do. I shall have to call in the cavalry."

Grace frowned.

"What cavalry? What are you talking about?"

Belle glanced at her, shaking her head.

"Nothing, my dear. Do not worry yourself about it."

For the remainder of the evening, she did not see James, and Grace contemplated what she had done or said to make him leave. By the time she, Belle, and Arabella returned home, she had come to the conclusion that she had somehow hurt him, but as she undressed in her room late that evening, she couldn't see how. Just because she was friendly with another man, didn't mean—

Oh.

The realization hit her suddenly and without warning. She was friendly with another man, while expressing her feelings for James, just as Catriona had done, right before abandoning him at their wedding.

Grace slapped her hand to her forehead. How could she be so insensitive? So blind to her own actions? Of course, James would behave strangely! He had lived this very situation before, only it had ended poorly for him.

As she got into bed, she couldn't let go of the fact that she had been so blatantly foolish. She would rectify this immediately. Tomorrow morning, she would apologize and hopefully he would forgive her for her supposed indifference. Because in truth, indifference was the furthest emotion from how she felt about James.

And tomorrow, she would tell him so.

Chapter Fifteen

JAMES AWOKE IN a sweat the next morning, having suffered some sort of nightmare he could barely recall. Something about a graverobber but they hadn't stolen a body? His hand came to his face as he rubbed the sleep out of his eyes and scratched his beard, considering not for the first time whether or not he should shave and be done with it.

Rolling out of bed, he went to the mirror that hung on the exterior wall, above the water table. The early morning light illuminated a reflection that appeared tired and discontented. He let out a snort. Of course he looked miserable. He was, and there wasn't anything he could do about it.

Bending down, he splashed the chilly water over his face, glad to have the invigorating distraction to try and dissuade visions of Grace from entering his mind. But having seen her last night in a gown that had all but demanded every ounce of his attention, well, it was difficult not to.

His hands gripped the edge of the porcelain bowl as his gaze wandered out his window. Her room was still dark, likely because she hadn't returned home until very late. Had she danced again with Mr. Milton? Had she finally realized that her even temper and clever speech could entice the entire city to fall in love with her if she so wished it? Or had she realized, just as Catriona, that perhaps there was someone better for her, more suited to her lifestyle?

Mr. Milton was a rich man, almost obscenely so, and while

new money wasn't particularly welcome in the upper social circles of London, he would undoubtedly be able to provide her with whatever she wished should she change her mind on marrying.

James splashed more water on his face, trying to force out the very word from his mind. He didn't care one way or the other if Grace suddenly realized what sort of influence she might garner by marrying a man like Milton. Yet, as much as his poor mood wanted to, he still couldn't shake the determination he had heard in her voice about marriage.

I will never marry anyone. Ever.

The statement was equal parts comforting and confounding. He believed that she never intended to marry, but there were situations where it would be necessary. Their experiment, for instance. While he had withdrawn from her before spilling his seed the first time, he wondered what might happen if he was too late the next time? If there was to be a next time, that was. Still, people changed their minds every day and he couldn't help but obsess with the idea of Grace spending a day with Milton, only to discover that she was in fact the marrying type.

A growl escaped him as he pushed himself up, away from the water bowl and decided to get dressed. In reality, it didn't matter. If Grace decided to change her mind and marry Milton, it would end whatever she sought to discover about herself and their tryst, or whatever she wanted to call it, would end and James would once again be left alone, although this time it seemed a far heavier burden.

With Catriona, he had been upset, angry even, and deservedly so, but having realized in the days that followed that she hadn't ever truly wished to marry him, he wondered if the feelings were mutual. She had been brilliant, not unlike Grace, but where Grace was honest and determined, Catriona had always floundered with her conviction. Particularly whenever her father was around, which, James had recently admitted, was one of the reasons he had proposed. His former mentor had been such an inspiration to him as a young doctor and he wanted to please him at all costs, so when Sir Ward had encouraged James to court Catriona, he likely did so in hopes to garner the approval of his former instructor.

That realization was difficult to concede, but it was the truth. As James finished dressing, he was left with the cold facts that Catriona had never loved him, and while he had believed himself to be in love with her, it was really more of a feeling of reverence for her father, because compared to what he felt for Grace, well, nothing had ever felt so visceral.

With Grace, James was constantly in awe. Not only did he find her clever and resolute, but she was humorous and genuinely kind. Easy to talk to and one of the few people who would push back when he became boorish. As a doctor, he had come to have a strong sense of self, to believe in his opinions and his abilities and rarely if ever was he pressed on his thoughts. Grace challenged him, however, and as much as it annoyed him at first, he had realized that he had become a better doctor for it and in turn, a better man.

She had made him a better person and for that, he couldn't help but love her.

It dawned on him halfway through his ride to his office and shook him to his core. He loved Grace, had loved her for weeks now, and it was only now that he realized it.

Stunned for the rest of the ride, he wondered how he should proceed with her. Their relationship had to remain professional, as she had dreams that he would guard and protect to ensure they came true, but how would he be able to go on living his life without at least admitting to her how he felt?

Would she be shocked? Horrified? Annoyed even, likely to believe that their coupling had led to his feelings. No. Perhaps he shouldn't tell her, lest she become uncomfortable and wish to leave to study under someone else. He needed to keep her close to him, if only to see her hopes become a reality because if there was one thing he could do, it was to guide her through her apprenticeship so that she would one day become a doctor.

Yes, that's what he would do. He would keep his feelings for her to himself and see her through her studies. Then, perhaps he would tell her how he felt, but he wouldn't do so now. Not when he held all the power. He didn't wish to coerce her into anything and so when he reached the office, he had decided that until the time was right, he would refrain from telling Grace how he felt.

Upon entering his offices, James could hear a number of voices coming from the back office. Curious, as he didn't have any appointments until nine o'clock, he took off his coat and handed it to Virgil, who came hobbling toward him.

"It's already a busy morning, doctor," he said, taking the coat. "The constable is here, requesting your presence at the Glasgow Necropolis as well as Dr. Cameron, who says he has something urgent to discuss with you, and Mrs. Felding is here." Virgil gave a little wave to the woman sitting in a chair just outside the doctor's office. "It seems her husband is in a terrible way and requests you accompany her to her house right away."

"What does the constable want with me at the Glasgow Necropolis?"

"It seems there was another attempt at body snatching and they believe there's some sort of clue that you might be able to help them with."

"You may speak when you are spoken to, Miss Sharpe!" Dr. Cameron's voice called out from the office, causing Virgil to turn.

"Dr. Grace is here too."

Instantly, James stalked toward the back office to push open the door.

There in the middle of the room stood Grace, a perturbed expression on her face, while Dr. Cameron, whose red cheeks and furious appearance caused James a surge of outrage. The constable, who was standing in between the two, seemed glad to see James.

"Ah, Dr. Hall, thank goodness," the policeman said, taking a step back.

"What is the meaning of this?" James asked, coming forward.

"Why are you yelling at my apprentice, Dr. Cameron?"

"Your *apprentice*," he spat with sarcasm. "Seems to believe that she is some sort of detective and has accused one of my students of several crimes—"

"I accused no one of anything," she argued. "I merely asked the constable if he had considered that there might be a connection between the missing persons in Gallowgate and the grave robbers at the Necropolis."

"Only to mention, by name, one of my students—"

"I was merely telling the constable what I saw."

"What you *think* you saw. Women are always so desperate to cause trouble and spread gossip."

"Ha!" she countered. "So, a woman cannot be stronger than a man, nor can we study as well as a man, but now we cannot see as well as a man? Good God, it's a wonder we're even capable of breathing without the help of your sex!"

"Insolent wench!"

Without thinking, without breathing, James was between the two, fists clenched at his side as he glared down at his former colleague, who stepped backwards with an air of self-preservation about him, bumping into the edge of James's desk.

"I will not have you disparage Miss Sharpe, here or anywhere. She is a student of medicine, a damn brilliant one at that, and one to whom you have shown little to no respect. As a physician yourself, it is your duty to teach others and yet you ridicule her based on the mere fact that she is a woman?" He shook his head in disgust. "It's not only beneath you, Dr. Cameron, it is in defiance of the very institution that you serve. It is your job, our jobs, as doctors, to teach those who are capable to learn."

Dr. Cameron's eyes went wide.

"You would defend this gossiping tramp over an innocent man?"

James's resolve snapped and he grabbed the man by his lapels.

"Call her that again, and I'll dissect you myself."

The frightening threat hung in the air, causing everyone to

remain still. It was like just before a storm, when the wind disappeared and everything became unnaturally quiet. James was breathing heavily, almost daring the cowering doctor to challenge him, but then the constable spoke.

"Sirs, I must implore that you settle this at a different time. Dr. Hall, you're needed at the Necropolis as soon as possible. We must make haste."

For a moment, James didn't move, still staring daggers at the older man, but then he released him and turned, quickly glimpsing at Grace, whose dumbstruck expression gave him no answers. He looked at the constable.

"Very well. Let's go."

"H-he threatened me," Dr. Cameron sputtered after a moment. "You heard it, constable. He threatened to dissect me."

"Only *if* you continue in your rude treatment of the lady, Doctor," the constable said as James moved around the room to fill his leather doctor bag. He would have to see to Mr. Felding after his business with the constable. "I suggest you heed his word."

Shaking with furious indignation, Dr. Cameron pushed himself off the desk and headed for the door. In a short moment, the bell to the outer door rang and he was gone, though the rage within James seemed untempered. He was nearly finished packing when Grace stepped forward, into his view.

"Thank you for that," she said softly, but he was in no mood.

"Do not thank me, Miss Sharpe. It is far from wise to accuse innocent men of crimes they did not commit."

"I didn't accuse anyone of anything, I merely mentioned that I saw Mr. Roberts—"

"Saw him what? Give some money to a couple of men in dirty clothes?" he interrupted, furious with her as well. "It was Gallowgate, Grace. There are a good number of people in stained and dirty clothes all over that neighborhood, not to mention it was raining."

"Yes, but—"

"But what? The truth is, you saw nothing of consequence. If anything, it could have been an act of charity. Not only have you offended one of the most prominent doctors in this city, but you accuse him, by proxy, of being involved with something truly heinous. Something that has caused fear and suspicion on our profession for decades. And with what proof?"

To his utter misery, Grace's bottom lip began to tremble as her eyes turned watery. God save him from witnessing her cry over his angry words. He shook his head.

"Tend to the patients today. I fear I will not be back until late."

With that, he was out of the office and the front door with the constable close at his heels. They both climbed onto their horses and after securing his bag to his horse, they were off.

This, this had been the whole reason he hadn't wanted Grace to apprentice with him in the first place. Because he knew his colleagues would think she was some sort of joke. He hadn't wanted to fight about the capabilities of the female sex, and he certainly hadn't wanted to put his hands on a man he had long considered a friend.

Yet, here he was. Without a doubt, news would spread about their argument, and before long James would be ostracized from his own community, all because he couldn't let Dr. Cameron belittle Grace. And it wasn't even because she was right. It was because James loved her and that was the worst of it. He had lost sight of his work, his duty to remain impartial and instead had chosen to champion her over common sense.

A small voice within his mind tried to reason that he wouldn't have done so if he didn't trust Grace, but it didn't matter. There was no proof of any foul doing and he was tempted to blame her imagination, but even then he couldn't bring himself to do so.

He would have to apologize to Dr. Cameron, and that, coupled with the memory of Grace's unshed tears, sent him into a foul mood indeed.

Perched on a small hill, the graveyard was a vast piece of land that had become the new favorite place for the well to do to be buried. Gates that were now locked nightly opened as James and the constable rode a short way into the cemetery, where a number of other police officers stood not too far from a large oak that reached out over an open grave.

James got off his horse and landed in the wet dirt. The grave had only been recently dug and then dug up again, leaving mounds of wet soil all round. Shuffling through a few police officers, James came to the edge of the grave and peered down.

The wooden casket had been pried open, but only partially as the bottom half was still nailed in. There wasn't much left, save a small pillow that must have been stitched by a loved one and placed inside, as a few tears of cloth that had been caught on the splitting wood were the only clues that were left behind. Frowning, James noticed the constable come up to his side.

"When did it happen?"

"Last night. They were in a bit of hurry, it seemed, as they left a hammer, supposedly used to pry open the coffin, thanks to the nightwatchman. Fortunately, they weren't able to get away with the body in tow. We found her near the front gates."

James's face contorted at his words.

"Is the hammer all that was left behind?"

"No. Davies!" The constable called out. As they turned around, James saw a young police officer, who was likely only twenty years old, scamper up to them, his police helmet almost too big for his head. "Where's the evidence?"

"Evidence, sir?"

"Yes, what was found within the grave?"

"Oh yes, sir." The young man pulled a small item from his breast pocket. "I have it right here, sir."

Taking it, the constable handed it to James. A small, hand carved cone shaped piece of wood with a rusty nail tapped into the base. His brow cinched together as he inspected it. He had seen this before.

"A child's toy," the constable said.

"How do you know it wasn't placed in the coffin by a family member? A child or grandchild."

"This is the grave of Pauletta Tidsale. She lived in the nunnery for the last ten years."

"Nunnery? Why is she buried here then?"

"Her parents were wealthy people. They would rather she be buried with the family plot."

James shrugged.

"Do nuns not work with orphans? Or even if she didn't, perhaps it was a toy she played with as a child."

"The Tidsales hardly seem the type to allow their daughter to play with such an inferior toy. Besides, we asked the nunnery if she had any dealings with children, and it seems she was more of a gardener type. She never spent any time with children and had been quoted to call them 'feral little beasts' from time to time." He sighed. "No, I believe this fell out of the pocket of one of our grave robbers."

It was likely that a wealthy family would have a spinner top made of something more substantial than wood. Tin perhaps? But as James twirled the small toy in his hands, he remembered where he saw it.

Mrs. Monty's child was playing with one of these when he visited with Grace the time before last.

"I have to inquire about something," he said, handing the evidence back to the constable. "Here. Do not lose that."

"Where are you going? Do you know something?"

"I may, but I'd like to be certain first."

With that, James walked toward his horse, hopped on, and rode straight to Gallowgate.

Chapter Sixteen

G RACE MEANDERED ALONG one of the crushed stone paths in Kelvingrove Park, hands behind her back as she followed her aunt, Arabella, and Mr. Milton from a short distance behind. It had been two days since the scene in James's office and while they had spoken professionally since, it had only been short sentences or single word answers, volleyed back and forth between them, in a way that strangers might speak to one another. She hadn't even the courage to ask about his investigation with the constable, but by his chilled attitude toward her, she could only assume that nothing of importance had been discovered.

It was crushing to be so distant from him, particularly working side by side with him, but then Grace was sure she deserved it. The reality of the situation was that she didn't have any proof that Mr. Roberts was in any way involved with the graverobbing and she was merely trying to thread two stitches of fabric together without any string.

"Come along, Grace! Don't dawdle."

"Yes, Aunt Belle."

If anyone's mood had improved as of late, it was her aunt's. She appeared positively chipper since Grace arrived home the day of her argument with James, calling the entire incident curious before ringing Mrs. Stevens to serve a rather decadent berry jam cake, layered with dollops of heavy cream. She had said it was to lift Grace's spirits, but she had appeared far too pleased with herself and Grace had gone to her room instead.

Even today, with a gloomy overcast sky above and the rumblings of a thunderstorm on the horizon, Aunt Belle seemed particularly light of foot, considering that she usually walked slower whenever it rained. But today she was on the arm of Mr. Milton, who was doing his diligence to keep his attention on Grace without crowding her, by peering over his shoulder every so often as they strolled through the park.

Mr. Milton would never raise his voice at her, Grace thought as she kicked a stone from her path. He probably wouldn't even know how to be cross with someone. But the guilt of comparing the two men seemed to swallow Grace up, pulling her deeper into her own misery. The truth was that it didn't matter if Mr. Milton was the kindest, most patient man in the world. He wasn't James.

Grace's footsteps slowed as the realization dawned on her. She would rather be in James's company, with all the tension and wretchedness she felt in his presence, than be with someone who was amiable and pleasantly tame at all times. What did that say about her? Was she a glutton for punishment, or merely too thick minded to realize what was best for herself? Surely she must be ill in the mind to want to be near James, even in this very moment, to try and work through their issues than stroll with a man who seemed so perfectly suited for her.

"Oh my!" Arabella exclaimed, causing Grace to glance up. "It's the largest glass house I've ever seen!"

There behind the tree line stood a partially finished building made of metal and glass. The top of the structure was pitched, with most of the iron set in place, but only half of the glass panes had been set.

"It will take another few months to be completed, if the snow doesn't stop us."

"Grace?" Aunt Belle called, turning around. "Mr. Milton has asked if you might join him for a tour of the greenhouse? He says he's something important to show you."

"Of course," Grace answered as she walked at a faster pace.

All four of them reached the open glass doors of the structure in just a few short minutes. Arabella seemed particularly excited.

"This must be six times larger than my greenhouse at home," she said upon entering. Twirling around slightly, her eyes widened. "I can only imagine the sort of plants that will be able to grow in here."

"We're hoping to have samples from all over the world," Mr. Milton said as he waved to a few men who were standing in front of an empty pond made of rocks. "Mr. Dalton?"

The man in the center excused himself from the others and came forward. He was a tall, somewhat gangly man, with a handsome face and honey colored hair and a smattering of freckles across the bridge of his nose, giving him a youthful appearance. Upon reaching their company, he bowed his head politely until his attention fell on Arabella. He stared for a moment, blinked as if awakening from an enchantment.

"Yes?"

"Mr. Dalton, may I introduce you to Lady Belle Smyth, Miss Sharpe, and Miss Scott," he said. "Ladies, this is Mr. Dalton. He is our lead naturalist."

"A pleasure to meet you," Arabella said, entranced herself as she lifted her hand for him to take, which he did instantly. "A naturalist?"

"Aye," he said as he kissed the back of her knuckles.

Aunt Belle leaned slightly back to make eye contact with Grace, who couldn't help but grin.

"And what does a naturalist do?" Aunt Belle asked. "I fear I've heard a similar word before, but I'm almost certain it isn't what you do here."

Grace coughed into her fist, trying to hide a laugh. Mr. Milton twisted back and winked at her.

"A naturalist is an expert in natural history. They would study the biology and environment of all matter of things, from plants to animals and the like," Arabella said. "Isn't that correct, Mr.

Dalton?"

"Quite right, Miss Scott," the young man said excitedly. "Although, I am more of the study of plants than animals. Particularly for this project."

"I'm something of a botanist myself, amateur as it were, but still, fascinated by the science of plants."

The young man's eyes widened.

"Truly?" Arabella bobbed her head emphatically. "Then perhaps, you might like to take a tour with me? I'd love to show you how we plan to arrange our findings once collected."

"Yes, please."

"Then take my arm. The ground can be uneven."

Arabella took the man's arm and they glided away, seemingly unaware of everyone else.

"Excuse me," Aunt Belle said, following after them. "I'm afraid my duty as a chaperone will finally be useful."

"Be careful," Grace said, though the old woman just waved her hand in the air as she went. Mr. Milton chuckled as Belle followed after the couple, leaving him alone with Grace. She swallowed as he offered his arm to her.

"May I?" he asked.

Grace took his arm as gingerly as possible.

They walked around the empty pond, out toward the part of the building that wasn't finished. Piles of metal beams, some thick and some thin, lined the paths. Flowerbeds were partially installed, with piles of black dirt nearly every few feet. Some native plants had already been planted, it seemed. One particularly large Scotch Broom bush, that towered over them, had been planted at the corner of a plot and as they rounded the bend, they were hidden from everyone else.

"It will be a jewel of a building once completed," Mr. Milton said. "In fact, I believe it will be the most beautiful building in all of Glasgow. Although I'm sure its beauty will not compare to yours."

Grace blanched at the compliment, feeling somehow worse

than before. When she didn't speak, Mr. Milton's steps paused.

"Are you feeling all right, Miss Sharpe? You don't seem your-self."

They had met a handful of times; how would he know what her true self was like? But she didn't say that. Instead, she shook her head.

"Indeed, I'm not feeling my best."

"Are you ill?"

"Possibly," she said offhandedly. Thinking of how much her heart hurt.

"Perhaps you should see a doctor."

"Ha! Er, I mean." She cleared her throat. "Y-yes. I suppose I should, considering I know so many."

Mr. Milton grinned, and for a moment neither of them spoke. A creeping sense of dread began to crawl up Grace's spine. Instinctually, she knew that Mr. Milton was about to say something and for the life of her, she couldn't bear to hear it.

"Miss Sharpe, I've been meaning to ask you a question," he said, eyes steadfast on her.

"Oh?"

"Yes. I was wondering, if you might consider allowing me to court you. I know we don't know each other very well, but that is something I'm very willing to fix. You see, I have spent many years traveling alone, building my fortune as I go, and it's come to my attention that it's rather lonely at the top. That said, I find you quite charming. Your intelligence, your bravery, your humor. All are qualities that I find attractive and while I will not belittle you with remarks on your beauty, I must say that it is truly mesmerizing to gaze into your eyes."

He leaned in slightly and Grace gulped, sure the feeling of dread was splattered across her face. She had been so cavalier in talking with James about Mr. Milton and her foolish experiment that she hadn't actually realized what it would be like to be face to face with him.

"T-that is kind of you, Mr. Milton. Exceedingly so, but I'm

not quite sure we are a good fit for one another." When he didn't speak, but instead waited patiently for her to continue, she nodded. "You see, I'm rather determined never to marry. Anyone."

He frowned. "Really?"

"Yes. Unfortunately, I believe that my profession will not allow it and as I'm determined to have that, I cannot entertain the idea of marriage, so I'm afraid a courtship between us would be fruitless."

"Huh," he breathed, seemingly unprepared for her dismissal. "And here I thought we shared a mutual attraction."

"Oh, I do find you attractive, Mr. Milton. That is, you are an attractive man, with many fine qualities and there isn't a woman alive who wouldn't be blessed to have you, but unfortunately for me, I'm afraid that my duty to the medical field is beyond my control. Like a priest called to serve the church, I feel I have been called on to serve the people, and marriage would hinder that."

His brows pinched together, trying to understand, though it appeared he didn't want to.

"It is a noble pursuit," he finally said after a long silence. "And unfortunately, it makes me like you all the more." He sighed. "Are you sure? I could build you your own hospital that you might be a patron of. You could help hundreds, if not thousands of people."

She smiled sadly and placed her hand on his shoulder.

"Are you trying to bribe me?"

"Possibly. Is it working?"

She laughed and her hand fell away.

"Would you allow me to practice medicine as your wife?"

Even before he answered, she saw the truth in his face.

"If I'm to be completely honest, no. I'm searching for a companion, one who might travel with me and I fear that would interfere with your work."

She understood and though she knew she should feel despondent about it, Grace couldn't muster up any regret at his honest words.

"Mr. Milton, if you did build a hospital, which I think you should, I would gladly take up residence there as an employee. I'm sure it would be a grand building indeed."

A small spark flashed in his eyes and Grace saw his attention switch.

"It would be, wouldn't it? Long, open hallways, spacious rooms. Running water," he said in a dreamy sort of way. "It would be the most modern of hospitals."

She smiled.

"I'm sure it will be."

His attention temporarily brought back to the present situation, Mr. Milton nodded.

"Well then, I am sorry for my loss, but happy for the city of Glasgow as she will gain you as a physician."

Grace couldn't stop herself from frowning.

"Perhaps one day, but not soon. I'm afraid I've insulted one of the most renowned doctors in the city and, well, generally made a mess of things." Mr. Milton waited for her to continue, but she shook her head. "Never mind. I'm sorry I couldn't say yes to your proposal, Mr. Milton."

"Me too." He paused for a moment. "Miss Sharpe, I know my next request will seem beyond outrageous, but I cannot seem to help myself. I will regret it the rest of my life if I don't ask."

"Yes?"

He hesitated and then shook his head.

"No. I don't think I will."

Seemingly reading his mind, Grace leaned forward and brushed her mouth ever so gently against his. He remained perfectly still and upon feeling nothing but friendship, Grace stepped back. A pleasured expression passed over his face.

"Thank you, Miss Sharpe."

"Thank you, Mr. Milton."

They continued their stroll through the unfinished part of the greenhouse, just as the skies opened up and it began to rain. As quickly as they could, Grace, Arabella, and Aunt Belle were loaded into their carriage and brought home, all the while listening to Arabella go on and on about Mr. Dalton, who apparently was preparing for a trip around the world. He was tasked with finding rare and beautiful specimens for the greenhouse and had fascinated Arabella with every word.

Once they had entered the house, Grace felt her previous melancholy surface once more and she was left with nearly a half day of nothing to do as she had told James that she would be out of the office for the whole day, but the rain had cut their activities short.

Now, as she wandered throughout the house, her mind reeled back to her brash accusations. Why had she been so insistent on telling the constable about Mr. Roberts, and in front of his professor no less? What had made her so sure of herself that she would do something so careless?

It had been instinctual, which of course meant nothing. But even now, after having been properly chastised for her rashness, she couldn't shake the feeling that something wasn't quite right about seeing Mr. Roberts in Gallowgate. Yes, James had said that he could be there on some charitable cause, but the amount of bills that had been handed over to those two men, it just appeared more like a payment than anything and what could a well-to-do university student want with two particularly rough looking men in the slums of Glasgow?

It simply didn't add up.

Not to mention that besides the grave robberies, a number of people were still missing and all of them had last been reported being seen in Gallowgate. It didn't make sense that people were disappearing in the middle of the city. Surely, if they were leaving or running away, someone, anyone, would have seen them leave. Particularly if they were from Gallowgate. The people there were dressed in near rags and if someone like them had been seen in any other neighborhoods, it would have been reported.

But it hadn't. They had all disappeared right in the middle of

Gallowgate.

Grace stared out the parlor window, watching the rain roll down the glass pane, arms folded across her chest as an outrageous idea began to form in her mind. If people were vanishing within Gallowgate, then there had to be some sort of evidence there. Evidence she could discover herself.

It was a dangerous idea, but then she had been there several times now. And she didn't plan on knocking on every door, but maybe she might ask a few of the families in the factory housing building. Surely they would have seen or heard something and if Grace could discover where these people were going, then she'd be able to bring evidence to the constable and, perhaps foolishly, show James that she was right.

Turning on her heel, Grace headed for the doorway when Aunt Belle appeared, followed by Andrews.

"Ah, my dear, there you are. Do you feel like a game of chess? This dreary weather has me in the mood for a game."

"I cannot, actually. I am going out."

"Out? In this weather? Where are you... Oh," she stopped herself suddenly. "Yes, dear, do what you must. But bundle up. I fear this rain may turn to sleet soon enough."

"I will. I won't be long."

"Take as long as you like," Aunt Belle said, waving her off.

Grace wasn't sure why her aunt was always so relaxed about her comings and goings. She was the complete opposite of her sister, Grace's Grandmother Alice, who had been a stickler for propriety. Grace and her sisters had never been allowed out on their own without at least a maid, yet here Grace was, acting as though she were completely independent, all with her aunt's support.

It was a strange situation, but one that Grace was grateful for. Her driver, however, seemed to blanch when she told him where she wanted to go.

"Are you sure, my lady? That is not an area I'm sure I should bring you to."

"I've been there a number of times before."

"Yes, but in the company of Dr. Hall."

"Unfortunately, Dr. Hall is busy at his office today and I have some pressing matters to attend, so if you will," she said with a definitive nod to end the conversation.

The driver hesitated a moment before agreeing, as he closed the door to the carriage. Soon, they were rushing down the cold, wet streets of Glasgow. It took some time to get there, as the rain had indeed begun to freeze, causing a slickness on the road that required an alternate route. By the time they reached the street that the factory housing was on, Grace tapped the roof of the carriage, signaling her driver to stop.

"My lady?" he asked as she hopped out of the vehicle, wrapped tightly in her wool cloak.

"Stay here but a moment. I shall return."

Without waiting to hear his pleas, Grace twisted around and hurried down the street. She didn't want the carriage visible, as it was rare to see one in this part of the city, and tended to make the locals suspicious.

Within a few minutes, she was pulling open the door to the factory housing building, and to her surprise, ran right into Mrs. Monty.

"Oh gads, now what do you want?" she asked, visibly annoyed. "Come to pester me kids with more questions about pieces of trash?"

Grace tilted her head.

"I beg your pardon?"

"Dr. Hall was here, not two days ago, asking about some silly little piece of toy that he found somewhere in your part of the city. Asked my boy where he found it and who gave it to him."

Grace was confused. What toy? And why had James come all this way to ask about it? Then, he hadn't even mentioned it to her. Of course, they had been on the outs, but still, it seemed to be rather important if he came all the way to Gallowgate to inquire about a toy.

"He did?" The woman bobbed her head up and down. "I'm sorry, I haven't any idea why Dr. Hall would have come. You say it was a toy?"

Mrs. Monty's shoulders dropped as she sighed, annoyed.

"Charlie! Get out here!"

The redheaded boy who had shown Grace his toy spinner during his first visit, came out of the room behind his mother. Mrs. Monty turned on the child, bent at the waist, and grabbed him by the face.

"Tell this lady where you got that top from, do you hear me? No more shrugging and saying that you don't know nothing. I'm not having my home invaded with doctors who think they can just show up whenever they bloody like."

Grace winced as the mother dropped the boy's chin. He came around his mother and hung his head.

"Sorry, doctor lady," he said quietly.

Grace knelt down.

"It's all right. Did Dr. Hall ask you about your top toy?" The boy nodded. "And you told him you didn't know where it came from?"

"I told him I just found it on the street."

"Was that the truth?" He shook his head. "Why didn't you tell Dr. Hall the truth?"

"Because I didn't want him to take it away from me."

"Oh," Grace said gently. "Well, if you tell me the truth, I promise, I won't take it from you."

The boy glanced up. Then, he pointed at the doors at the entrance of the building.

"I got it from them."

Grace craned her head around.

"Who is them?"

"The misters who stand outside that building."

"What building?"

"The one that has the picture of the bunny."

"Rabbit House?"

The boy nodded as his mother came up, placing a hand on his shoulder. "Heard enough?"

"Yes—"

"Good. Now I hope not to see you for at least a month. Come along, Charlie."

With that, the woman and her son returned to their room and slammed the door shut, causing Grace to jump. Well, that had been informative. Except that she had no idea why a toy had anything to do with Rabbit House. Or what James had been intent on discovering.

Leaving the building, Grace lifted her hood and through the rain, she saw one of the two men she had seen the day she saw Mr. Roberts. The bald one. He was leaning against Rabbit House, one foot up on the brick wall, while smoking a long pipe and staring daggers at her as she felt the hairs on the back of her neck stand up. Glancing down the road, she saw her carriage on the corner and cursed herself for being so careless.

Lifting her chin and staring back, she didn't let herself cower as she turned left. The bald man kicked off the wall and though she didn't turn around to see, she knew he was following her. At first she tried to walk at a normal pace, not wishing to appear nervous, but then her body seemed to take over and soon she was hurrying down the muddy streets.

The distinct sound of footsteps splashing in the puddles behind her caused her to grab her skirts and run. Thankfully, her driver was waiting on the side of the carriage, under an umbrella and saw her coming.

"My lady?"

"Hurry!" Grace yelled back and he opened the door as she dove into the vehicle, just as a meaty hand grabbed at her ankle. "Ah!"

She kicked the hand away and witnessed the driver turn his umbrella into a weapon, thrashing the bald man without mercy as she pulled her body inside the carriage and closed the door. Before she could sit up and push back the curtains, the vehicle was off. Gazing out of the back window, she saw the bald man stagger to his feet.

Heart pounding in her ears as she tried to catch her breath, Grace knew what she had to do next.

She needed to speak with James at once.

Chapter Seventeen

T HE GAS LAMPS that lined the tidy street that sat behind Grace's home illuminated the stone path that led out of the kitchens, into the alley, and out onto the road where James's house stood. It was late in the evening, at least for Aunt Belle, who had fallen asleep in the parlor after dinner, as usual. Arabella sat in the corner, writing frantically to someone, though she wasn't exactly eager to share who, as Grace had wandered down the hallway, down through the kitchens that had finally emptied out after the kitchen staff had finished cleaning, and out the back door. With Mrs. Stevens mending a gown, Andrews stationed by her aunt, and the cook, maids, and footmen all settling down for the evening, Grace had thought it a perfect time to confront James about the toy top.

It was strange, being out of the house alone at night. She had never actually been by herself on the streets during the dark hours and feeling somewhat daring, she hurried across the street, climbed the two stone steps, and knocked on James's door.

To her surprise, the door instantly opened to reveal James, staring at her with questioning eyes, as if he had somehow anticipated her arrival.

"What the devil do you think you're doing?" he asked, gazing past her. "Why are you sneaking out of your house this late at night?"

"I need to talk to you."

"And it couldn't wait?"

"No." He didn't move, obviously hesitant. "Are you going to let me in or must we discuss this in the middle of the street?"

Faced with such an unappealing offer, James reluctantly stood aside to allow her entry.

Grace removed her shawl and glanced around the foyer. It was a smaller entrance than Aunt Belle's house, with a black and white checkered floor, dark oak banister, and stairs that were covered in an ornate runner of carpet that curved up to the second floor. The walls were white, but two large paintings hung above a marble-topped hallway table, revealing a sight that stunned Grace.

"This is a portrait of Mrs. Fletcher," she said, stepping toward the painting. "And Dr. Barkley's office in Glencoe."

"Yes."

She turned to face him, noting something she had never seen before. Just above the top of his beard line, where his cheekbones showed, a faint blush had appeared. Grace tilted her head.

"I thought you… Well, I always assumed…"

"What? That I didn't care for my aunt or Glencoe?"

"No, of course not."

"But that's what you were thinking," he said, walking around her as he pushed open a dark, polished wooden door that led into another part of the house.

Grace followed and was rather taken aback at the size of the room. It seemed that unlike Aunt Belle's home, that had rooms on either side of the main foyer and hallway, and thus cutting the rooms in half, James's house had been designed to have all the rooms on one side, creating wide open spaces.

Guessing that this was the parlor, Grace noted the impressive crown molding that topped the tall walls. This room was also white, with dark wood furnishings. The settee and chairs and benches were all matched in a moss green velvet fabric, that had been embroidered with a heather purple stitching. The artwork in this room were landscapes, of all the mountains and Munros that encircled Glencoe.

He had decorated his home to match the Highlands.

Grace gazed at him, mouth slightly parted as it dawned on her. She had believed that the doctor disliked Glencoe, but it seemed he missed it terribly and this was his way of being surrounded by the home he had left, the place he had loved.

She shook her head.

"But you never speak of Glencoe, or Dr. Barkley or your aunt," she said. "You barely even mention the Highlands."

James swallowed, trying to appear unaffected.

"It's easier for me to be here if I have reminders of home. Like how annoying my aunt can be, or how pushy and hovered over I feel when I'm in Dr. Barkley's presence. He's really quite bothersome when we see a patient together. Right over my shoulder." James gestured to his own. "Constantly telling me the next step as if I haven't been a practicing physician for years now."

Grace smiled.

"He was your mentor. I'm sure he cannot help himself."

"More than that, he was my benefactor. When I came to live with my aunt, she was something of an outcast and not very wealthy, but Dr. Barkley had always paid for her lodgings. She was a healer after all, in the old ways, and he thought to keep her close."

"I didn't know that."

James sighed.

"I wasn't happy when I moved in with her. I was angry that my parents had died, angry that I had to live with someone who I believed, at the time, was a madwoman. Dr. Barkley began taking me on rounds with him. He was so normal in comparison. A professional man, well liked and well respected. A stark contrast to the woman I was living with, but he was always certain to instill tolerance in me for her bizarre behavior. For everyone." He stared absently into the space in front of him. "I owe them both a great deal."

Grace stepped forward, touching his arm in a comforting way.

"She's always spoken very highly of you. They both have. The little silver charm she gave me? She said to keep it on my person whenever I was working with you, as it would protect us both from illness. I know she believes that to be some sort of magic herb, but there have been studies about mint's cleansing properties."

James let out a huff of breath that almost sounded like a laugh as his mouth curved into a self-deprecating grin.

"I suspect she did that because she knows my fondness for water mint."

"Oh."

A moment passed and Grace dropped her hand from his forearm, feeling suddenly exposed. To be sure, when she gazed up at him, he was staring at her.

"Why are you here, Grace?"

Swallowing the sudden lump in her throat, she stepped away from him, in an effort to distance herself from what would surely be an argument.

"I went to Gallowgate this afternoon to ask some questions of the factory workers. I wanted to know if they had seen anything regarding the missing persons that have been vanishing from their neighborhood."

"You what?" James's voice sounded behind her, soft, yet enraged. "Have you lost your mind?"

"I am certain something is going on and I needed to know—"

Grace was instantly whipped around, as James reached for her elbow and spun her. His gray-blue eyes were wide with fury and something else. Fear?

"Tell me you did not go to Gallowgate alone?" When she made a grimace, he swore. "Grace, are you aware of what could have happened to you? The only reason I allow you to accompany me there is because I am with you."

"I am capable enough—"

He shook her slightly.

"No, Grace. You aren't. No one is. My own presence is only

tolerated because I serve a purpose and I know not to open my mouth about things that do not concern me."

She frowned.

"But that's dishonest—"

"It's a reality. I do not pass judgment on them, do not interfere with their affairs, and I'm left alone. Going there without any protection, to purposely try and find something out among them is a death wish."

"But I did find something out. Something you need to know."

"What?" he snapped. "What on earth could you have discovered that might be worth risking your life over?"

"The top toy that you brought there for Mrs. Monty's son to identify. He didn't tell you where he got it from, did he?"

James's entire expression froze. He released her at once.

"How do you know about that?"

"Because Mrs. Monty told me you went there searching for answers," she countered. "Not so unlike myself."

"It's different. They know me, trust me."

"Well then, why didn't Charlie Monty tell you where he received the top toy from?" James opened his mouth, then shut it, visibly contrite. Grace stepped toward him. "Because he was afraid. Afraid that you might take it away from him. So, he said he found it. But when I arrived, Mrs. Monty forced him to tell the truth, mostly because she didn't want me there, but that's beside the point. Charlie told me one of the men I saw Mr. Roberts paying, he was the one that gave it to him. He said he makes them out of scraps and bits of rubbish and hands them out to children in the neighborhood."

James's eyes widened at the revelation and Grace knew something had connected in his brain. His hand came up to his face and he rubbed his beard thoughtfully.

"Bugger me."

"Where did you find a top toy that would bring you to question Charlie Monty?"

"In the grave of a nun whose body had just been stolen."

Grace grabbed James's wrist.

"So, I was right? Those men Mr. Roberts was paying off, they've been stealing bodies from the cemetery?" She bit her lip with trepidation. "I knew something was amiss. I bet it was the man who nearly grabbed at me in Gallowgate, although to learn that I was correct, it was almost worth it."

James's brow furrowed, blinking several times as if he hadn't heard her properly.

"Excuse me?"

Grace stood up straight, releasing his wrist at once.

"Nothing."

"What happened in Gallowgate?" he asked, stepping toward her. She took a step back, but instantly the back of her legs bumped into an end table. "Grace."

"It was nothing really. My driver was able to beat him off with an umbrella."

"Beat him off?" he repeated incredulously. "You were attacked?"

A buzzing in her extremities told Grace that it was time to leave. She dipped into a curtsy and tried to move around him, but he reached for her arm and brought it up to his chest. Grace was breathing heavily as she stared into his eyes, and she had half a mind to push at him, only she didn't want to. Her gaze fell to his mouth and she thought about the last person she had kissed and how little it had affected her, while just being near James caused a riot in her chest. Before she knew what she was doing, she leaned up on her tippytoes and pressed her mouth to his, suddenly too weak to fight her urges.

Instantly, James pulled her against his chest, kissing her furiously. His mouth was punishing, likely to teach her a lesson about going off by herself, but Grace didn't care what he intended for her to learn from it. He was kissing her and that was all that mattered.

The aroma of citrus was now an aphrodisiac as she inhaled greedily, taking in the scent of him only for him to pull back, his forehead leaning against hers.

"What if something happened to you?" he asked roughly. "For God's sake, Grace, if you insist on going through this world alone, you have to take care of yourself."

"I know."

"No," he said. "I don't think you understand."

Her brow pinched, trying to decipher his words.

"I don't?"

He closed his eyes, his hands moving over her back, as if trying to memorize the feel of her.

"No." He exhaled. "You're too important to too many people and to think of you in distress, alone… It guts me."

Grace's heart expanded, aching at his confession. Ashamed for going to Gallowgate alone, she brought her hand up to his bearded cheek and pressed her mouth to his, slowly and deliberately. His kiss tasted like home.

When she pulled back, she saw such reverence in his eyes that it scared her. But then she spoke.

"I'm sorry for causing you distress." He dipped his chin to acknowledge her apology but it didn't feel like enough. "Truly, James. I do not wish to ever cause you anguish."

A soft laugh escaped him.

"Grace, every day I am in anguish." His hand came to her neck, his fingers gripping the back of her head. "Every moment spent in your presence is a special hell, knowing that I can't touch you, or even tell you what you mean to me."

Grace's pulse surged. She wanted to tell him that she felt the same way, but she knew it would only lead to conversations she neither was ready for nor wanted. She already had a dream and she didn't want to replace it and so instead of talking, she began to unbutton his shirt. If she couldn't tell him how she felt, she could at least show him.

But his hands wrapped around her wrists, stopping her. Gazing up, she feared he wouldn't let her, but then a hint of a smirk showed at the corner of his mouth.

"Mrs. Cramer might wake and discover us. Come."

For the second time, he took her hand and led her up a stair-case and she was grateful. All she wanted to do was to make love to him, curl up against his solid form, and sleep for ages. It was when they were alone together, naked and exhausted, that she had found the greatest peace of her life and she needed it now more than ever.

By the time they reached his room, she had noted a number of things. His house was well lit, but darkly decorated. Moss green hallway walls led to a large bedroom with a dark floral and vine pattern. A marble fireplace sat on the right wall, with a massive bed on the left, covered in an olive-green plaid blanket, woven with a blue and red stripe so intertwined it almost appeared purple, like the heather Grace had seen in fields surrounding Glencoe.

On the far wall was a window, familiar in shape as Grace had often stared at it after her baths, though it was always dark. She went to it and gazed out across the street to her own window.

"I've looked for you from my room, but you're never here."

"I've seen you."

She spun around.

"You have?"

"Aye," he said, reaching her. He took her hand and placed it against his chest. "A number of times."

Emotion crept up her and fearful of her own reaction, she kissed him, her hands going back to the unbuttoning that he had interrupted downstairs. He allowed her to take her time, his own hands moving over her as they kissed. Once his chest was exposed, she let her fingers touch his skin, but it wasn't enough. Finally, he stepped back and shrugged out of his clothes, while she undressed herself, thankful that she had worn one of her simpler gowns.

He was nude by the time she was only in her chemise, and staring at him in the dim firelight, Grace wondered if there had ever been a more perfect specimen. The way the shadow played against the contour of his muscles seemed to exaggerate all of him and she was in awe of him. From his corporeal gaze, to the clean line of his beard, the ripples of his abdomen and below, she was sure there had never been a more beautiful man. One who exuded care, intelligence, and above all, a touch that could not only heal, but could cause such a visceral reaction in herself.

She wanted to cause that same feeling in him and with a courage and audacity she didn't believe she possessed, she took a step toward him. Then knelt.

James let out a shaky breath. She didn't know exactly what she was supposed to do, but she knew what she wanted to do and reaching up to touch him, his hand instantly went to her cheek, his thumb moving back and forth as if she were some sort of pet.

Oh yes, a small voice echoed in her mind. Let her be that, just for tonight.

Grace leaned forward and pressed a kiss to the tip of his length, mesmerized by how silky he felt here. He let out a choked breath, and emboldened by this response, she brushed her tongue against the very spot she had just kissed, remembering how he had licked her. Her tongue swirled and she had barely closed her mouth around him when he spoke shakily.

"Grace."

A multitude of feelings could be heard in his tone. Pleasure, shock, surrender. She was kneeling before him, but he was under the spell of her touch and a burst of love and craving coursed through her body as she continued to do just as she wanted, exploring and tasting this man that she cared for so much.

All of a sudden, James's fingers tightened in her hair and he stepped back, holding her away from him as he panted, his chest heaving up and down erratically.

"Not yet," he rasped, as his hand dropped from her hair and reached for her hand.

He helped her to her feet, but then instantly picked her up and, moving around the room, he brought her to his bed. The moment her shoulders touched the plaid beneath her, a series of zings went through her heart and Grace had never been more certain of anything in her life. This was where she was meant to be, here in this man's bed, touching and kissing and discovering every part of him.

James's hands came up to the neckline of her chemise and without hesitating, he tore the thin fabric in half, causing her to gasp. She had half a mind to scold him for doing so, but then his mouth was on the tip of her breast and she was lost to her own pleasure. Her hips moved up just as his hand found her and he began to move his finger in and out while she panted with want.

"Yes," she breathed as he kissed down her stomach. Her back arched when his tongue replaced his fingers and she moaned. "*Yes.*"

He was not slow, but precise, and with his other hand high on her breast, teasing her nipple, Grace felt the pleasure she sought crash over her fast and heavy. Her body convulsed and she tried to pull away, but he held his place, until it subsided.

She wanted to fall asleep. Her body was boneless, but as he crawled up over her, he moved to her side.

"Not yet," he whispered, moving her arm over his chest. "I need you, Grace."

Dazed in a heady afterglow, Grace nodded and allowed him to pull her thigh up and over his body. When she felt the still rigid length of him enter her from beneath, her brow twitched. Her hands went to his chest as his went to her hips and slowly he moved her, teaching her how to ride him.

Now this was a position she had never considered, but as she began to move of her own volition, she began to chase the sensation that was once again building within her.

"God, Grace," he ground out. "You're perfect."

She smiled lazily, but soon her eyes closed as she began to move quicker. It was close, so close and she wouldn't let it go.

"Yes."

Grace's fingers dug into his solid chest and she moved in a bizarre way, not up and down, but not side to side either. It was a mix, a swirl of sorts as she felt him swell within her. Yes. It was coming again and she let it come over her again, crying out his name as it did.

James's body tensed beneath her and his fingers dug painfully into her hips as he moved her off him swiftly. Grace rolled onto the bed, the aftershocks coursing through her like little electric spasms while James's rigid back convulsed for several seconds until he finally slumped back. Reaching for her, he pulled her body close to his and they both fell asleep almost instantly, both seemingly aware that this was the only place in the world either of them wanted to be.

Some hours later, before the sunrise, Grace woke up with a jump. Pressed up against his naked body, Grace felt a finger circling around her shoulder.

"Shhh," James whispered, the dying fire giving the room a haunting glow. "You're all right. But you need to wake up."

She shivered and pressed herself against him, annoyed that her slumber was disturbed.

"I do not."

"You do. It's nearly three in the morning. You must return to your aunt's house, lest you be discovered missing."

Grace grumbled and buried her face in his chest.

"I don't care."

He kissed her shoulder and Grace felt her body melt. She smirked and, rolling over with her eyes still closed, she accepted a series of kisses down her cheek and neck. James paused after a moment.

"I'm sorry for getting angry with you the other day. I didn't mean to make you cry. Albeit, I'll admit I was rather taken aback by it."

Grace opened her eyes and gazed up at him, frowning slightly.

"Because you don't like when women cry?"

He shook his head.

"No. But as I recall, you once said that there was nothing in this world that I could do or say that would make you cry."

The words she had said to him in Lismore Hall months earlier felt like a lifetime ago.

"You remember that?"

"I remember everything concerning you."

She smiled and leaned up to kiss him, and was met with equal enthusiasm, but as she reached for him, he pulled back. Frustration rolled within her and she pouted, causing him to laugh.

"We need to get out of bed."

"No."

She plopped back down to the mattress defiantly.

"You must. If anyone discovers what we've been up to, they'll force us to marry." The threat was enough to set her rigid, and he felt it beneath his touch. "See? Now you must wake up."

Lifting her head up, she stared down at him, his eyes barely visible in the shadowy room.

"It's not as though you want to marry either." But even in the dark, Grace could see the unmoved muscles of his face and she suddenly felt uncomfortable. "You don't wish to marry, right?"

"I was ready to do so before."

"Yes, but not now."

"Why are you so sure?"

"Because I don't."

"I'm aware."

She frowned.

"But you don't wish to marry me. Correct?" He did not answer and as the silence dragged on, Grace sat up. "James, you don't want to marry me, right?"

"Grace, you don't wish to marry and I understand the reasons why."

"Yes, but that is not what I asked."

"What do you wish for me to say?"

"Tell me you do not want to marry me. Tell me that this, whatever this is, tell me that this is enough."

Another beat of silence followed and Grace's nerves began to vibrate with anxiety.

"Would you like me to tell you that this is enough or would you like me to tell you the truth?"

Grace's hand went to her face, puzzled by his words. How could he be telling her this? And why was he so calm?

"But then, this must be a less than desirable arrangement for you?"

He shook his head.

"I don't see it like that."

"How can you not?"

He pulled himself up, the edge of the sheet that covered them slipping down his chest to reveal the taut muscles of his chest and abdomen. Grace had to force herself to pay attention and was temporarily distracted when his hand reached out for hers.

"Grace, I am aware of your reservations about marriage and as much as it pains me, I happen to agree with you."

"You do?"

"Yes. If you were to marry, your chances of becoming a doctor would be drastically diminished. Even if it was to someone like me, who would afford you every freedom required to pursue it. I cannot, in all honesty, tell you that I would not eventually change my feelings about it, should we marry." He paused for a moment before adding, "And as much as other men might promise to allow you to achieve your dreams, I would take their words with a grain of salt."

She frowned.

"What other men?" When he didn't speak, she blinked. "You mean Mr. Milton?"

"I'm sure he will try and tempt you with promises and whatnot, but I know your desire to become a physician and I'm not telling you to not believe him, but I wouldn't put it past him to promise you all sorts of things and then change his mind once he has what he wants."

Grace glanced down at their joined hands.

"He offered to build me a hospital."

A moment of silence.

"Did he?" James asked, his voice gruff and she gazed up at him.

"But for me to be a patron of, not a doctor. He was honest with me. He told me he should want a wife first and foremost and I cannot give that to him."

James stared at her.

"So, you will not marry Mr. Milton?"

"No."

James's hand tightened around her fingers, his countenance suddenly relieved and Grace felt her heart beat with pleasure. He breathed deeply after a moment.

"Then you will see this apprenticeship to the end. I will make sure of it."

"And after?" she asked, unable to help herself. "When I become a doctor, what will we do then?"

He shook his head.

"I do not know." He leaned forward and gently brushed his lips against hers before pulling back. "But I should like to be near you, however possible, for a very long time, indeed."

Although Grace had always prided herself on her ability to refrain from crying, James's words affected her in a way no others ever had. He wanted to be with her, regardless of marriage, all so that she might realize her dream. It felt as if her heart were breaking and mending all at once.

She reached forward, kissing him with all of herself, her hands going to either side of his face. He leaned back, allowing her to have her way with him until they were both breathing unevenly.

"Wait," he tried. "Grace, you have to leave."

"Later," she muttered in between kisses.

"If you wait any longer, we will be married, and as much as that would please me, it's not what you want."

She paused, leaning her forehead against his and she tried to calm her breathing. Then, she pulled away.

"Yet. It's not what I want yet."

He smiled at her, but it felt uneasy.

"However this turns out, Grace, I'm here for it."

She was still for a moment before she slid off the edge of the bed to get dressed. He did as well, and with the next quarter of the hour, James was walking her across the street and opening the back door that led into the kitchens. He wouldn't let her go alone, which was as annoying as it was sweet.

"Wait," she said suddenly, remembering why she had gone to see him in the first place. "What are we going to do about Mr. Roberts and the men in Gallowgate?"

James shook his head.

"I'm not sure. There's obviously something going on, but without evidence we cannot do anything."

"But we have evidence. The top toy. You must show it to the constable and tell him everything."

A strained expression shone on James's face.

"To accuse a student of medicine of something like this is to accuse his professor, Grace. I need more evidence, something to confirm what we suspect, before I bring it to the constable, lest we get it wrong and are destroying several people's lives in the process."

Grace nearly stomped her foot.

"But we have enough evidence."

"Let me handle it."

"But—"

"Please, Grace," he said, effectively silencing her. "Good night."

"Good night," she said coolly as she turned and entered the kitchens.

James closed the door behind her and she stalked across the room, up a small flight of stairs, and down the servants' hallway until she reached the foyer. To her surprise, however, a light shone in the parlor. Nervous that someone was still awake, she tried to tiptoe to the staircase. Upon putting her foot on the first step, a loud CREAK echoed around her.

"Grace?" Aunt Belle called from the parlor.

Oh no.

Chapter Eighteen

WINCING, GRACE TURNED.

"Yes?"

"Come see me for a moment."

Shoulders dropping, Grace walked toward the parlor door. There, sat behind a desk not unlike the one she possessed in Lismore Hall, was her aunt. Andrews was standing behind her, his eyes drooping and to Grace's amazement, there was Penguin the cat, sat on her desk atop a stack of papers, purring loudly as Belle rubbed her bejeweled fingers on the cat's cheek.

"Good evening, Aunt Belle. It's late, is it not?"

"I could say the same thing to you." She turned her head. "Andrews, you are dismissed. Grace will help me to my room tonight."

Andrews bowed his head, though only Grace saw it, and he left the room without issue.

"Are you feeling well?" Grace asked, coming farther into the room.

"Well enough, except for the fact that I've a wayward niece."

"Wayward? That's rather harsh I should say—"

"Driver told me you went to Gallowgate. Alone. That you were attacked and that he had to fend off the attacker with an umbrella. Then, when I wake up in the middle of the night to have a nibble, I'm overcome with this strangest feeling. I have Andrews check on your room and alas, you're missing. What's more, I've received a letter from a Dr. Cameron, personally requesting that I remove you from the city, or else he threatens to sue you for libel."

Grace cringed.

"I'm sorry, Aunt Belle, but Dr. Cameron is exactly why I had to speak with Dr. Hall about a police case—"

"For four hours?"

Grace dropped her head, mortification sweeping over her.

"I'm so sorry, Aunt Belle. What you must think of me, I'm sure I cannot bear it."

A moment of silence passed and then.

"I do not judge people, my dear, least of all women. Come. Sit down and tell me what's troubling you."

For a terrible moment, Grace felt her emotions rise up within her, but then she allowed herself to take a deep breath and followed her aunt's instructions. She sat on the settee before the fireplace. Hands clasped together, she spoke.

"Dr. Cameron, the chief constable, and myself were in Dr. Hall's office a few days ago, waiting for James-er, I mean Dr. Hall to arrive. The constable mentioned that he was there regarding another grave robbery and I foolishly mentioned that I saw a Mr. Roberts paying two men dressed in dirty clothes, in Gallowgate while I was attending Dr. Hall. Mr. Roberts is one of Dr. Cameron's students and when I called out to him, he saw me, but hurried away. I thought it was suspicious, and so I spoke about it. Dr. Cameron became suddenly enraged, saying that I was accusing Mr. Roberts of grave robbing and in turn, accusing Dr. Cameron as well as the entire Andersen University. I argued that I did no such thing and it turned into this whole fiasco." She shook her head. "James told me that it was rash of me to speak on such things, but I *know* Mr. Roberts wasn't in Gallowgate on any sort of charity mission."

"And why are you so sure of that?"

Grace's shoulders dropped.

"That's the crux. I didn't have any evidence, so I went to Gallowgate to find some. I went to question the factory workers and learned that one of the men that had taken money from Mr. Roberts carved small toy tops and handed them out to the children."

"Toy tops?"

"Yes, those little toys that spin around and around? Well, there was one found near the last grave that was decimated. That places at least one of them who was being paid by Mr. Roberts at the crime scene."

Aunt Belle shook her head.

"But how does that connect Mr. Roberts or Dr. Cameron to any of this?"

Grace's hand lifted to her head, rubbing her temple where a headache was forming.

"It doesn't, at least, not yet. That's what I was speaking about with James tonight. He thinks we don't have enough evidence, and that it would be irresponsible to go to the constable at this point, but I'm positive that we should."

Aunt Belle's face twisted as she soaked in everything Grace had said. After a moment, she nodded.

"Grace, you are one of the brightest women I've ever known, and I've been on this earth a long time. If you believe that you have enough to go to the constable about this, then I support you."

Grace stared at her.

"You do?"

"Yes."

"But what about James?"

She sighed.

"Dr. Hall may be too familiar with Dr. Cameron to see what's going on. He isn't on the outside, like you, able to take in the entire picture."

"But am I seeing the whole picture?" she asked, standing up. "I've gone over it a dozen times and a dozen times more. I can't be sure anymore. I would be remiss if I accused an innocent man of something."

"But you have a lead. You must follow it to discover if it's true, regardless. If anything, you may prove the doctor's innocence."

She shook her head.

"I just don't trust myself anymore."

"Always have faith in yourself, my dear. Always. There are forces in this world that try to silence our instincts. That would call us hysterical, or foolish for trusting ourselves. Believe in yourself. Most of the time, you're the only person you can trust to know your feelings." She tilted her head. "I believe in you, my dear."

Grace smiled, though she wasn't sure if she could.

"Then, perhaps I should go to the constable?"

Aunt Belle smiled with a firm nod.

"I will go with you if you wish. Now, tell me about your relationship with Dr. Hall." Grace blanched and a chuckle escaped Aunt Belle's mouth. "It's quite all right, my dear. Remember, I was a king's courtesan."

This was true, but even so, Grace felt wildly out of her depths. Inhaling, she decided to be honest.

"I am fond of him. Very much so, and he wishes to marry me." Aunt Belle's eyes widened with glee. "But he believes that his mind may change over time, about what he wants in a wife and so he's decided to respect my wishes to remain unattached while I finish my apprenticeship."

Aunt Belle's smile vanished.

"That's three years from now."

"Yes."

"But after that, he will propose?"

Grace shrugged.

"If our feelings remain the same, I suppose he might."

A strange "Boh!" sound escaped Aunt Belle's lips as she slapped her hand against her desk. It was obvious that she was annoyed, angry even, but then she shook her head and seemed to calm herself down.

"Men," she spat as she stood, causing Grace to step forward to help her. "They never do what they're supposed to." Grace tilted her head in question, but Belle waved her free hand as she allowed Grace to escort her. "Never mind, my dear. Never mind. Take me to my room. I'm in want of sleep. And I suggest you go to sleep as well. We've an appointment with the constable tomorrow."

"Yes, Aunt Belle."

"Oh yes, and dear? You've misplaced this." Belle pulled from her robe pocket Grace's silver chain.

Grace felt her cheeks warm as she stepped forward and took it from her.

"I had been looking for this. I must have forgotten it."

Belle watched as she replaced it over her head with a knowing expression.

"I thought so. Come, walk me to my room."

Grace helped her aunt out of the parlor and down the hall to her bedroom, followed by Penguin, who seemed to have taken to his new role as favorite with pleasure. After helping her into bed, she exited the room and climbed the stairs before reaching her own room. Once there, she leaned against the door and let out a sigh.

She was going to go to the constable's office first thing in the morning and tell him everything she had learned. Surely James would be annoyed with her for going around him, but she felt it in her gut that this was the correct thing to do.

As she dropped onto her own bed several minutes later, staring up at the ceiling, she wondered if marrying James was a possibility after her apprenticeship. This could be a passing fancy, one that she might one day regret, but she couldn't see doing so now.

At some point, Grace's eyelids became heavy and she fell asleep where she had dropped, her mind awash with worry about tomorrow's task and all that might result from it.

Chapter Nineteen

JAMES WAS SLOW to rise the next morning, taking his breakfast nearly a half hour later than usual, to the great irritation of his housekeeper, Mrs. Cramer, who had sent his toast back three times to reheat before she finally just sat down at the dining room table and waited for him to appear. After which, she served his breakfast in silence, but James didn't mind. In fact, he couldn't think of anything that would ruin his mood this morning, after last night.

The image of Grace's half-opened eyes and dark hair draped around her shoulders seemed to be permanently burnt into his memory, as if her very name was branded on his heart. She had been every bit as amazing as the last time and while it had felt fundamentally wrong to wake her from her slumber and take her from his bed, he instead focused on what the day might bring anew in her presence.

He had frightened her by admitting that he wanted to marry her, but he had approached the topic with a cool disposition, for which he was grateful. Because if she understood just how greatly he wanted to keep her in his bed and marry her as soon as possible, she might have gone running all the way back to Glencoe.

The truth was, he was desperate for her. Nothing before had possessed his mind so earnestly. He wanted to marry her, to love her openly and without worry, but he was also aware of what that might entail. He had been infatuated with Catriona, after all, and while he was sure his feelings for Grace were something else entirely, he was cautious not to try and pressure her or force her into marriage. He wanted her to want it equally, if not more so, and she would only resist or push him away if he insisted upon it. He knew that about her and he had made the decision not to burden her with a proposal. He would wait, quietly and by her side for as long as it took for her to realize her dream, and he would help her along the way in any way that he could, solely because he loved her and wanted her to have everything she wished.

The housekeeper plopped the rewarmed teapot on the table in front of him, a droplet of light brown water dropping to the white tablecloth below. James glanced up.

"I am sorry for sleeping in late, Mrs. Cramer, but might you refrain from slamming things down?"

"I'm not mad about you sleeping in, Doctor. I'm upset to receive visitors in the middle of the night without warning."

James stared at the old woman, partially surprised that she would be so daring as to bring up his private life, while also feeling a sudden need to lie, if only to protect Grace's reputation.

"I wasn't aware that you heard…"

"Not heard? I'm awake at five o'clock every morning, aren't I? And not two minutes after I step out of my room, do I hear a knock at the door."

James frowned, confused. Who had come to call so early? He opened his mouth to ask when the sudden footfall sounded from the staircase and before he could stand up to see who was in his house, the dining room door opened and there stood his aunt.

"Mrs. Fletcher?" He nearly choked, dropping his napkin on the table, and coming around the table. "What are you doing here?"

Flora Fletcher was in her late sixties, with wild, gray hair that was always braided and rarely pinned up. She wore a gingham pattern dress, nearly a decade out of style, with a lace choker that just peeked out over the edge of her collar. Her eyes were bright green and always slightly wide, as if she was constantly surprised, which had caused a great many children in Glencoe to tease and taunt her, as she did appear rather wild, but she had never cared for the thoughts of others.

"My presence was requested," she said as she moved into the room, taking a seat at the table without invitation.

She was a slender woman, but in a way that always caused James to worry. She should eat more, he always told her, but she was a sound believer in eating only vegetables and breads.

"By whom? I did not call you here."

"No, and I wouldn't expect it of you. You never call when you're in trouble."

He laughed, stunned that she was here.

"What is this, one of your premonitions? I'm fine, truly, there was no need to come all this way."

"You've not been home in over two months."

Ah, that was why she was here. She was cross with him. Very well, he deserved whatever bitterness she was feeling toward him.

Sitting down next to her, he took her frail hand.

"I am sorry, but I wrote to Dr. Barkley that I was busy. Training your prodigy is rather taxing, you know."

Her green eyes flashed at the mention of Grace and her hand flexed against his, almost in a panic.

"You must believe her. Whatever it is she's telling you, I can sense that you do not trust her and if you don't, she will be next."

James had never liked when his aunt became like this. She hadn't always been so outspoken about her senses in the natural world. Hell, in his youth he had tried to call her crazy himself, arguing with her or outright ignoring her whenever she became pensive, but however he felt about it, it didn't matter. His aunt had a knack for calling things out before they happened, and whether he liked it or not, she seemed to be having a feeling about Grace.

"What is it?" He leaned toward her, his voice low. "What's

wrong?"

Just then a knock at the front door sounded, causing Mrs. Cramer, who had been eavesdropping, to jump.

"Jesus, Mary, and Joseph," she said while crossing herself. "I'll answer it."

James wanted to press his aunt further about what she sensed, but before he knew it, Dr. Cameron was standing in his dining room, red-faced and furious.

"Dr. Cameron?" James said, standing up as he dropped his aunt's hand. "What are you—"

"Your apprentice has ruined me!" he shouted, waving his hand about. "Ruined my reputation, my school, the lives of my students. Everything!"

"What are you talking about?"

"Your little harlot went to the constable this morning and told him about some silly stupid toy that supposedly links Mr. Roberts to the graverobbing and in turn me. But I will not go down quietly, oh no. I will sue you and Lady Belle and every bloody person in this city to see justice brought forth."

The harlot comment was not lost on James, who was finding it difficult to not react.

"Have a care with her name, sir," he warned, his tone lethal. "Or I will ask you to leave."

"I will not! You should be ashamed! Your practice, your profession, all wasted so that some chit might pretend and play doctor! And for what? She's ruining the lives of actual professionals."

"I have had enough," James bellowed. The doctor stared at him, stunned at his explosive reaction. "Grace has not done anything wrong. There is an open case about graverobbing, she's aware of it, has been following it. I've been working with the constable for weeks now as well."

"That doesn't give her the right—"

"She saw Mr. Roberts—"

"She thinks she saw—"

"For the grace of God, man!" he said, slamming his fist on the table. "She saw your student paying certain people who have been, or are very close to being linked to the participation in bodysnatching. Now, if you are innocent, what are you worried about? It is a lead that must be followed. If your students are involved in something dastardly, then they don't deserve to be doctors anyway. However," James stated, stepping toward the old man. "If your students have been doing this on your behalf, then Dr. Cameron, you have some things to explain yourself."

The old doctor shook with either rage or fear, for after a few sputtering curses, he turned and stalked out of the house. After a long tense moment, the housekeeper spoke.

"Never enjoyed his company anyway," she said, turning to Mrs. Fletcher. "Tea, mum?"

"No, I should like to see Grace," she said as she stood up. "Where is she?"

"Probably just returning from the constable's office. I should like to speak to her as well."

The two were quick to ready themselves and decided to walk around the block to use the front door, since it wasn't particularly polite to enter through the kitchens. Though they were quiet as they walked, James felt a sinking feeling in his stomach that told him something wasn't right and by the time they reached the front door, Flora seemed to feel it too as she was gripping his arm tightly.

"Something's not right," she whispered to him as the door opened to reveal a distressed looking Mrs. Stevens.

"Hello, Dr. Hall. Madam," she said with a curtsy as she stepped back to allow them entry. "It is good that you are here."

"What's happened?"

"It's Grace. She's gone missing."

The pit in James's stomach pulsated at her words as he and Flora stopped.

"Gone? Where? When?"

Mrs. Stevens pressed a kerchief to her eye to wipe away a tear as Arabella appeared in the doorway of the parlor.

"We don't know," she said, coming forward. "Aunt Belle arrived home, having gone with her this morning to the constable's office. Grace told her that she wanted to go to your offices, Dr. Hall. But that was over an hour ago, and when Andrews went there, he only found Virgil, who said Grace hadn't been there since yesterday."

Releasing his aunt, he stalked into the parlor to find a visibly shaken Belle who was seated before the fire, her fist pressed to her mouth while Andrews hovered over her like a protective guard dog. The black and white cat that Grace had named Penguin sat at her feet, seemingly on guard himself.

"Did she say where else she might go?" he asked. "What did the constable say when you told him about the toy top?"

"He said it was evidence enough to bring in Mr. Roberts for questioning, but doubted that he would reveal who his contacts were. Grace insisted that she knew where they were, Rabbit home, or something, but the constable was more interested in Mr. Roberts and Dr. Cameron, considering that the bodies were likely for the use of students at the university. The constable said it was probable that the men were already gone." She tapped her mouth with her knuckles. "You don't think that she would be foolish enough to go to Gallowgate alone? Not after yesterday, do you?"

A grim mixture of worry, fury, and the like rose up in James's throat.

"I intend to find out. Excuse me."

He took off, stalking out of the room, down the hallway, and through the kitchens, causing the maids and footmen to jump out of his way as he headed for the back door. There was no time to waste. He needed his horse ready and mounted as soon as possible, for if his instincts were right, Grace was in a truly grave amount of danger.

Chapter Twenty

G RACE KEPT HER hood up, sure not to let her face appear to anyone who might recognize her as she approached Rabbit House. She had taken a hackney to just a few blocks over and walked the rest of the way so as to not appear suspicious.

It was perhaps the most foolish thing she had ever done, coming to Gallowgate alone particularly after what happened yesterday, but she was determined to see everyone involved brought to justice and, after stealing the letter opener on the constable's desk and tucking it up her sleeve, she felt ready to defend herself if needed. But if the constable was correct, the men were likely already notified of their impending arrest. This was really just an attempt to gather whatever information she could, like their names and places of residence, things some people might not wish to share with the police.

Taking a deep breath, she knocked on the door of Rabbit House and not a moment passed before a redheaded woman with foreboding eyes and yellow teeth opened the door. She glared at her, up and down, before frowning.

"We ain't got any beds. Move on."

She tried to close the door, but Grace stuck her foot out.

"I can pay."

Grace spoke in a coarse Scottish accent, but knew that it didn't sound quite right. She tucked her hand into her sleeve and revealed several bank notes.

"Wot did I just say…" The woman's eyes lit up at the sight of

Grace's money. "Oh, aye, ya can, I see. Well, come in, come in."

Grace followed the woman into a dark room, with dirty wood floors and dozens of laundry lines strung up from one side of the room to the other. All manner of clothing were set out to dry as if after being washed, although they didn't look particularly clean and Grace had to duck her head several times until they reached a plain wooden desk with an open ledger book on it. The woman scooted around it.

"How long might ye be staying with us fer?" she asked, glancing down at the pages.

"Ah, two nights."

"Is that all?"

"Well, er, I may be staying longer, depending."

The woman winked.

"Sounds like ye're not too familiar with the area. Are ye new in town?"

Grace shook her head but didn't answer. She was already speaking too much and she worried her accent might not be as convincing as she hoped.

Her silence seemed not to bother the old woman who scooted out from behind the desk and nodded her head in a "follow me" way as she turned around, opening a door. Grace was close behind her when they crossed another threshold and revealed a room crammed together with long, wooden boxes. Grace's heart dropped at the sight of it. It appeared as though rows and rows of coffins had been built, but upon closer inspection, they were slightly wider than coffins and there were people moving around in them and each one had a number carved onto the foot of them.

These were four-penny coffin beds. Grace had heard about them while reading Aunt Belle's pamphlets on the poor conditions of the housing problems that had been happening all over the country. In recent years there had been a boom in population and there simply weren't enough homes to fit people. In some cities, they had tried to build affordable houses, such as tenant housing, but these buildings had quickly become overcrowded. Some boarding houses had ceased renting out single rooms and had instead installed wooden box beds, much like these ones, and rented them out by the night. There were also hangover benches, where people would be about to sit and lean forward on a rope to sleep, or a penny sit up, where they weren't allowed to even sleep, but sit all night. Sometimes, that was all they could afford and a far better prospect than getting frostbite in an alley.

The number of miserable people moving about the room slowly made Grace's heart ache, but she had to focus on the task at hand. As she followed the woman to the end of the room, where the 19th bed was, she tried to ignore the cries of two children, huddled against their mother.

"Hush, hush," the young woman cooed.

"Ye shut those brats up or you'll be out on the street tonight!" the yellow-toothed woman threatened. "These people pay good money to sleep in peace. Ah, here we are." She held out her hand as if to present the bed to Grace. "Home for the night."

"Thank you."

For a moment, the old woman squinted.

"Where'd you say you were from again?"

Grace shook her head.

"Nowhere important."

The woman lifted her chin and glared at her.

"You're familiar…"

One of the other lodgers started coughing abruptly, distracting the old woman for a moment. Grace sat down on the edge of her small bed and hung her head low, hoping to end their conversation. It worked, for in the next moment the woman let out a curse of sorts and left. Once she had gone back to the front of the house, Grace glanced around the cramped room. She needed to ask someone about the bald man; surely someone here had seen him.

One of the children that clung to her mother wailed, causing the poor woman to cover the child's mouth.

"You must be quiet," she insisted.

"But I'm hungry."

"We haven't any food, so you must hush, or we'll be frozen and hungry as opposed to just hungry."

Grace stood up and walked over, kneeling before them. The mother wrapped her arms tightly around her children, as if to protect them from whatever Grace was about to do or say.

"They'll be quiet, I promise."

"Oh, no," Grace said, shaking her head. "I just, I overheard they were hungry and I don't have anything to eat, but I do have some coins that you could use at the market, down the street?"

The woman glared at Grace.

"I'm not leaving my children with ye."

"Oh, no, I don't want you to. I just, here," she reached into her pocket and handed it to the woman, who took it with caution. Several people surrounding them turned to stare. One even got up and left the room, and Grace felt suddenly uneasy. Instead, she focused on the woman, who was wide-eyed. "Sorry."

She got up and turned, worried that she had just made a mistake when the far door opened. There in the doorway was the bald man, staring directly at her. Panicked, Grace glanced at the back door, then back at the man. In an instant, he was pushing people out of the way to get to her and she jumped up on the edge of the wooden bed and leapt over a sleeping person before jumping to the ground and rushing to the back door as the bald man shouted. Thankfully it wasn't locked and she bolted out the back into a small courtyard that was filled with crates and rubbish.

Whipping around, she saw a narrow walk that led out against the neighboring building. Without thinking, Grace ran toward it and tried to squeeze through as her dress caught on a number of things. The sound of the door slamming open only hastened her attempt to get away. Glancing behind her, she saw the bald man ripping away old crates and pieces of wood to try and make room for himself, but she was too far away. In the next instant, she was free and out the other side, stumbling into the street until a crushing set of hands gripped her arms, causing her to cry out.

"AH!"

"Keep 'er mouth shut," the unseen man growled into her ear as the bald man finally reached her.

Panic like she had never known before finally seemed to settle into Grace's heart as she realized just how precarious this situation was. Never before had she ever been handled so crudely and when the man placed a dirty palm over her mouth, Grace was forcibly dragged back into Rabbit House, and she felt a pit begin to grow in her stomach.

The bald man walked around her and opened the door. Out of the corner of her eye, she saw the yellow-toothed woman glaring as the man behind Grace began to drag her upstairs. She tried to kick and wrench out of her captor's arms, clawing at his hand that covered her mouth if only to scream out for help, but he was holding her too tightly and the bald man only sneered.

"A right mess you've gotten yerself into, innit?" he asked as he followed them up the narrow staircase. "But I reckon yer won't be making much more noise fer long."

"Yeah," the man who held her agreed, talking into her ear. "We've a gentleman who will pay us twelve pounds sterling for a pretty little pigeon like you."

Grace stilled in her fight to be released as the bald man nodded slowly.

"Oh, aye. You didna think we were digging up the dead, did you?"

"But Bill, we do dig up the dead."

The bald man glared at the man behind Grace.

"Shut up, Barley," the bald man snapped, before refocusing on Grace. "It doesn't much matter. I have a feeling our friend Mr. Roberts might throw us an extra little something for knocking this bird out of the sky."

"What do you mean, twelve pounds sterling?" Grace asked, her hackles drawn up.

"A new body is worth twelve pounds. Dug up ones are only worth nine," Barley said.

"Shut it, Barley!"

"Oi, who's she going to tell?"

The man holding Grace kicked a door open and dragged her backwards into a sparsely decorated room. Wood floors, wood walls, a small straw bed, and the dingiest of windows barely let in any light.

"He didn't like you snooping about the other day, little miss," the man named Barley spat as he tossed Grace onto the straw bed. "But ye're not gonna be a problem fer him anymore, is ya?"

Both men took a step toward her.

"Remember," Bill said. "No broken bones. The doctor likes 'em intact."

"Strangled as usual, I know."

The realization that these two men were not only employed to rob graves, but they were also providing newly killed persons to Mr. Roberts set Grace's blood cold. All the missing persons in the newspapers, all having been from Gallowgate. Had they been killed by these two?

"Wait. The people in the newspapers, the ones who've gone missing in this neighborhood," she said with her hands up to stall them. "You didn't…"

Bill the bald man's brow lifted.

"Looking for a confession, pigeon? Aye, we did them all in and were paid a pretty penny for it too."

"Not a penny, Bill. Pounds."

"Will yer shut up, Barley?" he snapped. After a second, he turned back to Grace. "And now, it's yer turn."

Without hesitating, Grace reached up her sleeve and pulled out the letter opener she had stolen from the police station. Holding it up before her to defend herself, both men began laughing.

"Is that supposed to frighten us?" Bill asked, reaching for it.

But Grace was too quick. She slashed at his hand when she

was suddenly rushed by Barley.

"HELP!" she shouted at the top of her lungs as a pair of meaty hands wrapped around her neck.

The fingers tightened and the air she struggled for wouldn't come, but for the briefest of moments she could have sworn she heard someone calling her name.

Chapter Twenty-One

JAMES HAD EXITED Lady Belle's home just as the constable arrived, having been summoned to investigate Grace's disappearance. Evidently, the constable had a soft spot for Lady Belle and had come as a personal favor. Although James didn't speak to him, the two men were quick to climb onto their horses and take off down the street in an effort to reach Rabbit House as soon as possible.

The fury that had surged through James's body at the idea of Grace going to such a place alone was only dampened slightly by the existential dread that consumed him as he hurried his horse to move faster. Ducking around corners and cutting off pedestrians and carriages alike did not bother him, though he did hear the faint call of the constable behind him. It was dangerous to ride at breakneck speeds through a city, but James did not care. His only concern was for Grace, who he would promptly put over his knee the moment he reached her for daring to do something so foolish.

He and the constable arrived in Gallowgate quicker than he ever had. Without hesitating he jumped off his still moving horse and ran directly to the front door, banging on it with ire.

"Open up!" he demanded, as the constable climbed off his horse. "Now!"

"We're full up!" a muffled, female voice called out.

"It's the police!" the constable called back.

But James's hands were already holding onto either side of the doorjamb. Bringing his knee up, he kicked the front door open with the booted heel and marched into the small entrance.

"Now see here—"

He grabbed the person, a woman as it were, by the collar.

"Where is she?" The woman snarled and barely let out a word when someone from above called out for help. Dropping her, she fell to the floor as he glanced upward. "GRACE?"

"Quick! She's upstairs!" the constable yelled, but James was already two steps ahead of him.

He climbed the staircase two steps at a time only to find a dozen doors in a narrow hallway. He held his hand out to stop the constable and upon hearing a scuffle behind the first door, he took a step back and rammed his shoulder into the thin wood, bursting through the room. There on a straw bed was Grace, eyes bulging from her head as she reached out toward James while two men hovered above her.

James's vision went black. In an instant he was grabbing both men by the collars, tossing one to the floor as he attacked the other with a series of blows to the abdomen. When the other man stood back up, a bald man, James threw the other at him, knocking them both down before he leapt on top of them and continued his shower of fists and cursing to rain down on them like a monsoon of fury.

"James!" Grace's voice called out, but he could not stop.

It was as if the devil himself had come to possess James and he would not end his reign until both men were dead.

"Hall! For the love of Christ, you're killing them!" the constable yelled, and it was only after the police chief wrapped James's arms up and yanked him backwards, causing the doctor to fall on him, was he stopped.

After several minutes of heavy breathing, James rolled to his side and, upon seeing Grace, hair tussled, neck red with finger marks, and tears streaming down her face, did he finally go to her. He grabbed her, holding her in a painful hug, pressing her body to his and he kissed her forehead, cheeks, ears, and mouth, every inch he could.

"You foolish," kiss. "stupid," kiss. "outrageous," kiss. "damning," kiss. "woman!" Kiss. Kiss. Kiss. He held her back by the shoulders, shaking her. "Have you any idea what could have happened to you? They were going to murder you!"

"I know," she cried, nodding as she leaned forward, accepting his biting words with humility. "I'm so sorry."

"What would I have done without you, Grace? What sort of world would you have left me in?" He kissed her again, this time softer before stopping again. "When I think of what else they might have done to you..." He turned, almost ready to start his campaign of vengeance again, but at the squeezing of Grace's finger's he stopped.

"Please, James. I have to tell you. And the constable," she said as the chief of police looked at her. "The missing persons in Gallowgate. These men were killing them, by strangulation. They said Mr. Roberts was paying them twelve pounds a body. On top of the graves that they robbed at the necropolis."

The constable's eyes widened.

"Is that so?" She nodded vigorously. "Would you mind coming down to the station to give a testimony?"

"Yes—"

"No. She's going home."

"But—"

"As your doctor, I demand you return to your house at once where I can properly examine and diagnose you. Until you are deemed fit, I must refuse any statements delivered to the justice of the peace until you are no longer under duress."

"But—"

"Grace."

Swallowing, she eventually nodded, evidently seeing something in his face that told her not to test him.

"Take me home, please."

With that, she was wrapped up with his arm just as a number of police officers came into the room. They moved down the steps, out of the boarding house, and onto his horse, where he held her close to his chest, keeping the animal below at a steady pace.

Though they didn't speak the entire ride home, James had to admit that he wasn't sure what to say or where even to begin. Since learning that Grace might be in danger and then finding her so close to death, he had sensed his entire foundation shift. No longer was he concerned with the thoughts and ideas of his fellow physicians, colleges, or patients. All that mattered to him was Grace and as dangerous as that was, he knew it was a feeling that would never leave him. He loved her. He loved her so much that he was willing to put his entire life, his entire profession on the line if only to be near her and to make sure she was safe and close.

But did she feel the same?

Upon their arrival to Lady Belle's home, James helped her off the horse and walked her in through the front door, only to be immediately met with the thankful sighs and yips of joy from the household.

"Oh, my goodness, Grace!" Arabella said, coming forward. "Are you all right?"

"Where did you go?" Mrs. Fletcher asked. "Are you hurt?"

"My dear, that was a terrible idea," Aunt Belle scolded. "You should be ashamed—"

"She needs rest," James yelled at the lot of them, causing everyone to quiet down. He continued to help her up the stairs. "I need hot water and blankets. Mrs. Stevens? Send someone to retrieve my doctoring bag from my house at once."

Everyone began to follow him upstairs, but he turned on them, with Grace still in his arms.

"I will see the patient alone."

Aunt Belle spread her arms as if to block everyone behind her from passing.

"As you wish, doctor," she said matter-of-factly. "Everyone! Give this man some room!"

James was down the hallway and in Grace's room within

minutes, sitting her on the bed as he knelt before her. He touched her chin as gently as possible and turned her face to the side as she winced. The red marks on her skin sent a rush of fervor through him and he wanted to be back in that room at Rabbit House, pummeling those two men again.

"Bastards," he said as he gazed up to her.

Her tears had dried on her cheeks and as furious as he was, he was also grateful. So grateful that she was there. Without thinking, his head fell to her lap as his arms reached around her waist and pulled her toward him. For a moment she didn't move, but then her hands began to rub his back and he felt his spirit break.

"James, I'm sorry," she said as he glanced upward. "I'm such a fool."

"I can't have anything happen to you, Grace. Not anything."

She tilted her head, her brow furrowed.

"Why?"

"Because I love you. I love you as surely as the air in my lungs keeps me alive. I love you beyond reason, beyond measure, beyond clarity." He paused, the emotion of his confession causing his throat to tighten. "Please, Grace. Promise me, you'll never do anything so foolish again?"

"You love me?"

"Grace, please promise—"

"Do you really love me?"

"Yes," he said in a huff. "Of course I do."

"I love you, James. I do," she said, sliding off the side of the bed to kneel before him. "I knew it, for a while now, but I didn't think… I'm sorry." She wrapped her arms around his neck as his spirits lifted. "I love you and I'll never do anything so wild ever, for as long as I live."

She loved him. What a world it was.

After Mrs. Stevens returned with his doctoring bag, he set to work. Grace was bathed behind the silk screen and dressed in the softest, frilliest night rail and placed beneath the covers. Once they were alone again, he did a full examination and prescribed her a week's worth of rest, which was met with arguments, but he insisted. Once he finished, there was a knock at the door.

"Enter," James said.

Mrs. Stevens entered the room scowling as she was followed in closely by Constable Murphy. James opened his mouth to speak, but the constable held up his hand.

"I know you have your work, Dr. Hall, but I do as well and I need to question the patient at once."

"Now listen here—"

"James," Grace said gently, causing him to turn. "I can manage."

Although it was obvious to everyone that James would rather she didn't, he only nodded stiffly. He didn't leave the room, however, and while the constable appeared annoyed, glancing at the door several times to suggest the doctor leave, James refused.

Sighing, the constable came forward and looked down at Grace.

"Can you explain, in your own words, what led you to Rabbit House and what transpired there?"

"Yes. I went to Rabbit House in hopes to confirm a suspicion I had about one of Dr. Cameron's students. You see, I saw Mr. Roberts paying a man outside Rabbit House a few weeks ago while doing rounds with Dr. Hall. It seemed odd that a medical student would be in Gallowgate without accompanying an attending physician, so I was suspicious. When Dr. Hall told me about the spinning top toy being found at the grave of Pauletta Tidsale, I remembered Mrs. Monty's son playing with something similar. I was sure that the grave robbers were connected with Rabbit House."

"And you knew about Dr. Cameron's involvement?"

Grace shook her head.

"No. I suspected that Mr. Roberts was doing something nefarious, but I didn't think Dr. Cameron knew about it." She paused and glanced at James. "He didn't, did he?"

"I don't know," James said, looking up at the constable. "But he was in a foul mood this morning about the entire ordeal."

"Unfortunately, Dr. Cameron's involvement seems to be a little more complicated."

"How so?" Grace asked.

"Well, it seems the doctor was paying a premium for bodies, but had specifically instructed his students not to involve outside parties. Dr. Cameron has been paying for stolen corpses for well over a year now. His student, Mr. Roberts, found the work too strenuous and decided to employ a few fellows from Gallowgate, who also didn't particularly care for digging up graves. When one of the occupants at Rabbit House died in his sleep, they handed his body over and were paid extra for the, er, well, I suppose the freshness of the body." The constable shifted from one side to the other, visibly uncomfortable with his own words. "It sparked an idea and when Mr. Roberts offered to pay them extra for clean, fresh corpses, they decided to take matters into their own hands."

Grace's hand lifted to her mouth and James took a step forward.

"I think you've asked enough questions for now. Please, allow her some rest."

"Well, we didn't get to what happened to her in Rabbit House."

"She was attacked. Nearly killed, what else must she tell you?"

"Dr. Hall, if you're going to interrupt me, I'll have to ask you to step outside."

"Not bloody likely."

"Please, the both of you," Grace said, lifting her hands to stop them. "I'm perfectly capable of speaking. Now, Constable Murphy, continue."

The constable asked several more detailed questions, things that certainly didn't seem like they were important, at least to James. Things like what her assailants were wearing and exactly what time she arrived at Rabbit House. Eventually though, the constable finished and with a nod, thanked the both of them before leaving. Grace fell asleep soon after and he waited until he heard the gentle snores coming from her before leaving her to sleep in peace.

Upon exiting the room, he found Aunt Belle with that damn cat at her feet. It seemed she had climbed the stairs unassisted and was watching him with intent.

"Yes?"

"How is she?"

"Bruised but otherwise unharmed."

"And?"

"And what?"

"What are your intentions, Dr. Hall? I know I am a senile old woman, but I am not blind. You care for my niece a great deal and I wish to know your intentions."

James sighed, scratching his beard for a moment.

"I doubt anyone would ever accuse you of being senile, Lady Belle. In regards to Grace, however, I am fond of her. More than fond, actually. I love her." Belle smiled. "But she does not wish to marry. At least, not until her apprenticeship is over with and she is a fully fledged physician."

Belle frowned.

"Yes, I thought so. Well then, I suppose there is no helping it. Grace will have what she wants. But afterwards, Dr. Hall. What about when she reaches her goal, what then?"

He shook his head.

"I do not know. But I promise that I will only ever be in the business of making her happy. I do not care if she ever marries me. I just wish to be by her side always. I want to be there for her as no other person can or will be."

Aunt Belle smirked, seemingly satisfied.

"Good. Then I believe you will be."

He let out a soft, pitiful laugh.

"Until she realizes how much better she can do."

Aunt Belle's smirk vanished.

"Do not question the loyalty of a Sharpe woman, Dr. Hall. Grace is her own person, but she looks at you the same way Hope sees her Graham or how Faith sees her Logan. I believe you will have your own bride, given the time and the gentle touch I know all you doctors to possess."

With that, Aunt Belle turned, as did the cat, and before he could stop himself, he hurried forward.

"Let me help you down the stairs."

"What a dear. I shall be very happy indeed when I get to call you my nephew-in-law."

Epilogue

Three years later, Lismore Hall

THE WARMTH FROM the parlor fire's blaze was enough to make Grace second guess her wool plaid dress that was trimmed with gold thread. It was a fine gown, far fancier than her usual attire, but one that was expected for Hogmanay celebrations.

Glancing around the room, it was a sight that would always warm her heart for years to come. Wedged between a frail Aunt Belle and Dr. Barkley sat Hope and Graham's eldest of three children, a girl named Fiona as they read from a large book. Grace could not see, but by the look in Aunt Belle's eye, it was something exciting. The twins, Elanor and Gregory who were barely two, were cackling with glee at Andrews, who was making faces behind a paper mask that he kept moving in front of his face, causing the two to giggle wildly.

Graham was speaking to Logan and Faith, who were swinging their own child, a two-and-a-half-year-old boy named Ian, by the arms back and forth, as it was proving to be the only thing to keep his attention for very long. Mrs. Fletcher was in a conversation with James as well, as a pregnant Rose, Aunt Belle's former secretary, tried to gather the McTavish clan together so that they could be ready to sing in the New Year. Of course, she was finding it difficult as they were all scattered throughout the room, dancing and chatting loudly amongst themselves. Penguin the cat chased Jaco the dog around the chairs, causing a great fit of laughter, and Arabella chuckled from the corner of the room. The elderly Mr. Scott was telling her what appeared to be an amusing story, judging by her smile.

It had been a long time since everyone was together like this. For the past three years, Grace herself had been working tirelessly on her career. Having finished her apprenticeship six months ago, she had just returned to Scotland the day before from a surgical stint in Italy, where she had studied under the very surgeon who had performed Aunt Belle's surgery five years earlier.

She had barely been able to speak to James privately upon her return before they had to embark on a journey north to Lismore Hall.

James had stayed in Glasgow during Grace's time in Italy, and while their correspondence had been strong during her time away, the atmosphere between them had felt somewhat strained since her return. Of course, they had been traveling with James's aunt the whole time, as she had come to live in Glasgow with James in recent months. But even after their arrival, dinner and whatnot, Grace couldn't help but watch him and worry that perhaps his feelings for her had lessened over time.

Staring at him now, he must have felt her gaze, for he turned back to look at her.

Grace's heart began beating wildly, just as it always seemed to do when she was the center of his attention. Excusing himself from his company, he came across the room, reaching for two goblets of wine as he reached Grace, who was leaning against the window seat that overlooked the snow-covered garden.

"My love," he said, handing her a glass, which she took. "Are you all right?"

"Very much so. Why? Do I not appear it?"

He shook his head, a touch hesitant.

"To be honest, no. You've a look of melancholy on your face and it's causing me to worry about you."

Grace grinned.

"When have I ever caused you to worry?" The obvious expression on his face made her chuckle. "Well, I suppose I have from time to time, but you needn't be worried now."

"Oh? Why is that?"

"Because I've decided on something. Something I hope you might assist me with, since I will be lost without you and I can't very well do it on my own."

James sighed.

"If this is about the hospital again, I already told you, I will allot as much of my time as I can, but it will be difficult considering my new position at the school and everything."

"It's not about the hospital."

He gave her a suspicious glance.

"Then what is it?"

Grace placed the wine glass that she had not sipped from on an end table.

"Well, I've been thinking recently and it has been several months since I've been granted the title doctor and I was rather curious... I mean, I once asked that we might wait to further our, well, relationship until I reached this goal I had and since I've reached it, I'm not sure if you were still... I mean..."

She shook her head, staring at her hands while the words formed clumsily from her lips.

"Grace—"

"I just want to know if you were still of the mind to propose, or if your feelings have waned in the years since you made that statement."

When he didn't speak right away, Grace felt her throat tighten, but then he grabbed her by the hand and pulled her straight out of the parlor, in the view of everyone. Mortified, Grace tried to pull her hand away, but he had such a grip on her that he did not let her go, even when they were in the hallway.

"James," she tried. "Please—"

"You think my feelings have waned? That it is you, who has been waiting these months to hear about a proposal?" he asked incredulously. "For God's sake, Grace, it is I who has been waiting for you."

She stared up at him.

"Me?"

"Yes. It was three years ago that you told me that when you finished your schooling, your studying, that you would come to me. But that wasn't true. You went to Italy instead."

"To shadow a surgeon."

"Yes, I understand that. But to assume that you were the one waiting, when you specifically said that you would be the one to come to me, well, Grace. You've cut me more than you know."

Grace, realizing that she had indeed told him such a thing, reached for him.

"Oh, James. I am a fool, aren't I?"

"The smartest, most clever fool I know." She smiled, tears stinging her eyes. His hand came up and his thumb brushed against her cheek. "Well? Are you going to ask me?"

A bubble of laughter came from her throat and she nodded quickly.

"James Hall," she started, gripping his coat lapels. "Will you marry me?"

"Yes," he whispered, leaning down so that their foreheads touched. "Finally."

He kissed her for the first time in months and Grace was stunned that so many cheers and whistles sounded within her soul when he suddenly broke away. To her horror and combined pleasure, the entirety of their friends and families stood in the doorway, cheering them on.

In the next moment, the bells chimed and more cheering came.

"*Should old acquaintance be forgot,*" Andrews began to sing, surprising everyone as they all joined in to sing the rest of "Auld Lang Syne", all under the tired but gleeful gaze of Lady Belle Smyth. Her nieces were all joyfully on their way to their happily ever afters, just as she promised her sister she would help with, all those years ago.

The End

About the Author

Matilda Madison lives in the Pocono mountains of Pennsylvania. A history lover, she finds immense joy in knowing useless facts, exploring the woods around her home, and drinking copious amounts of tea. When she's not writing, she can be found researching obscured periods for her books, refurbishing old furniture, and baking.

Catch up with me anytime on my socials.
Website – www.matildamadison.com
Instagram – matildamadisonbooks
TikTok – @matildamadison

www.ingramcontent.com/pod-product-compliance
Lightning Source LLC
Chambersburg PA
CBHW072107300726
48975CB00003B/737